Notes on Anna

By Corri van de Stege

Creative Gateway

First Published by Creative Gateway 2014

Paperback Edition: ISBN: 978-1-908636-30-0

Typeset in Minion Pro 11/14 font
Published in Great Britain by Creative Gateway, Norfolk, UK

Creative Gateway is an imprint of Creative Gateway Ltd
A company registered in England, number 4684923
Registered Address: Edwinstowe House, Edwinstowe, Notts
NG21 9PR

Birth pangs

Your rural idyll
cloaks the secret burial of
armoury beneath the fields of
desolation.
My birth unnoticed
until the attempted flight
from the gods, worshipped
by the defences of the local army
dressed in their Sunday best.

The tangled webs of disconnected
limbs and groping branches
secure me to your embrace
your spell prevents escape.

Tied to your eternal
godly whispers,
your grip the cob
webs of loss,
the umbilical cord
twisted round my neck
forever.

Chapter One: 1977

Iran

I wake up with a shock from a deep black sleep. It's too early. The alarm clock shows 4.55 and I groan into the quietness of the room. Mike is fast asleep still. Fierce, glassy and transparent thoughts flit through my mind; I cannot capture any one of them long enough to focus on. I toss and turn and then fall back into an uneasy dream.

The green parrot flies up from the corner of the pillow on my shaded bed and I am surprised. "It's here," I say. But I don't know where the other bird is and now the parrot has gone, disappeared with a fleck of orange on its feathers. I join the party, a gathering of many people. They're all very friendly and they're people I know, but I don't know anyone in particular. I'm happy because it's the end of the week.

There's an anteroom with a table covered by a white cloth ready for the food. I look for my little girl who's playing very self-confidently with wooden toys in the corner and doesn't need me. A lanky young man, no, a boy really, comes in with the food for the three of us, me, my girl and my husband. Only I don't know who this husband is.

"Put the food on the table," I say to the boy. "We will have a proper meal."

1

The boy floats off with the covered food as I search for change in my wallet, and only after shaking all the coins out of it do I find the pound coins to give him as a tip.

"That much?" he says.

I nod. My husband that I don't know and I are the only ones having a sit down meal, everyone else is milling around a buffet in a corner of the room. "This is the only time I get to eat," I explain. "Eat properly I mean and it's worth it."

Our daughter floats towards us, sits down and says she doesn't need us.

The loud bell of the alarm clock on my side of the bed makes my husband, our daughter, the food, and the table disappear into thin air and replaces my dream world with the realisation that I am somewhere else altogether. Mike stretches out his arm over me to silence the clock and then rolls away to get up.

I look around me, where am I really? I recognise the bedroom, the new bed, the still freshly painted walls, the bright light filtering in through the sides of the thick curtains and already I can feel the air warming up quickly at seven-thirty in the morning. We have lived here for three months and I still feel like a guest in what is now my home.

"What are you going to do today?" Mike asks as he gets out his clothes from the inbuilt wardrobe; a clean pale blue shirt with his light brown suit, and a bundle of socks and underwear from one of the drawers. He throws the suit over the bed, the rest on a chair and on his way to the bathroom he asks, "Do you want to go into town? You could get a taxi from the campus gate across the road, the guard there will stop one for you."

"No," I say. "I'm going to write. If I don't start I never will. I've been dilly-dallying for too long, I'm simply going to make it my job being a writer."

He laughs. "Well, you'll have plenty of time. Have you seen my tie anywhere?"

He's forever losing his tie, still unused to having to wear one after years of avoidance when he was a student. It's lying on the floor under the chair in the corner. I point at it and he says, "Damn, it's all dusty," while he shakes it around for a bit.

"You might buy another one," I say, "This one is beginning to look quite tired already."

"I'm going to try and introduce casual wear in the department," he says and grins at me. "Iranians are too self-conscious about their own image. About time we relaxed the rules. However, today's not the day. We have a professor's meeting this afternoon, our weekly one, and the Dean is very keen on his staff looking professional and tidy, and that includes wearing a tie."

We have breakfast at the small table in the corner of our kitchen and when he's gone I tidy away the remnants and sit down again at the wiped table with the notebooks that I bought in Tehran before we travelled to Neshnafad. I've made a very good start already.

I look at these notes, while outside the sun warms up the dusty air. It's difficult to imagine the small village tucked away in the east of The Netherlands where Anna lives, and where life seems to have stood still ever since the Second World War ended. Anna lives in a village in a western country, in the fifties, and that village seems as cut off from the rest of the world as some of the villages in this country that I live in now, on the threshold of the east, barely twenty years later. The two countries have very different gods, different climates, with dramatically different cultures, so that everything is different except for one thing, that woman is subject to God and man.

3

My dream, which has become a recurrent one over the last few weeks, has unsettled me again and I know that I have to write Anna out of my system. Moreover, living here provides the opportunity to draw a comparison between the two settings, between that of Anna's in the fifties and that of mine now, and to discover who I am in this country, whether it is so different from the one I've left behind.

I start to write.

Chapter Two: 1957

The Netherlands

The wind blew her short, blond hair across her face and then swooped it back again. Anna was flying as the wheels of the bicycle whirred with the pumping of her legs up and down and round, faster and faster. Her thin cotton skirt flapped against her legs, then wafted up and she pushed it down with her hand and held onto the handlebar with the other.

The country lane was still and empty on this warm afternoon, and the few farms dotted along the lane were deserted, except for a farmer's wife on the forecourt of a large and sprawled farm building. She was talking to someone invisible behind one of the barns, whilst holding a big pan with both hands.

Anna was queen of the road. She was thrilled with being in charge of her sister's brand new bike, far too large for her, and the saddle too high. She had difficulty keeping the bike straight as she momentarily let go of the handlebar with one hand to push her skirt back.

The bike had stood there, leaning against the house, unlocked and taunting her.

Here I am, not yours, you'll never have one like me, I'm far too good for you, you'll get me when I'm old, have lost my shine, when my light is broken and my brakes don't work so well. My gears, yes I have gears, will be lousy by the time you get me, they'll tick over, unwilling to go up or down smoothly. And when your sister needs a new one then you will get me!

She'd moved towards the bike, caressed it with her hand, felt the saddle, the smooth chrome of the frame. She'd been worried that someone might come, jump on it and disappear with it, looking back with a big grin on his face. And then her sister wouldn't have a bike anymore, would she? And what if she took it? Why had her sister left it there, unlocked, inviting?

What is it with her? These impulsive actions, always contrary, never thinking clearly, jumping in at the deep end without fail. She's daft, she's a bitch, she's difficult, and she's selfish. She's always out to draw attention to herself. She's been called all of this by just about everyone she knows. Sometimes they add that she's also clever, and she buries it all deep while knowing that God hovers over everything she does, and that escape is impossible. Whatever sinful act she carries out, her father on behalf of God will punish her. He will shake his head, shout or worse, say nothing, and will then send her to her room, no food, no playing, no books. It's best not to think about any of that.

So she'd carefully placed her hands on the handlebars; the handbrakes fitted her hands perfectly, and her thumb reached the lever of the gear switch, so smooth. She'd put her left foot on the pedal and slowly moved away on the bike, turned the corner of the house, looked back to check that no one was knocking on the windowpanes of the front room to call her back. Then quickly she'd steered the bike out of sight and disappeared from the view of the house along the village main road. The few pedestrians walking along the road didn't take any notice of the seven-year-old girl on a large ladies bike.

The farmer's wife was still talking to her invisible husband behind the barn when she heard the screeching followed by a loud wail, looked up and saw the girl crumpled in the middle of the road, a bike on top of her. The woman walked up the drive and along the road towards the crying child and pulled the bike off her. A few cows were moaning in the distance and provided the chorus to the unfolding drama.

Tears of pain and guilt flowed over Anna's cheeks; she sobbed and bit her lips.

"The bike, is the bike alright?"

They would know, they would find out, she would be punished.

"Oh forget the bike," the woman said. "Let's have a look at you first. You're going to need some bandaging dear, you'd better come with me. What happened?"

"I fell." She cried out louder now.

"Ay, does it hurt much child?" the woman asked, her face in a frown as she bent and carefully helped Anna to sit and then get up on one leg. "We'll get you a drink, and a biscuit. You'll be all right, no broken bones by the looks of it."

Anna pushed her short cut, blond hair out of her face, leaving wet strands smeared across her cheeks, and hobbled along with the woman, tears streaming down her thin face. She held onto the woman's skirt with one hand and held her right arm with the bloodied scrape sideways and away from her body. The woman pushed the bike, which rattled with the front wheel scraping along its protective frame, the chain ticking over noisily, click clack, click clack. Anna's right knee showed the bright red flesh, and dirt and blood were smeared across her clothes and face.

"What's you name now child?"

"Anna," she sobbed. More tears were now streaming down her snotty nose and cheeks. "Anna Dent."

"Ah, you're one of Dent's daughters," the woman said, nodding, and pressed her lips together. She suddenly looked stern and her eyes clouded over. She put the bike against the wall of the farmhouse, next to the kitchen door and pointed for Anna to sit down on a bench placed under the kitchen window. "There now child, sit down," she said quietly.

Where she'd been before, a pan of half-peeled potatoes was on the tarmac in front of the bench and a bucket of water next to it. There were two large pots of rhododendrons on each side of the bench with large pink flowers that were well cared for. Everything in this courtyard was tidy and neat, even if the asphalt covering was old and cracked in places. A man came around the corner of the house, her husband, curious about what was going on and why his wife had suddenly stopped talking to him.

"The front wheel's a bit bent," the woman said, examining the bike. "There are a few scratches here and there and the bell is dented. You'll need a new one."

Anna wailed louder, as much with the stinging pain of the gashes in her knee and elbow as with the realisation of what she'd done, and now the inevitability that she would be found out. Why had she taken the bike? How could she get out of this one? The farmer shook his head compassionately and cluck-clucked his tongue, carefully extracting a pipe from his pocket, which he put in his mouth, then sucked it hard.

"*Arme meid* – Poor girl," he said. "That probably hurts real bad."

The woman went inside, whispered something to her husband as she passed him, and returned with a glass of cool orange lemonade and two biscuits. From a pocket of her striped apron, worn over a flowery summer dress, she pulled a jar of ointment, which when she opened the screw top, revealed a brown looking mixture smelling vaguely of liquorice and something else, iodine.

"She's one of the Dents," she nodded to the farmer. "Must be a younger sister of Liesbet. You remember, the one that was here playing with our Letty last week."

"Ah, yes," he said. "*Die Dent* - That Dent," and again he sucked long and hard on his pipe, producing a gurgling sound as if it was a water pipe being unblocked.

What did he mean? Anna looked at the two people in front of her through her tears, and swept away her hair again with the back of her dirty hand, leaving more streaks on her blotchy face. She couldn't remember having seen these two in their Calvinist church, so they probably weren't people her father would approve of. Would that make things worse for her? Would her father be even angrier with her? She sobbed again with a heaving shudder, while the woman went about her business carefully washing and dressing her knee. The ointment looked black and viscous and it stung when the woman applied it. She watched with her tongue outside, ready to scream again. The ointment made her forget all her other hurt and worry. Then the woman wiped her elbow clean with a cloth and some more fresh water that she got from a pump in the yard.

Half an hour later, the farmer, still sucking on his pipe that now hung from the corner of his mouth, put the bike on his tractor and took her home. Anna did not much enjoy the majestic view from the top of the vehicle. All she could think of was the punishment and the anger of her father, for having taken the bike, for having fallen, for having ruined it and then for being taken home on top of a tractor by someone that her father probably didn't approve of at all.

"This is where you live, isn't it?" the farmer said. He stopped outside the village shop where garden furniture was piled up outside and the shop windows were full of curtain material on rolls and household goods, china, pans, pots, jars, buckets, anything that a village wife might need. The farmer picked her up from her majestic seat and put her down next to the tractor. "Stay here, I'll get your father or your mother."

He went inside and a few minutes later returned with Johannes, her father, and her mother Greta not far behind them.

"Go inside," Johannes said. "No, not through the shop. Go round!" He pointed to the side where a path led to the front door of their house behind the shop. His face was red as if he suffered from high blood pressure, and he managed to look both angry and apologetic. His lips were pressed closed and he made a movement of apology with his hands to the farmer, who stood aside.

"Here she is," the farmer said. "She's hurt her knee and arm. The bike's a bit bent, that's all."

Johannes was not a very tall man, with a round fleshy face that gave the impression of a larger man, as if the proportions of his body were not quite correct. He was going bald except for a ring of black and grey straggly hair around the back of his head. Anna had seen photos of him in which he was much younger and had a head full of black, shiny and straight hair, combed flat across his head to the back and with a lean face in which brown eyes burned straight at you. Age, and the responsibility of an ever-increasing number of children, was beginning to change him without mercy. His brown eyes were large but looked dull, his eyebrows were bushy and greying along with his hair and the skin of his high coloured face was covered in small purple veins on his cheeks. Despite the

10

summer warmth, he wore a blue- and black-specked suit jacket over a brown V-neck sleeveless jumper that revealed the collar of an open necked dress shirt that was beginning to fray slightly. His non-matching dark grey trousers were baggy and appeared a couple of centimetres too short because they were pulled, high up and tight, over a slightly protruding stomach. Although he was barely forty years old, to Anna he looked ancient and threatening, and his breathing, which was short and sharp as if he was perpetually behind breath, did not soften this impression.

The farmer looked at Anna and put his thumb up as if to say 'good luck' or perhaps 'you'll be fine.' She wouldn't be, she knew that much. She backed away then turned, pulling her painful leg, which was throbbing underneath the bandages.

Greta, her mother, followed her into the house. As if in imitation of Johannes, she also pursed her lips together but she glanced over at her daughter and the bloodied knee, and once they were out of sight of her father, she smiled at Anna. "Poor you," she said and took Anna's hand, pulled her forward into the house, out of the way.

Greta was slightly taller than her husband, only a few centimetres. She was a trim woman considering the number of children she had borne and raised, nine live births in total. Only six months ago, Rienske the baby had been born. Although she'd been quite ill after this last birth, she was again helping her husband out in the shop, irreplaceable and essential. The doctor had given her a clear warning though and had repeated it to Johannes. "No more or you'll die."

Greta's complexion was clear, but her facial skin evidenced a daily scrubbing with soap and very few applications of essential creams. She always managed to look smart though and dressed well, if conservatively, in a long-sleeved cream blouse and dark

11

blue pleated skirt with grey and blue buckled low-heeled comfortable shoes. Her light brown hair had turned grey already. She regularly went to her brother in law's hairdressing salon in the village for a perm and her hair was set in neat curls and waves, away from her forehead but covering her ears. She wore a thin gold necklace and a small gold watch, the only jewellery she possessed apart from two rings, all given to her by Johannes, perhaps when they got married or when she delivered her first child, a son. Anna didn't know.

Greta looked at her watch, as she tended to do every time she interacted with her children or her husband. "Why on earth did you take that bike?" she asked. She didn't sound angry, just tired. "You know it's far too big for you. What a silly thing to do. It's Liesbet's bike. Why are you so thoughtless always, and get yourself into trouble?" She sighed and then stopped to look at Anna's knee and said, "Well, your father will probably punish you enough. You'd better stay here and wait for him."

Greta smiled her half smile as if to apologise to Anna. She had that peculiar facial expression that indicated kindness that was disconnected from the world around her, an inherent gentleness that was more inward focused than related to the people surrounding her. Anna sucked back the mucus that clogged up her nose again and wiped it on her skirt. "Don't do that," her mother said.

How should Anna know why she did these things? They simply happened as if nothing to do with her own volition. She just wanted to try that new bike, feel its speed and try the handbrakes. Her own bike was old and didn't have handbrakes, only the backstep brake that would clumsily bring you to a halt, not as brisk and fast as the brakes on this new bike, which made her skid and lose control. She couldn't say any of this, shrugged her shoulders and said, "Don't know."

Henry, the elder of her two younger brothers and two years younger than Anna, came running into the kitchen. "Mother, I…" then stopped and looked at Anna, and shuddered at the sight of her knee. "Did you fall? Does it hurt?" he asked.

He came up closer and his eyes shifted from her knee to her elbow and he shuddered again at the sight of the bloodied bandage and the smears across her leg and arm. His mouth pulled down as if he was going to cry, but then he suddenly grinned, and ran off quickly through the backdoor.

Then Bert, her eldest brother, who at thirteen usually considered himself far beyond and above Anna, came in from the front room. He'd clearly followed what was going on outside, watching through the large windows as she came into the house with Greta. He shook his head as if to say, 'silly you, you know it's not worth it.'

He said, "Silly you, you know it's not worth it. That's what you get, that bike's far too big for you."

Bert was a war baby; only Anna wasn't quite sure why that should make him so special, so different and beyond the rest of them. Or maybe it was simply because he was a boy and the eldest child. He appeared mature for his thirteen years. Sometimes he was kind, though, and said things that sounded as if he cared after all.

"'Hope Father isn't going to be too hard on you. You know what he's like, especially when other people get involved. He won't like it." Bert gave her an encouraging smile, "Got to go now, good luck. Mother, I've arranged to meet with Dan, I'll be home before we eat."

He walked out quickly into the hall and then out through the front door, which he slammed shut behind him.

Anna was left alone as Greta also disappeared, following Bert out of the kitchen and into the shop. She'd forgotten to clean the rest of Anna's leg; her socks and skirt were crumpled and dirty. Anna sat down on one of the old wooden, cushioned chairs that were arranged around the large dark-brown dining room table. After meals, when the table was extended, it was reduced back to its smaller size, the middle extension bits folded underneath, and it was covered with a thick, dark red and brown and green flowered tablecloth to hide the scars and the grooves of the top. She held her leg in front of her and bent down over the knee to examine the bandage.

Her father came in, opening the door hard. "I have not got the time now, *geen tijd*, to deal with you," he said. "But you cannot go out. Stay here and I'll talk to you after we've closed the shop later on today. It's busy in there, your mother is needed, there's no one else to help out. Why did you do that? You deserve a beating, *een pak slaag*, but I see you've been punished already." He looked at her knee. Blood began to seep through the bandages. "I'm ashamed of you, you've been disobedient again and what you've done is not right, it's being dishonest. You realise that? On top of that this farmer..." He trailed and did not finish his sentence.

Punishment was severe, although her father did not actually slap her as he sometimes did with the boys when they'd been disobedient or done something that was considered bad. She was grounded, no playing outside after school for a fortnight, no library books, but none of it would make her any different, she knew.

Her little saving box, a green and square tin with coins for books and for small toys or an ice cream in the summer, was emptied to pay for a new bell, but there wasn't really enough to pay for all the damage at the bicycle repair shop. Her father shook his head in dismay, swallowed and checked himself and said, "Hope you've learned your lesson."

14

Twelve-year-old Liesbet glowered at her. "You're such a nuisance, always jealous, why can't you keep your fingers off my things?"

Liesbet was very pretty in her anger. Her large, clear blue eyes were ablaze, her mouth round and red, her brown, curly hair had recently been cut short in preparation for going to secondary school, cycling along with Bert to the next village, some seven kilometres up the main road, and she would need a good and reliable bike to ride back and forth every day, summer and winter.

A few weeks later, when Liesbet's anger had somewhat cooled and she decided to talk to her again, Anna asked about the farmer and his wife. "They know you, you've been to their house," she said.

Liesbet looked around quickly, making sure that no one was there to hear this. "Ssshh," she whispered, putting her right forefinger to her lips. "They don't know I hang out with Letty; she's my best friend. Besides, it's none of your business." You could see she was worried, that she'd said too much to her, the smaller sister. "Letty is going to the same school as I'll go to and so they can't really forbid me to talk to her, can they. It's not our fault we don't go to the same church." She shrugged her shoulders.

A few days later the bandages were removed and Anna carefully, almost lovingly, picked at the thick granular scab that was beginning to form. Fibroblasts would do their work further, and the scab would be replaced by a stronger type collagen in the form of scar tissue. Collagen deposition was important because it increased the strength of the wound, contracting it, stretching the skin, and for it to do its work properly she would have to keep off picking at it, let the tissue repair so that the strength of the wound increased, and with the reduction of

15

activity at the wound site, the angry purple-red appearance would reduce. The scar stayed, however, as a white and thin-line reminder of her impulsiveness and inability to stick to the rules. More would follow, on her arms and her other leg because she remained impulsive and thoughtless for a long time, as Greta said.

*

Neshnafad

I reread what I've written about Anna who in some respects resembles me and my own childhood. Not all of it is true of course. This is fiction after all, and all I want to do is give you an idea of what it was like to be a girl in that confined and claustrophobic environment, where God and father ruled.

I can't help but smile when I remember my own glorious feeling of being master of the road on a bike, those ten minutes of pure enjoyment and my own greed as a child for a new bike, having that summer wind in my hair and racing along a lane all on my own. I haven't changed that much really. I can still feel ecstatic about a new experience, about the sense of freedom when I'm running, swimming or playing tennis in the open air, as if no one can stop me from doing what I want to do.

I'm Katie though and I've done away with the child that resembles Anna and I no longer live in a village similar to that where Anna lived. Anna isn't even me, not really, not all of her. I don't even live in that country anymore. I'm writing a book about Anna because I want to tell what it was really like. I mean, what it was like to live in a place that you have become to hate, but which at the same time has left you with so many cherished memories. How can you hate and love your own childhood so much? How can you hate your parents and also in your own mind make excuses for them because they were as much caught up in it all as their children were? All this God fearing stuff – they didn't know anything different. I can't forgive them though for what they did, but then they always believed that the sins of their fathers and of them would be our own sins. All I'm trying to do is forget it all and live my life differently.

They really believed in all that God and Jesus crap, for example that He sat there high up in the sky just watching them and their children and their family and the rest of the world, as if He would be able to keep track of every one of us, and they put the fear of God into me. I was very afraid as a child of what He might do to me and I was afraid of the burning pain in Hell. My parents, at least my father, couldn't cope with a changing world that encroached on their lives after the War in which they had fought so valiantly against evil, the Germans and the Russians and the Japs and the Communists. They couldn't cope with an ever-increasing number of children who, one after the other rebelled against so many things that they held sacred and which provided their own sense of security as well as their predetermined place in heaven. That's the way it was.

I'll carry on with my notes on Anna, and by doing that I'll discover who she is and then perhaps I'll find out what part of Anna is really me. I'll write about what I know, if that makes sense. I'll use this opportunity of being jobless in Neshnafad and without much else to do, to become a writer. I'm a bit stuck on this new housing estate on a hill outside Neshnafad and I don't really go out very much. I don't like going out on my own in this country, in this town. I'm sure that my life and our life together, Mike's and mine, would have been better if we'd stayed in London, but who knows, I might even like it here in time.

Perhaps I should explain who I am and why I'm here in Iran before I continue with writing about Anna.

Chapter Three: 1970-1976

London

I met Mike in London quite by accident. It wasn't as if friends or fellow students introduced us, or that we met because we were members of the same club or because we had a love for the same sport or we happened to be at a party together. No, the first I knew of Mike was when I heard a man say in a quite posh-sounding English accent, "Excuse me, can I share this table with you? It's pretty full and I won't take long."

I looked up and I saw a man, a student probably, with black hair, dark thick-rimmed glasses, and dressed completely in black; a black jumper, black trousers, a black overcoat and a black scarf and there was even a black woollen hat that stuck out of his coat pocket, stuffed in probably when he entered the warm college cafeteria from outside. It was November and cold. He smiled at me, a tray with food in his hands, and he was about to sit down in the vacant chair opposite me. I looked around. He was right. The place was full and there was not a single free table, people were crowding around looking for seats. I hadn't noticed, I was reading my book, as I usually did during my lunch hour break, when it was either raining or too cold outside to go for a walk. I preferred going for a walk and would then eat my sandwich in the park.

"Of course," I said and pulled my tray away, which I had left on his side of the table, and piled up my cutlery and plate back onto it. I closed my book. "I'm leaving anyway."

"You like Iris Murdoch?" he asked. "I've got some of her books. She's quite amazing. I've also read that one, the Unicorn."

I nodded and half smiled. I felt quite shy all of a sudden and wanted to get away from his eager face and his interest in what I was reading. He was nice looking though and seemed genuine, not someone who was taking the mickey out of me because I was reading Iris Murdoch. Nevertheless I slipped my book into my shoulder bag. His English was impeccable even though he didn't look English, perhaps Greek, Pakistani, Indian or Arab? At the time, I couldn't tell the difference between all the nationalities and faces I came across in London and I felt caught out and shy. He took off his coat and draped it behind him on the chair. There was a white shirt just visible underneath the black polo neck jumper and his jeans and jumper were tight fitting around a slim but solid looking body. He pushed up his jumper and shirtsleeves before he picked up his knife and fork.

"I've got to go," I said. "Back to work I'm afraid."

"Didn't mean to chase you away," he said. "Sit a bit longer. Have a tea. I'll get it for you."

He put down his knife and fork again and got up. He drew me out of my perpetual aloneness in London. He seemed nice enough, I told myself, and he soon returned with tea in the usual plastic white cup, made with a teabag and hot water from a container at the side of the cafeteria. He sat down to eat his food, talking all the time to prevent me from getting up again. I didn't want to be rude.

"I'm Mike," he said. "Actually my name's Mehrdad, it's Iranian, but here in London everyone calls me Mike, and even my own family do, sometimes."

"I'm Katie," I said.

He continued talking in that BBC English accent. "Actually, I don't know that many people in this place. I've only just started my course at my uni. Not this college by the way. I'm here to see a lecturer after lunch, and am still finding my way around. I'm at King's College now; I transferred there after doing my A-levels here in London. Are you a student here? Not so, I think, because you said you had to go back to work."

No, I wasn't. I was working as a secretary to one of the Professors in the Engineering Department. I'd come to England on a work visa; you still needed visas then before England joined the EEC, before it became the EU, even coming from The Netherlands, and initially I worked for a Dutch couple and their small engineering company. I left them though after a couple of months, hating the claustrophobia of the small office they had, hating the commercial environment which was selling machinery, hating the boring techies who needed a secretary to type out all the dull specifications, the letters making offers, the invoices, the ledgers and the tedious telephone calls about different models of equipment, I hadn't the slightest interest in. I hated the nine-till-five existence with only the end of the day to look forward to. So I searched and found the advert for a secretary in this college for one of the Professors and they took me on. My English was very good by then, I'd passed my Cambridge language exams with flying colours and now rarely spoke any Dutch at all. I liked the academic and scientific environment, the professors in their offices and the research students in the labs, and I even liked typing out research reports and taking shorthand letters that were about discoveries. I set up meetings between staff in universities across the world. I was good at it and the Professor didn't seem to mind that I always had a book in my bag, or that I took off to the park at lunchtime to read. He would tease me, saying I should become a student, but how would I manage to live? I could only just about afford the small room in the shared flat, with the shared bathroom and shared kitchen in Willesden.

"You could get a grant," the Professor told me. "You'd have to work for three years to pay your tax here and then you'd be eligible for a mature student grant." He said he would support my application, whatever I'd wanted to study, even if I wanted to study engineering, his subject area. That's how much confidence he had in me.

Mike looked interested when I told him all this. He told me about his studies; he was in his first year as an undergraduate, something in medical biology, and wanted to do a PhD. He had another five years or so ahead of him studying in London. Once he'd finished, he said, he wanted to go back to his native country which was Iran, and perhaps I would like to have dinner sometime, or we could see a film? Did I like films? He was a film buff himself, as well as a lover of classical music and literature and...

"I've got to go now," I said. "I'm late."

"Let's meet tomorrow, here, same time. I can come over again, easily. I like talking to you," he pleaded. "We can perhaps arrange to go and see a film this weekend?"

"Okay," I said, nodding, and moved away. I really wasn't sure what to think or do.

"Wait! Here's my telephone number. This is where I am in the evenings and you can reach me if something comes up." He quickly jotted down his name and a number on a piece of paper he pulled out of his bag.

*

We had lunch together the next day; he just sidled up to my table again and sat down with me as I was eating. We arranged to go out on a Saturday night to see a film he said he desperately wanted to see, Bunuel's Discrete Charm of the Bourgeoisie. I can't say I completely understood that film at the time, because I had to read the sub-titles quickly as my French was not up to the task of following the rapid conversations, and not even the not so rapid ones. I remember that I enjoyed the visuals and the surreal plot with the portrayal of the middle class people who somehow or other missed the point of each other. It was all fairly new to me. My world in the Netherlands had been so very sheltered and removed from much of this kind of worldly imagery, except perhaps for that last year I spent in Amsterdam, but that was a different story and the reason I was in London. I still had a lot of catching up to do and I loved it that Mike took me to see films.

Mike said that it was the second time he saw the film, so perhaps it was not too dumb not to understand all of it immediately. Later we went to a nightclub, where we danced and could barely hear what the other was saying because of the din of the music and people shouting at each other over the blasting noise, but we clung tighter and tighter and it was great to just let go. I deserved a break.

He paid for everything, although I said that we 'should go Dutch'. He just wouldn't have it and I couldn't insist for too long, too awkward somehow. Afterwards, sweaty and breathless, we moved to the back wall, and well let's say that we clung face to face and his tongue came quite deep into my mouth. And I let him.

He said, "Come back with me. Let's get a taxi. I get you back to your flat afterwards or tomorrow morning. In time for work — promise."

So at three o'clock in the middle of the night we crept up the stairs of the house he shared with four other students where they each had their own room. Mike's was at the top of the house.

He fumbled with a condom, but I said, "Don't worry, I'm on the pill."

He looked at me in the dim light of his room and I thought I saw a slight hesitation. He said: "Yes, but you should be careful really. I don't want to get you in trouble."

I giggled. "I don't think so," I said. "Definitely not. I'm on the pill for medical reasons."

I'm not going to give the details of that night, but it was good.

*

That's how we fell in love. Mike was gentle and clever and he read a lot and we talked endlessly about the authors we both liked, and over the following months and years he bought me books, mainly by oversees authors such as Thomas Mann, a Tolstoy and some poetry anthologies.

I told him there wasn't much to say about my family background except that I'd fallen out with my parents. He never really asked further questions, I mean he didn't insist on wanting to know more, not then and not later. He didn't probe, judge or assume. It was as if parents were unimportant and I liked it that way. We went out together, hung out with friends of his, and listened to music played loudly on his gramophone when we were in that room on the top floor of his student house. I had always associated classical music with Calvinism and church, the Bach, the baroque and all the others, even

Mussorgsky and Chopin. In my ignorance I assumed that all classical music was church music, because my father used to play the organ so loudly and insistently, Sunday after Sunday. Bach, Handel, everything I knew was played full blast on church organs and the organ at home, and I associated it with everything forbidden and glorification of something that I didn't want to know about, and associated with a world full of men in power, directed by God.

Mike made me aware of the beauty of the music irrespective of religious beliefs and feelings, and he hummed along with Handel's Water Music and Mussorgsky's Night on a Bare Mountain. He was really good at imitating conductors, turning up the music loud and waving his arms, clutching a ruler in one hand and then he'd bow to me at the end of his performance. The more I listened with him, the more I began to appreciate the music for its evocation of beauty and people, not just men, and when he took me to classical concerts, I began to recognise the different pieces and relished the calming effect they had on me. They still do.

Over the next months and year he told me about himself, his family and his two younger sisters. He told me about his mother, Parry, whom you could tell he admired deeply, although she really was overprotective and absurdly proud of who they were and who her husband was. Mike said that Parry would have a fit if she knew her only son was serious about a girl who was not Iranian, let alone approved by her or his father Sharrokh. It would be hard to make Parry agree that he had a girlfriend who was neither Iranian nor from the minority religious tradition of the family, and Parry would try hard to prevent it from going any further.

Later, after we'd moved in together in London, he said. "You see I don't want to hurt them, I would want them to accept you for who you are, a wonderful person, the girl I'm in love with, because I am in love with you! And I want them to realise that you are the woman I want to live with for the rest of my life."

He never talked about former girlfriends, and to begin with I was shy to ask. After all, I wasn't exactly forthcoming about my own past and then it no longer seemed to matter. I listened to him talking about his love of his study area, the medical biology course but that he veered more towards microbiology, and his interest in literature. We talked about what was going on in the world, the Paris insurrection, student rights, political justness, freedom of the press, liberation from oppression. Don't forget that this was the early seventies, and after all the mayhem of the sixties in England, the truth was that a lot of the liberties that we later associated with that decade were only introduced in the seventies. I was on the pill, and it only became really easy to get it in the seventies, let's be honest. And then we had the endless strikes of course, with an economic crisis following in '73, just when I was about to start my undergraduate life as a student and Mike embarked on his PhD.

All I want to make clear is that Mike seemed interested in just about anything you could think of going on in the world, and also that he was very discreet about probing into my background. I did not want to think about my own situation too much, where I'd come from or who I was. Although I had twitches of doubt about whether our relationship would work, I just pushed these thoughts away. I've never been one to think very far ahead into the future. I worried about his parents though and what they would say, or how they would react if they never got to meet my family. Would they understand that there was no compromise possible? That my parents would simply refuse to meet them? I'd already lost all contact with my parents by then and my father didn't want to know about me any longer, and my mother would not go against my father, so that was that.

Mike talked a lot about his own father, Sharrokh. He was very proud of him, an American trained specialist in internal medicine who had a private practice in Tehran. Mike implied that he worked very hard to provide the best for his family and that he was generous. Sharrokh was well versed in Iranian literature, and Mike said he'd inherited his own love of books and literature from him. Sharrokh could afford to send his son to a university abroad, pay the fees and would probably come to visit his son in England sooner or later. Even though he'd wanted Mike to go to the States for his studies, Mike had wanted to go to London and had set his eyes on University College to do his PhD. His father, in fact, came from a poor background, but a distant relative had helped with the fees for Sharrokh to go to America to study and at the time there had been a special government grant. Sharrokh had worked himself up from someone who was 'a nobody' as a child to becoming a wealthy professional with a significant standing in the medical world.

About his sisters, he said that they expected that someone would ask for their hand back in Tehran; there were plenty of suitors. However, the older of the two sisters, Taraneh, had already announced that she would not marry because she wanted to become a doctor like her father, and did not want to be hampered by a husband who might object to his wife being cleverer than him. Sharrokh had laughed, but Mike knew that he was really very proud of Taraneh, and that he would have liked it if Mike had gone into medicine. His younger sister, Susan, would probably marry soon, that was what she wanted. She refused to go abroad to study, even though she regularly travelled to see relatives in America and in England.

I wondered about such expectations, how simplistic all that sounded. Mike would talk a lot about his relatives, his aunts and uncles, most of whom lived in Tehran, but there were also others who lived in London, in New York and even in France somewhere. He said he wanted me to meet his cousins, but unfortunately none of them were in England at the time, although his cousin Parvaneh would soon come to London to start medical school, followed a year later by his own sister. He insisted that all of these cousins and relatives would like me, and that I would like them.

He didn't tell me all this at once, of course. But this is how I was introduced to his family those first few years in London. He would make comments and observations after he'd been on one of his lengthy telephone calls to his parents, once a month. It wasn't easy to ring Tehran at the time, and often the line would go funny he said and then a coherent conversation was not possible, but he always related to me the goings on of his family in Tehran, however brief the conversation had been.

Once or twice, he asked me about my siblings, about my childhood, what it was like to grow up in Holland, where I went to school and what had made me come to England. I always said it was unimportant and that my background was uninteresting.

"My parents are very religious and I couldn't stomach it any longer," I said and then added, "I should've married someone that they approved of, it was already happening and they were happy with the religious boyfriend I had. I walked away however, because I would have been stuck for the rest of my life with no exit. I would have had rows and rows of kids, no using contraception, and then ..." I laughed and tried to make a joke of it. I combed my hair back from my forehead with my fingers, picked up the plates from the table and avoided eye contact with Mike by carrying the dirty dishes to the sink in the kitchen.

"You see, I hurt Paul, that was my boyfriend's name, by walking away. It probably sounds ludicrous to you but I decided that I wouldn't go to Hell if I never went to church again. At the time that was quite a conclusion to come to, I'd been brainwashed so badly in believing that Hell was just waiting round the corner for me. And to walk away from the church I had to walk away from Paul, they were linked in my mind. That was difficult for me at the time."

I didn't tell him about what happened exactly, about who I really am and how I ended up in England. I was afraid of the consequences. He might have thought again and I was in love with him. It was too difficult to explain my temporary madness and so I spun my story — how I decided to leave home because of religious disagreements and my parents' anger, or rather my father's anger at my disobeying his orders. The fact was that they only heard later from one of my brothers that I lived in England.

"You don't know what you're talking about," Johannes, my father, said when I announced that I was leaving home and the village and also the church. He implied that I would go to Hell when I died; he was a frightened man, unless I admitted my sins and asked forgiveness. It's not exactly what he said, but something like it. He contacted the church elders and the vicar to talk to me, and I just sat in stubborn silence.

I told Mike that when my father realised that I wouldn't give in, and that I wouldn't marry the boyfriend they all approved of, that I refused to be part of the church, and worse, that I had taken a job in Amsterdam with a large international company as a junior secretary and that I could just about afford to pay the rent for a small room, and that I would not want to come home every weekend and definitely would no longer attend church, he went white and said that I needn't come back to my parent's house ever again. As a matter of fact, my father said all that much later. Initially, I think he hoped that I would come round and see the waywardness of my behaviour. I think he hoped that if he allowed me to live in Amsterdam and he made sure that church elders there were aware of my existence, I would 'come to my senses.' Explaining it my way helped to shorten the story for Mike, however. I did not want to give him all the details.

Mike shook his head in disbelief but he liked my professed atheism, I think, as he then confessed to his own anti-religiosity, even if his family would not accept this but quietly let him be until he would see sense.

When I look back at those first few years in England with Mike, I'm still surprised at my own audacity. I never doubted my self-worth and it was only later that I realised why his parents were so set against me to begin with. It was not so much that my family were religious or that I had broken off contact with them; no the real problem for them, especially for Parry, was that I came from a much poorer background and they shivered at what Mike told them. Parry would undoubtedly have been furious that after all the hard work they had put in, building a solid middle class background for their children, that their first and only son would then not take advantage of that by marrying into another wealthy family, one of their own caste. Especially now that I know Parry better I realise that I was a very hard story to swallow for her.

Mike said he didn't care about my family, however strange they were, and that he wanted to be with me, not my family. Surely they would meet with him when I insisted? I think we both felt that it would perhaps be less complicated if we had to deal with his family only, once we'd decided that we wanted to stay together. We'd moved into a flat in Hammersmith by then.

*

The Hammersmith flat had a small bedroom off a sitting room, a kitchenette and a bathroom. The bedroom had an old double bed, more like a large single, Mike said, when we tried it out. But we agreed that it would be cosy, and there was also a large old-fashioned wardrobe with creaking doors that you had to slam shut. Sometimes in the middle of the night, it would fall open again, first slowly and quietly and then with a rattle and a bang.

In the sitting room, there was just about enough space for a grey-green sofa that sagged in the middle and which had lumpy cushions alongside a small bookcase and a chest of drawers. The tiny kitchen, without a door, was off the landing and the kitchen and landing walls were yellowing, some of the paint peeling badly; there was a dirty electric oven with years of neglect engrained into the walls and bottom and racks and a gas stove on top of it. The pink bath had a plastic shower unit attached to the cold and hot water taps and the bath curtains had a wide, brown border along the bottom edge.

On the ground floor of the house lived a single girl, the agent said, when he showed us around. We only came across her once or twice when we lived there. She was always out and worked during the day. The landlord lived a few streets away, but we had little to do with him. The agent said that if we wanted the place we would need to sign for the inventory and he advised us to note down all the visible shortcomings so we wouldn't be held liable when we moved out. There was a three-month notice period and we needed to pay a month's deposit up front.

We didn't have enough money even after we'd pooled our resources, so Mike telephoned his father for some extra cash. It certainly was nice that he had a father who helped out even though Mike didn't tell him at the time that the money was intended for a flat for the two of us.

I had scant possessions, as I had not brought much with me from Holland except for some clothes and a few books. I had truly started from scratch once I arrived in England. Mike lined his study books on the small bookshelf in our sitting room. The rest of our paperback novels and poetry went onto the bottom shelf and on a pile on the floor, in the corner.

"This'll do just fine," Mike said. "We can look around for a better place now that we've got a base. I'll be doing most of my studying in the College library anyway, or I may go to the British Museum library, I'm quite used to that." And in those first few years we spent together I was out during the day anyway, working.

*

We moved a few times across London, finding roomier or more economical flats, in Gloucester Road and then in Willesden. At the end of our first year of living together, in the summer of '72 Mike travelled back to Tehran, to attend his younger sister Susan's wedding.

"I'm expected to visit them once a year anyway and I'll have to prepare them for you, for us," he said. "I can't just show up with you. We'd have a bad time. They have their own ideas about who I should marry and why."

When he'd gone from Heathrow, I came back to the flat alone and threw myself on the bed and howled in my pillow with an unbearable emptiness inside me. I was suddenly alone again after a year of living with Mike, and I wondered, this man that I'd fallen in love with, who he actually was. Perhaps he cared more for his family than for me and would tell me it was all over when he came back.

He'd talk to them on the phone almost every week, in a language I didn't understand, although he never excluded me and he always gave an account of what they talked about, what his sisters were up to, weddings his parents had been to, but sometimes these tales seemed to become more constrained. There were times he was reluctant to give me details and he'd try to distract me.

"I've told them about you, not exactly about us living together, but I think they realise," he'd say. "They're not very happy, but they'll get used to it."

I knew it was important for him that they gave way about me. He would never walk away from them in order to be with me. He needed a compromise, and I was the last person who knew how to go about that. I hadn't yet outgrown the black or white of Calvinism.

Once he actually said, "They've found a girl they want me to marry."

I stared at him with my mouth open. What would he do? Was that going to be the end of us, is that what he was trying to tell me? I didn't want to be alone again.

"Don't look so worried," he said. "If I ever get married I won't marry anyone but you. We're made for each other. If necessary, I'll simply stay in London after I finish my PhD, find a job here and then they'll have to get used to you or simply throw me out. And they won't do that, they couldn't." So perhaps he wasn't willing to compromise forever. Perhaps I needn't be so worried.

I knew that he missed his country and his extended family and his former life in Iran, however much he enjoyed living in London and however much he liked his studies and his friends.

He made a lot of friends during those years in London, and especially to begin with, he had many more friends than I had. But I caught up.

He and his friends seemed to come together like bees to a pot of honey from all over the world, meeting up in someone's flat or over a cup of coffee in campus cafeterias. They were all foreign students, or students who had a non-English parent or two non-English parents and who lived in London for some reason or other. Unlike my own friends who were mainly English, although I had an Australian friend and a Scottish friend once I went to University.

Mike's friends came from all over the world. There was Aristo who was Greek and studied social anthropology at King's College, there was Raoul who was from Bolivia and studied engineering, there were fellow students on his course who came from South America, Asia, Iraq and Iran, and who had parents who could afford to pay the fees so that their offspring received what they considered to be the best education possible. Some of these friends came from seriously wealthy backgrounds, and I was amazed at their casual approach to money. Sometimes I felt quite unequal but no one seemed to notice much. Of course, some of Mike's friends were English nationals, but they all had some kind of link abroad, with one of the parents being Spanish or German or South African.

As I said, it took me a while to see how genuinely matter-of-fact Mike was about all this. He introduced me to his friends quite casually, over a coffee, or a meal out, or when someone threw a Saturday night party when they would gather and bring their bottles of cheap wine and beer, eating French bread, cheese and celery sticks, smoking Gauloises that made me cough and brought tears to my eyes, but I persevered and pretended to abhor the peppermint cigarettes that appeared to be the only acceptable alternatives.

Sometimes at these parties, I was quite tipsy but Mike appeared to find this amusing, especially when I philosophised about what we would do and how we would never get married but would live happily ever after, wherever we would end up. I'd be quite argumentative about the right of women to decide whether or not they would want babies, or whether they wanted a career, or perhaps even wanted to have both. I would quote Simone de Beauvoir about what and who women are, although I admit that I had some difficulty reading the whole of her book, The Second Sex, but I'd underline a few things that seemed to express everything constantly mulling around in my mind.

"*I am awfully greedy,*" I once declaimed loudly and drunkenly, reading from my little notebook that I had started to carry around in my handbag. "*I want everything from life. I want to be a woman and to be a man, to have many friends and to have loneliness, to work much and write good books, to travel and enjoy myself, to be selfish and to be unselfish…*" I continued, "*You see, it's difficult to get all that I want. And then when I don't succeed I get mad with anger.*"

Mike would pull me over to him and once or twice we ended up at Trafalgar Square where we'd sit down on the steps in the middle of the night and there we would kiss and watch the world go by.

"You shall have it all," he'd say. "Everything you want." We giggled a lot and made comments about the people roaming about so late into the night, the drunkards and noisy groups of young people.

At the end of the summer we'd go the Albert Hall and queue for cheap Proms tickets. We'd be part of the crowd swinging sideways in front of the orchestra, clapping and stamping our feet in appreciation. Mike loved to sink into Mahler's misery and complaints, but always with a happy and intense face as if he was listening to party music, and we'd love the dark mysteriousness of Mussorgsky's 'Night on Bald Mountain.' We'd sing along 'God save the Queen' with the rest of the crowd, although neither of us, nor most of our friends for that matter, felt much allegiance to either this English queen or her country.

Once, Mike bought tickets for a Karajan concert when he conducted in the Royal Festival Hall. Mike was, in fact still is actually, in awe of this conductor, the tall grey slightly stooped figure that we could barely see because our seats were so far back. When we returned to the flat later that night Mike stood in front of me humming loudly, gesturing that I should sit on the edge of the bed, and he imitated Karajan by gently moving his arms up and down on the beat of the music until we collapsed with laughter and excitement and he pushed me back on the bed, where we stripped each other naked, Mike still humming away.

Increasingly I began to think of London as my home, as the place where I wanted to live my life because I felt comfortable. In London, I could be oblivious to what other people might think of me. As far as I was concerned, there were no gods or devils hiding behind trees, trying to trip me and to make me feel bad, nor were they hovering across my dreams during the night.

It was clear to me though that Mike retained a certain reserve about living in London. He had a longing for all the things he couldn't have there, the easy family relationships, a get-together on a Friday in a relative's garden in Tehran, the home cooked Persian food, the kebabs and the saffron rice, the stews and the dishes prepared for Nou-Ruz, their New Year celebrations. He'd talk about this and about his suspicion that he would always be an outsider, and that the English would always consider him a foreigner because of his looks, he was too dark skinned. Mind, this was the time of Enoch Powell and all that dreary racism, and Mike clearly felt that he did not need to accept the infrequent taunts or put-downs that he encountered.

As I listened to him, I realised he suffered from homesickness, but I tried to fight it. I tried to laugh some of his worries away because I wanted them to go away. I wanted to be with him in London and I didn't really want to share him with a country and people that might be hostile to me and to where I came from. Wasn't London neutral territory for both of us?

"You'd miss the concerts, the films, your friends, wouldn't you?" I asked.

"Of course I would. And I'm not saying that I definitely want to go back. It's another four years or so before I'll have to make up my mind. It'll also depend on getting a job and what I'll be able to do there. And if you definitely wouldn't want to…"

You see, he hesitated and then he added. "Well, I don't think I could live anywhere near my parents anyway; that wouldn't work. We'd have to live somewhere outside Tehran. Now there's a new university in a town further south, Neshnafad…"

We did not talk this way very often. We pushed it back and let it simmer, this huge monstrous decision we had to take some time in the future. We were too busy with our day to day lives, Mike with his studies and keeping up with the lectures, working in the lab, socialising with his fellow students, wanting to achieve that first class degree, or minimally an upper second. And for the first two years of our life together, I worked and would leave the flat early in the morning, catch the Tube, and come back at the end of the day, either to the flat or we'd meet somewhere in town or with friends.

I was also determined to make the most of my time, and I joined a couple of evening classes in English literature and philosophy. I was greedy for books, words, thoughts, ideas, films, and discussions. I read and listened and read some more, translations of German and French books, Herman Hesse, more of Simone de Beauvoir; I read Tolstoy and Dostoyevsky and read them again and I felt sad for Ana Karenina, the tragedy and loss, and would wait year on year for another Iris Murdoch to be published, so that I'd be one of the first to pick up the paperback version in a bookshop. I wanted to make use of this opportunity to do what my parents would never allow me to do, go to University. After three years of working I managed to do just that and enrolled in an English Literature undergraduate course at King's College.

Once or twice, I dropped the name of one of my siblings in conversation, when telling Mike selected bits of my childhood, always carefully censoring, shrugging off his questions; he never probed too deep. We loved each other in the present and neither of us thought it was important to hark back to the past. We'd lived such different lives anyway and we had so much in common that it didn't matter to us.

*

The summer that Mike visited his family in Tehran, I went on holiday with my friend Tessa and we drove from England, across France, all the way to Spain. Tessa's parents were well off, with a large farm in Northamptonshire, and her father had bought her a small mini. We took it in turn to drive.

Tessa and I became friends when she worked temporarily at the same college I worked in, before she joined a posh legal firm as a secretary, and we stayed in touch. Usually we met up together, without boyfriends, for lunch or to go shopping. She was clever and determined to earn her way and be independent from her parents, however much they tried to keep an eye on her. She had an actor boyfriend, who lived with her but who also seemed to live a separate life from Tessa's and who'd often be away for performances in the country. I only met him once or twice at a party and a Sunday lunch. Tessa invited me to the big farm in Northamptonshire where she grew up. Her parents were welcoming if somewhat remote in my eyes, and Tessa's younger sister was the only sibling that still lived at home. I never met her brother or older sister. Tessa still had her own bedroom in that mansion, large and sprawling, with an old fashioned record player, toys in boxes at the back of a cupboard, a desk and even an old black and white television. Photos in frames on a bedside table, on the wall and in drawers, provided memories of the kind of happy and protected childhood that I envied.

"I know I'm really, really lucky," Tessa said, grinning, when she showed me the house and her room, pushing her long, thick blond hair behind her ears. Her face was set in a constant smile, mischievous and daring, as if she was always trying to engage people in a world that only knew of fun and secrets that she could tell them. I loved Tessa with her bubbly self-assurance, and she was fond of me.

I only realised later we actually looked a little like each other as well. At the time, I had also let my hair grow to shoulder length, we were both tall and slim and although Tessa's hair was a light blonde and mine was closer to being light brown, plus the colour of her eyes was a sharp blue whereas mine were closer to grey, nevertheless there was a similarly that others noticed. Mike commented on it and said I had befriended my non-identical twin sister even though Tessa is a year older than I am.

That summer, when Mike was away, Tessa and I took the ferry to Calais in France and drove in her Mini, past Paris and down to Spain, where friends of Tessa's parents had a house on the coast just outside Altea. The elderly couple were spending part of the summer in England with their children's families, escaping the August heat. For one month their house would be empty and they offered it to Tessa and me, to housesit during the time they were away. A maid lived nearby and she would give us the keys when we arrived and also keep the house clean.

"I need to get away," Tessa said, when she telephoned me a few days after Mike announced that he would visit his family, alone. "I don't suppose you can bear to be separated from your other half, can you?"

Tessa had quarrelled with her boyfriend, she said, and she wanted to have her holidays away from him but didn't want to be alone.

"He seems to believe that it's perfectly alright to go out with other girls and once or twice I've caught him out," is all Tessa would say over the phone. "I need some time to think and I want to do that when he's not around. Also, I need your advice."

She sounded dejected and angry when we met over spaghetti in one of the many Italian places that had mushroomed everywhere across London. She'd lost the smile on her face, and there was tiredness around the puffy eyes.

"Well, that makes two of us then," I said. "I'm not too sure I'm happy that Mike feels he needs to get his parent's permission to live with me."

I knew I was being unfair to Mike, but I grabbed at the opportunity to give vent to my unhappiness. Tessa wouldn't take it the wrong way and would never mention it to Mike, I was sure. We took it out on the Mini during the first day of driving and pressed it into ever more performance along the way and we slept in a small motel just outside Bourges, exhausted but glad we'd come that far. After a quick meal in the motel cafeteria, we fell asleep without talking much.

When we crossed the border into Spain the next day, the little Mini nearly gave up the ghost, spluttering once or twice and reducing speed, whilst the water gauge moved dangerously close towards the red. It had become very hot and we decided to give the car a rest and to let it cool down during the midday heat. We parked at the side of the road in a small, deserted picnic area with a wooden table, a broken bench and beyond that some woodland, which also appeared to be deserted. There were few cars on the road during the heat of the day. We sat down on a blanket that we spread out on the dry twigs and hard soil. We took out the bread and cheese we'd bought in the morning and that we kept in a large cooler box in the boot of the car, and also some water and fruit.

Tessa threw some paper plates, plastic knives and forks and a box of salad on the blanket and said, "I'm so glad you've come with me, Katie. Things aren't so good. I'm devastated really. I never thought Jim would let me down and would play me along, the way he has. What is it with us girls, or rather what is it with the boys? Free love and all that! Jim wants the world, me and my house for his convenience, but also wants his freedom. He's not very successful you know, he can't get the parts and half the time he doesn't even earn enough for his keep, let alone contribute to the house."

I knew that Jim, so far, had only managed to secure some bit parts with regional theatre companies, but not enough to live on and he'd moved in with Tessa for the times he spent in

London, in Tessa's small starter home that again was subsidised by her parents. On her own salary, Tessa couldn't afford her lifestyle. Her parents weren't keen that Tessa had moved to London, but once they realised that their daughter had made up her mind they tried to support her financially wherever they could, and Tessa was happy to accept their help. She would not accept their advice on any of her personal affairs though, and so when Jim moved in with her, her parents could only watch and shake their heads, presumably hoping it would all end well. Jim was dark and handsome, slightly shorter than Tessa but with a self-confident stride and a heavy voice that made people oblivious to his somewhat diminutive stature. I could see how Tessa was attracted to him. He was charming and handsome, full of life, and matched Tessa's usual cheerfulness, two people constantly in a bubble and laughing at the rest of the world.

As I watched Tessa unpack some of the bread, ham, tomatoes and fruit, I saw her unhappiness; her eyes were dull and her face withdrawn. She sighed and then I saw the tears and I understood.

"Oh no, you're not," I said. 'You're not, surely!"

"Yes, I'm afraid I am. I'm pregnant. I've got to decide whether I have an abortion or whether I keep it."

She suddenly cried out loud, drowning the sound of the crickets further back in the woods, and it was as if even the leaves started to shiver with her despair, in a sudden and very slight breeze that came from across the other side of the road.

"But you're on the pill. You didn't come off it, did you?"

"Forgot. Forgot one weekend and didn't think it would matter. How stupid can you get? And how unlucky."

She screamed again, a loud 'aaahh …' trumpeting into the empty road stretching out all the way into Spain and then echoing backwards into France.

I wondered whether to tell her about Anna, but coward that I was and am, I didn't. It wouldn't have made any difference to her decision anyway.

*

When we returned from Spain just a week later, Jim had moved out of Tessa's house and Tessa had an immediate abortion. I spent the rest of my three weeks holidays with her, helped her organise and cooked for her and held her when the day after the abortion she suddenly cried and screamed and shouted and then, exhausted, went back to bed.

The Monday after Tessa returned to work, she telephoned her parents to say that, yes, we'd returned from Spain and had a lovely time. We'd left the friend's house much earlier than planned but that was so that we could travel around a bit, see some more of Spain. She told them that we'd been to Madrid and stayed in a cheap hotel and went to the Prado, that we saw the Goya's and the Velasquez and she would tell them all about it when they saw each other next. Yes, she said, Katie was fine too and was in fact staying with her for a couple of days because Mike was not back yet. She would come and visit them as soon as she had a free weekend.

When Mike returned from Tehran he said, "I've convinced my parents, I think. They know I'm serious and that I won't marry any of the girls they conjure up."

"And?"

"My father will be in London for a medical conference in November and my mother will join him. You will meet them," he said, as if that settled it.

"Tessa's had an abortion," I said. "Jim was cheating on her. As you know, I went with her to Spain; she needed someone to talk to."

"You're kidding," he said. He was shocked. He raised his eyebrows high and he stopped what he was doing. "Why would she do that? That really is taking it a bit far. Couldn't they have made up? How can she terminate a life, just like that? She and Jim have been together for years."

He shook his head and looked worried, but he was still too full of his own stories, of his Tehran adventures and of his homecoming. He didn't really wait for my answer or further explanation, and we never again talked about Tessa's abortion and what he thought about it. When we met up with Tessa a few weeks later we didn't mention it and Mike acted as if he didn't know anything. The abortion was Tessa's and my secret, and after that even when we were together we didn't talk about it anymore.

"My sister Tara told my parents she had a secret lover," Mike said. "They were horrified and actually believed her at first. It just seemed strange as she's always maintained she doesn't want to get married and wants to focus on becoming a doctor. However, she is full of these sorts of pranks. She subsequently denied it all, but I'm not too sure. There was something going on, they wouldn't let me in on it. Maybe that's our luck. They really have their hands full at the moment, they now worry about Tara and she's a girl, a daughter…"

When Mike had mentioned Tara's remark to Parvaneh, who is a close friend of Tara's as well as being their cousin, Parvaneh just laughed and had said that if Tara wanted to tell him what she was getting up to then she would, and that she, Parvaneh, wasn't going to tell tales.

"So, to be honest, I've no idea what's going on. Still don't. Anyway, everyone was too pre-occupied with Susan's wedding, which took up two full days. The preparations they go through…"

He showed me photo's of the wedding which appeared to have been a very sumptuous affair, with women in evening gowns, men in evening suits and white shirts, children in party dresses and outfits, long tables piled up with food and servants with trays full of drinks. "Mainly non-alcoholic," Mike said. Susan looked very pretty in a sumptuous white wedding dress; she is petite and dark haired.

He was full of news about Iran, about the way the country was picking up, how different everything was from when he'd left, even if that was less than four years ago.

"The oil income is making a lot of people very rich and Tehran is becoming a very mixed up place," he said. "There is a strong urbanisation and the gap between the rich and the poor is becoming more like a chasm. There are some fantastic places, you know, up in the north of Tehran, really beyond belief. I've seen them. We drove past some of those gated houses when we went to my uncle's garden in the north. My uncle's family often spend their Fridays there, inviting close relatives who live in Tehran, and they have a servant who lives in this garden with his family. In a separate building of course," he chuckled, before continuing. "I can't imagine my mother and the *xales*, the aunts, staying in the same place as a servant, when they visit."

He stopped for a moment and sipped from the mug of coffee I put in front of him. "In the south of Tehran it's quite different. People there are poverty stricken, most of them. They've come from the countryside outside of Tehran in the hope that there's work for them in the capital, but there rarely is, not the kind of work they can do. They live from hand to mouth, large families in one small hovel," he said. "There is a lot of inequality there." He frowned. "Whatever, Iran will be a country full of opportunity, and perhaps I can help make it better. I've decided that I want us to go back there when I've finished my PhD and make use of these opportunities. There will be plenty to do for the likes of us, for me especially, as a western educated scientist."

He looked at me and must have noticed my sharp intake of breath and he continued before I could say anything. "Really, now that the Shah is so clearly in favour of liberating women, forcing open all kinds of opportunities for them, it'll be a good place to live, even for western women. Yes, there are rumours and there is mullah opposition to this modernisation drive, but nothing can stop a country that can afford to modernise in the way Persia, or rather Iran, can. The oil will help, now that at long last the British have given up their stranglehold and America is friendly towards the Shah and the country. There will be lots of opportunities and we would have a really good life there."

I listened, but it all seemed so far away, this Iran and its factions and religious discontent with a monarch who was driven to modernise a backward country and who wasn't liked by the poor and the mullahs. I was far too busy building up a strong and interesting life right there in London with Mike and with friends at work and later with my fellow students. I wanted to achieve something in my life before I would even remotely begin to think of living somewhere else. What I really wanted was to feel at home somewhere.

"I don't want to get married in a hurry," I said. "In fact, I'm quite happy as we are. Why do we want to go through all that? I want to get my degree and who knows what will open up for me here."

"Of course," he said. "That's fine for now. We have a few more years to go anyway. I also have to finish my PhD before I can make definite plans."

*

45

In November I met Mike's father, who was kind and friendly to me. "Yes, yes," he said, looking me up and down. "It's very nice to meet you. Are you all right? How are you?"

I wondered if he thought I had been ill, but then I realised that he was just saying what first came into his head, without much rationality, and that this was his way of being polite. He was just as shy and uneasy as I was.

Mike's father took us out for lunch a few times to a Persian restaurant in Kensington, where the owner and he talked very animatedly with each other, in Farsi.

"Are you alright Dad?" Mike asked when we sat down. "Is it not too lonely being in your flat, on your own here in London? Or are you meeting fellow medical men? You can always stay with us if you'd like. When's Mummy coming?"

I kicked him under the table.

"Oh I'm fine. I can look after myself, I am used to it. And yes, I am busy as well as on holiday." He smiled as he looked around him at the décor, the miniatures on the wall, the photos of Iranian singers and of Iranian dishes and dancers and musicians. "I like eating here. Our flat is not so far from here, as you know."

He said to me, "I'll order for you too. We must have kebabs, and polo, that's rice, and perhaps you would like to drink some dough?"

"That's buttermilk, kind of," Mike mouthed. "Just eat what he orders," he said out loud. "The food here is very good. Look at the menu."

The pictures showed the dolmens in their wrappings, the kebabs on skewers and the cutlets. There was the basmati rice, and the other rice dishes, the havij polo and the baghali polo, with chicken, and the sabzi polo mahi with fish and the lubia polo with spring beans.

46

"Mehrdad's mother will cook all those," Sharrokh said. "Now we will have kebab and plain rice."

"He calls you Mehrdad?" I whispered to Mike. "How confusing our names are."

Two weeks later, Mike's mother, Parry, arrived in London, and we were again summoned to the same restaurant to meet with her. She was much more forthright and watched me carefully, her eyes half closed as if she was ready to pounce the moment she discovered a fatal shortcoming or weakness. She opened her mouth once or twice to say something but then she quickly checked herself, and turned away to search for her handbag. When she found it right next to her, she took out a small mirror to check her lips, searched around some more until she found a lipstick and proceeded to apply it, a hard red colour that set off her pitch-black hair. I was sure it was dyed. She was at least ten years younger than Sharrokh, I realised then. She had a beautiful skin and looked much younger than the fifty-four years or so she was. She wore an expensive looking black and red long-sleeved dress, tight fitting, although she wasn't at all slim, and with matching red shoes and a black leather handbag. I felt quite underdressed and plain next to her in my Laura Ashley best dress and non-matching brown handbag. However, the new Vidal Sassoon shop had just cut my hair and I looked good in the bob.

Later, I noticed that Parry often tied a colourful scarf around her head to protect her thick and glossy black hair, immaculately coiffed, from the English drizzle, sleet and wind that was a perpetual feature that winter. She grumbled about the chilliness of London, and about the cold apartment her husband had invested in and where they stayed.

"Why don't you move into our flat?" She asked Mike one day when they visited us. "It's not very large, only one bedroom, but it's in a much better area than where you live." She looked around as if she suddenly discovered herself in some unpleasant and very distasteful back street hovel. Parry's English was heavily accented which emphasised her disdain, a curt and final judgement on the state in which she had found her son. She disapproved.

"Because there is always someone staying there in your flat," Mike said. "If not you and Daddy then there'll be an aunt or a cousin or another distant relative. They all come and go, and if I live there with Katie we'll be expected to host everyone. At least no one expects me to put them up in our current flat."

I was aware of Mike's rather clever ploy to choose to live with me in some less-than-snooty apartment so no one would come to stay, and I laughed, but then had to pull my face back into straight mode when Mike's mother looked up sharply. She made no further comment though.

"Anyway," Mike said, "We'll only move if we can find something bigger and cheaper, and that is unlikely to happen."

"Maybe we'll buy something bigger then," his father suddenly said. "We'll sell our apartment. We'll buy a house. It would be good if you were living somewhere so Tara can live with you when she comes to London to study."

I surreptitiously shook my head at Mike, but there wasn't much either of us could do to thwart this plan. I didn't particularly want to be living with Mike's extended family, even though I hadn't met his sister at the time and she sounded perfectly all right. I was worried about his mother's attitude to me, and how that might extend to other members of the family. We consoled ourselves with the thought that it would be some time before his father would be able to sell the flat and then buy a house that was just right, somewhere in London. It might be better if Taraneh stayed in student accommodation or with an aunt who lived in London.

At the end of their stay, Mike's mother thawed out a bit and even exchanged pleasantries with me. I carefully worked my way around her when they visited. I cooked dinners even though I was often tired at the end of the day, and the trail back home on the Tube and the winter darkness were getting at me. I fought off the depressive suspicion that this was all somehow inevitable. I was caught, after all, in a kind of spiral of domestic inanities and polite family relationships that didn't mean much to me. I was just glad that we could keep a distance simply because we lived in separate parts of London, but Mike was on red alert every time the telephone rang, and even when it didn't ring he seemed to expect the inevitable call to come over for dinner, to spend the Saturday shopping in the West End, to take his mother to a doctor or dentist, to find out where she could best buy presents for an uncle who liked specific trinkets, or a distant cousin who wanted a particular set of crystal glasses.

I couldn't get used to the demands this family made on Mike and therefore on me. Their closeness and their irritations with each other, their expectations of total dedication, their possessiveness, all of it required accommodation and compromise. I hadn't bargained for any of this when I fell in love with Mike and when we moved in together.

Parry insisted on a *'real English Christmas now we're in England'* and so we bought a turkey, took our small foldable kitchen table into the sitting room, and rather than spending the time with friends as we'd planned, we decorated a small Christmas tree and bought presents, wrapped them and went through all of the jolly festivities. Mike's mother didn't actually understand that I'd never before celebrated Christmas in the way the English did, and that this was all a new ritual for me as well.

"The Dutch celebrate St. Nicholas," I explained, "And that is on the fifth of December, not on the twenty-fifth of December. St Nicholas is really for children. He's a good man who has a black servant who will chastise naughty children. The Dutch don't eat turkey for Christmas, at least not many do. In fact my family always celebrated Christmas as a very religious event, nothing to do with presents. We went to church, usually twice on Christmas Day and then again on Boxing Day which in Holland was called the second Christmas Day." I realised that Parry didn't understand what I was talking about and so I let it go and concluded that I was happy to help prepare a Christmas meal for them.

I did my best to find a recipe for the turkey and got up early to put it in the oven but I forgot to take out the little plastic bag with giblets, which I only found when I poked a spoon inside after it had been cooking for hours and Mike had proudly placed it on a board in the middle of the table. He realised what had happened and I secretly discarded the plastic greasy blob when Mike diverted attention to the television, which was on in the corner of the room with some kind of comedy programme followed by a broadcast of the Queen's speech, because Parry wanted to hear it. Mike cooked all the trimmings and the vegetables, he made a starter and a dessert, and between the two of us we drank a bottle and a half of wine. Sharrokh only sipped from a small glass, half full and Parry only drank water. They spoke Farsi most of the time and I felt like an intruder in my own house.

New Year's Eve was spent in front of the television and afterwards I told Mike that I never ever wanted to do that again, and that next year if his parents wanted to visit over

Christmas and the New Year I was going to stay with Tessa or another friend and Mike could take care of his parents all by himself.

Tessa gave me all the details of her New Year's Eve party that lasted till early morning and they all had a jolly good time. Of course, we'd been invited and Tessa was very disappointed that we were not able to come to the festivities.

When Mike's parents left for Tehran in the middle of January, I sighed with relief when quietness descended again and it soon seemed as if it had all been a dream. Mike proclaimed that his mother actually liked me, she'd told him so, but I wasn't at all sure and wondered whether he was trying to make me feel better.

"Your father probably likes me. He's nice and doesn't comment on anything we do or how we do it, except for the fact that he was horrified one night when I couldn't just give him ten pounds for a taxi because I never have more than five pounds in my wallet." I laughed at the memory of his face, shaking his head when I said I couldn't give him a tenner. "He was really surprised that we, or I, didn't have a great pot of money somewhere, that we could just pull out when we needed it."

"That's a bourgeois Iranian for you; or at least, that's my father's Persian-ness," Mike said, laughing. "In Tehran, he hoards money all through the house, including jewellery. He's ready in case there is an unexpected revolution, a war, an air attack or whatever, so that he can grab his little goody bags and then jump in his car and have enough money for petrol and supplies and which will take him somewhere where he can go and hide with his family. It's a leftover from when he was a child also, they were dead poor and he never had any money and he never wants to be in that situation ever again. Having the cash around makes him feel better, more in control."

*

After they left something had changed between us. There was an undercurrent in everything we planned and did, and we couldn't shake it off. The parents later let us know that they expected Mike 'Mehrdad' to return to Iran after he'd finished his PhD and if necessary they would accept me as long as we returned to Iran. It was then that I realised how important home was for Mike. England, however pleasant at the moment, was not home to him and probably never would be. I had plenty of time to get used to that thought however.

In September I got a place on the English literature course in one of the London colleges and Mike started his PhD. Mike's father put his expensive West End flat up for sale, and we temporarily found a larger house to rent in the cheaper Hammersmith area. They helped with the rent, bought additional furniture and we agreed with them that we would have a permanent guest room made up for Iranian visitors, most of them relatives, who came and went and who brought stories from Tehran and Iran and who took back suitcases and bags full of Marks and Spencer clothes, sales bargains from stores in Bond Street, Kensington and other west end stores and toiletries, make up, and specialist creams that were unobtainable in Iran. I got used to it all and it became a part of our living in London.

When the lights went out all over Britain and London with the power cuts, and the newspaper headlines screamed that Iran and the Arab countries were to blame for the increasing oil prices, the number of visits from Iran reduced for a while and despite the inconvenience of long queues and the lack of electricity and heat, we actually breathed a sigh of relief.

Although Sharrokh managed to sell his flat, he didn't buy another larger house in London. He decided not to invest in London anymore. He told Mike that he felt uncomfortable with what was happening in England, the economic unrest, the miner's strikes, the electricity cuts, and perhaps there would be a backlash against foreigners investing in property in London. Mike said he didn't know, but it might be wiser to buy something in America. And so the family no longer threatened us with extended visits and stopovers, and the rare visits became rarer still when other relatives, who lived on the outskirts of London in larger properties, started to put them up. Once, Taraneh came and stayed with us, but she also preferred to stay with her cousin rather than with us because 'you're never at home.' I'm not sure that we got on that well together, she wasn't exactly hostile but she certainly wasn't warm and friendly to me, most of the time.

*

When I was in my second undergraduate year at university and when Mike was half way through doing his PhD, he announced that his parents wanted us to get married in Tehran.

"Why would they want that?" I asked. "They don't even like me. Why would they want us to get married?"

Mike shrugged his shoulders. "They know that we're serious, that I'm serious about you. We've been together now for over five years." He told me then that they'd tried again to convince him to become engaged to a girl they had their eyes on, an Iranian girl, a distant relative of theirs.

I was quite upset and angry. I had not been aware of these renewed discussions. Until then, I'd simply tried to ignore Mike's family in our day-to-day life. Just as Mike rarely asked me about my family, I tried to avoid them as the topic of our conversations. At least when they weren't around.

Once, my brother Bert made contact when he was in London and we met over a meal in an Italian restaurant. Mike actually got on quite well with Bert, whom I had not seen for about six years, not for all that time I'd lived in England. I exchanged a few greeting cards with some of my siblings, for Christmas and birthdays, and not even with all of them and anyway the messages usually were quite banal.

Bert had changed and was a grown up man, not the haughty elder brother who looked down on me with disdain. He had mellowed. He had a family, a son and a daughter, and he and his wife appeared to live a comfortable existence. He was a finance wizard, a professional who had done well. He talked about his work in London, the finance conference he attended on behalf of his bank back in Holland. He was in London with colleagues and was only free for the one evening when we met. We talked a bit about our studies, about what Bert did and about Bert's wife and new family and he showed us some pictures of his beautiful blonde stay-at-home wife and their two children, a pretty little girl and a very cute boy.

"Pity you couldn't come to our wedding," Bert said. "Well, your father would have had a heart attack if you'd been there. He knows that you two live together of course and you're a complete anathema as far as he's concerned, someone not even talked about. As it is, they only came to the reception of our wedding and left immediately after. There was no church service, you see, and we had a lot of friends and my colleagues they don't know. Mother asked though why you weren't there. I don't think she agrees with Father, she looked unhappy."

Afterwards, Mike wondered why Bert called me Anna and not Katie.

"Leftover from the past. You know that my full name is Anna Katarina. Well in Holland they used to call me Anna and I changed my name when I came to England," I said.

*

I was sure that a wedding, our wedding, would cause trouble. There would be the inevitable requirement for invitations and then explanations as to why none of my family were going to turn up, especially not if we got married in Iran.

"I don't want to go to Tehran to get married," I said. "I'm happy the way we are. At most I'll have a civil ceremony somewhere here in England, simply saying 'yes I do want to marry you' and nothing related to obedience or what have you. No blessings either. I don't believe in that, we're good as we are."

"It can't do any harm, us getting married in Tehran," Mike said. "After all, I'm their eldest son and they have accepted you, have agreed that is what I want. You've met them often enough here in London, after all."

"Can't we get married here first, if we must?" I wondered. "Besides, you haven't even asked me if I want to marry you."

He looked really surprised.

"Why would you not want to get married?" he asked. "We've been together for almost six years now. I'll finish my PhD soon and you'll get your degree and then we'll have to decide what we're going to do anyway. Stay here or go somewhere else. I'd like to try and live in Iran again. Surely that's not a secret to you? Life is good in Iran now with lots of opportunities for highly qualified people, the economy is really picking up and we'd have prospects we could only dream of here."

He stopped and then added. "We couldn't live together in Iran, not being married, you must realise that."

The problem was that I didn't want to move away from London, where I felt very comfortable and where my friends were. I'd built up a wide circle of university friends and had kept in contact with people I used to work with in London, before I became a student. Tessa was still my best friend, and there were many others now. I liked living in London, being able to see a film whenever we wanted to, go to a concert when we had the money, meet up with friends in a pub or at a party. I particularly liked the anonymity of the big city, the underground, the throngs in the street, the unknown neighbours, and yet feeling part of this one vast living organism that I was sure you could only find in London. I shuddered when I thought about the small villages in the east of The Netherlands, or anywhere in that country.

In the end we compromised, and we had a registry office ceremony in London joined by our friends, bottles of wine, snacks and sandwiches at our rented house, just the way I wanted it. Mike looked smart in a light suit he'd bought for the occasion and I wore a floating long silky dress bought in Kensington High Street at Bibas. No other frills, just a toast with student friends and others.

The compromise was that afterwards we'd go to Iran for a month, and we'd submit to his parents' proposed wedding ceremony — a wedding party with an official blessing in their temple and a huge reception and dinner attended by people I'd never met before, all of them dressed fit for a party in the palace gardens and of course with tables laden with food. Prior to this ceremony we had evenings out in Tehran with cousins and cousins twice removed, and also old friends of Mike's and his relatives, no one I knew apart from Mike's sisters and a few faces I recognised from photos. This was a Tehran that was as good as London, with its nightclubs where we danced to

Iranian music and I must admit I softened somewhat. I didn't even inform my own family, although afterwards I sent some photos to Bert, the twins and to Liesbet, all of whom had married as well in the meantime. I hadn't attended any of their ceremonies either.

*

"See, it wasn't so bad," Mike said at the end of our wedding ceremony and dinner in Tehran, when we sat on the large double bed in the guest room, shoes kicked off, with a bottle of imported expensive wine that Taraneh had smuggled up into the room. I've no idea how she got hold of it, but she had a good giggle when she whispered to Mike that the room was in order. In a kind of ceremony of our own that had nothing to do with where we were, we threw the glasses back against the wall where they left a dirty smudge.

"Are they going to check the sheets for blood?" I wondered before we rolled back on the bed in our wedding outfits, and started tearing them off, to be rid and rediscover our bodies beneath the now clammy and creased clothes.

Chapter Four: 1977

Iran

So here I am, it's the spring of 1977 and I'm living just outside Neshnafad in our house in a compound up on a hill not far from the university campus, writing up Anna's story, or at least putting together my notes on her, trying to find her as well as some of my own past.

Early in the morning when it's still relatively cool and late in the afternoon when the heat subsides, I sit on the balcony upstairs, outside our bedroom, and watch the glass blue skies taper off to white and blank sheets of paper, as the days wear on and summer heat washes out all memories of where Anna comes from. I like this sensation of being absorbed by the dry landscape, with its cultivated flowerbeds that imprint themselves inside my skull as if this is their home turf, where the flowers, the earth, the dust, the dry twigs, watered greens and my own body transmogrify into one. The hot intensity acts as a catalyst, burns out the past and unravels the blank page of a new and different world, still mostly unknown, to be filled in by who I am now and what I am going to be.

I easily sink into the stupor of this heat and allow it to wipe out the reality of what is going on around me. Both this world and the one of my childhood are equally strange and diaphanous, and every so often I get up and walk through our house, to touch the books on the shelves, to lie down on our bed, to sit in the Habitat chair and to open cupboards and see our clothes hanging side by side inside two equally large wardrobes, one for me and one for Mike. These are all part of my life now and confirm the physical reality of who I am, as if these possessions assure me of my own legitimacy here in this country.

We live the life of the privileged, of well-to-do professionals; the doctors and professors and lawyers and lecturers with their wives who don't really need to work if they don't want to because the husband's income is sufficient for the middle class existence that we lead. Most of the wives aspire to get a job, even if part time, to shake off the loneliness of the 'foreign wife' existence. A job, any job, will also give the additional legitimacy we crave, and wards off a sense of futility that will inevitably raise its head when we have too much time on our hands. Nevertheless, ours is a carefree and careless paradise as long as we don't listen too much to the stories about dissatisfaction amongst the local communities, as long as we ignore the rising clamour against the Shah and his dreams of creating a bourgeois western society, where women are free to the extent that they can dress in western clothes and be beautiful. We claim our rights to live the Shah's dreams, even if we don't agree with all of his policies and abhor the stories about secret police and their torture of people that won't submit to the Shah's illusions.

I am one of those that lay claims to the beauty of Neshnafad's architecture and gardens, the harsh climate, the summer heat and relentless autumn winds and I want an untroubled existence. After all, I am Mike's wife and we are rightful inhabitants of this country. Having moved here I realise how much Mike is a part of this country as he never was part of the London life to the extent I imagined. We and our friends, the foreign wives of Iranians, are different from other foreigners who've come to live here, the many immigrant workers, the professionals, consultants and advisers, who have come to work on a temporary basis. They'll live here for a while and will take advantage of the boom economy that's been unleashed on the instructions of the Shah. These foreign workers, the Americans, French, English, Germans, use the Shah's largesse to their own ends even if they sometimes laugh at his unlimited desire to make this country great and equal to any western society. We, the foreign wives and their Iranian husbands, who work in the University and the hospital and who live on specially designed housing compounds and in other large houses around the University and the hospital, we belong here and are here to stay, whereas they are like vultures picking what they can when the going is good.

"Some of these foreign workers ignore the locals altogether and show scant respect to the local and national culture," my American friend Betty says one day when we're in our local shop for groceries. We're witnessing an angry exchange between two American women and the grocer, Ali, who sells everything from local fresh meat, fruit and vegetables, if available, to imported American packets of Jell-O and pampers, the new throwaway nappies for babies. The two women raise their voices when they talk to Ali and seem to assume that they'll be understood better if they shout with their heavy American accents and drawls. Betty tries to intervene and explains to Ali what it is that they want. Betty's Farsi is near fluent, much better than mine, and she always speaks to Ali in the Farsi language. Ali says they should not be rude to him and Betty agrees. He huffs, '*farangi*', foreigner, and turns his back on them.

They rarely mix in social settings with locals or even with us, these foreign professionals and their wives. They live in a different bubble, far removed from the day to day life of the people in the country, a bubble in which they are oblivious to the increasing resentment of the shopkeepers and local workers who cannot afford the cars, the clothes, or even the food that these *farangi*, these foreigners, want to buy.

"We're different, we're here to stay. We're here to build new families with children that have mixed parentage but nevertheless will be Iranian," Betty says. "We're not like them. We haven't come to make a quick buck and to bully the native Iranians around. We plan to live here forever and ever. We're part of the family."

Betty is as much trying to convince herself as she is us and will say that she's proud to be Iranian as well as American. I've come to realise that it depends on her mood and that, like most of us, she often is violently homesick and would love to leave again to re-join her American life, family and friends.

Our children will be beautiful, Rosa, another American friend agrees. She claims that with a mixture of the genes of their very different parents, our future children will be more beautiful because of this cooking together of characteristics that have not previously been mixed, the darker and the fairer skinned, the blonde, brown and black haired, the round and the angular, the short and the tall, which all mixed together will conspire to produce something more beautiful and attractive. I'm still not sure what it all means. Even after having been here for a year, I find it somewhat overwhelming, and although I claim to want to live here for the rest of my life, I am not quite ready yet to give up my western identity, whatever that is, and submerge myself into being Iranian. After all, I'm suspicious of belonging, of being one nationality rather than another. I'd rather not think about it.

Living here I've learned about gods I didn't know existed and what they stand for and who worships them. There isn't just Allah and God, but here there's also Ahura Mazda and then there are the Baha'is and others still, and of course all their ramifications. My head spins when I think about Christianity and how in just those little villages across parts of The Netherlands, the kind that Anna lived in, there would be three or more churches, denominations they called them, and the children whose parents belonged to one of these would group themselves into a kind of gang, fighting each other after school, or trying very hard to avoid each other, afraid of being bullied. Their enmity was as much due to ignorance as to a real fear of the unknown.

Here you have the different Muslim creeds, the majority Shiites but also some Sunni and the difference between the two seems to be about who is the anointed leader, just like the Jews refuse to acknowledge Jesus and the different Protestant and Catholic churches insist that their reading of the Bible is the correct one. Crazy really when you think about it all, how differences in interpretation become so important, so much so that people start discriminating and fighting each other about it. I've asked Mike about the variations in Muslim beliefs but he's not that interested in the subtleties, not the way I am. I'm amazed to find all that religious obsession here too because I always thought it was peculiar to the Dutch nation and their obsessive Calvinism and Catholicism, but I now realise that you find it equally strongly in other societies and cultures. It all depends on where you were born and on how much you take for granted that what you're told by your parents and their communities is the truth.

62

I'm surprised that many Iranians know about the variations in Christian religion of our western countries, whereas I, who've come to Iran to live here, know so very little about their different belief systems and feel quite bewildered by it all, and by the power and hold the ayatollah's have over the vast majority of the people here. Very much like the pastors and elderlings in small Dutch villages in the fifties.

This country is so enormous and so different from anything I've known before or imagined. It's so diverse and magical that it conspires in making me forget my past, which seems irrelevant and small. I'm beginning to find it quite easy to write about Anna, as if I've outgrown that world for good and can observe it as someone else's story, one that I'm inventing as I go along. I sometimes wonder what Anna's heartache is all about, Anna's and mine. My parents' belief system was so damning and so cruel, but not that different really from a Muslim's belief, and it turns out to be just one of many belief systems, where poor humans and in particular children are caught up in a web of hand-me-downs from great grandparents, where stories are twisted and re-interpreted, naïve and consoling in their terrors and fears of life and death. I ask myself how it damaged me and how it could have had such a grip on me, and still has on some of my siblings; how I nearly got lost in it, in the fear of it and the soul searching ambiguities that would haunt me. And, if I had not escaped, I might never have known about these many different worlds, nor live here and understand their relative cruelty.

When we first arrived from London in Tehran, it was midnight when the plane landed, and Sharrokh was waiting for us to drive us to their home in one of the side streets in the middle of Tehran. As we entered the gate, a fire was burning in the courtyard and I was told to jump over it to clean my spirits and chase away the demons, and so their new gods welcomed me and purified my being. It was rather nice, if quaint, to imagine that all your wrongful actions and thoughts were being eradicated simply by jumping over a fire, avoiding the burns and making sure you did not hurt yourself — if only it had been this easy in the past. If only my parental beliefs had not been so damningly judgemental and unforgiving.

Allah is a different matter though and I don't like him much. He is another male god who comes down hard on non-believers, and as far as I can see around me he tries to keep women down even more so than Calvinism does, and whole swathes of the country will, if let, then be ruled by men and their dictates. I shiver when I think of it. I ignore Allah and I'm actually quite happy that Mike's family have no truck with Islam and I don't have to try and fit into a culture that I'm not comfortable with.

It's quite strange to see the behaviour of some of my friends here, Betty and Rosa for example; women who, like me, have come from a western country, America or England or France, but who are married to Iranian Muslims and who now live some of these curious rituals of covering themselves when they visit relatives. I'm horrified at the thought that I'd have to cover myself, as if simply being a woman is sinful.

I admire the beautiful mosques and cloths, I enjoy the smell of the spices and flowers, I enjoy the taste of the kebabs, the bean stews and saffron rice, but I pity the women, even if the Shah seems to have it in mind to change all of that and has decreed that women must not cover themselves in universities and other public places.

"Oh these poor women," Betty says one day when we walk up together to see Rosa.

"Some of them are just treated like trash, so much trash. Behmand's family is quite liberal in comparison and they wouldn't dare say anything to me. I just wear a scarf sometimes, out of respect for his elderly mother, but never a chador. You probably don't know, but poor Rosa really has to put up with some when she visits her family. You know, she actually wears a chador when she goes visiting them. Farzman's parents live in some half forgotten small village just outside Neshnafad, and he actually encourages her, well he commands her really. He thinks it's perfectly normal for a woman, even an American woman, to be covered from head to toe here in Iran."

"I don't mind," Rosa says, when we ask her. "It's all quite harmless. They know I don't wear a chador when I'm not visiting them; they're just worried about their neighbours and are too old to change their ways. It's such a small village. I just indulge them, it's easier."

Farzman, Rosa's husband, is the eldest son of the family. When it turned out he was clever at school, his parents sent him to America to do better. The whole family paid towards his education on top of a special grant he received from the government, and he is back now to do them proud, an engineer and a University professor in the family. He owes them, he says. He seems a gentle man, with kind brown eyes and a soft smile. I guess that he's about ten years older than Rosa, and when he looks at her his eyes go all swimming with adoration and he fools around with their two children, a two-year old boy and a very pretty four year old girl, who squeal and pat him when he's on the floor pretending to be a horse that they can ride. I've never heard him raise his voice at his children and he always talks to them softly, even when he tells them off for being naughty. It's difficult to imagine that he's so adamant that Rosa should wear a chador when she visits his family.

Betty shakes her head. "Don't think that all you see is all there is. There is much more to this, but Rosa has sworn me to silence."

Listening to their stories and conversations I'm very glad that Mike's family is quite different from these relatives of my friends in Neshnafad. Mike's parents and uncles and aunts send their sons abroad and sometimes their daughters too, for their education. There's an uncle who is a surgeon and who studied and lived in England; there's a cousin who's a lawyer and who studied in France; and there are female cousins who study languages and architecture. When we visit his relatives in Tehran the conversations are often in English, with a few odd French and Farsi comments thrown in. Family members who have not studied abroad have picked up enough of the English language during lengthy stays and visits in England or America.

That's enough about me and where I live. I want to discover more about Anna and tell you about her.

Chapter Five: 1957

The Netherlands

The village called Armitan, where Anna lived, lay hidden from the main road, which connected the nearby provincial town Gelen to the north with another smaller town some seventy kilometres south. Along this newly asphalted, winding road were other villages, some smaller, some larger, peas in a pod straddled by woods and fields. The road was the lifeline along which lorries, buses and vans distributed their goods and services, connecting the villages to a larger world about which most of their inhabitants, in the late nineteen fifties, had little awareness, except for the news brought by the local and national newspapers and, of course, the regular radio bulletins.

These villages and the road were part of a large, naturally low lying, nature reserve with a few high peaks from which brooks flow to the lower parts of the area. Some of these waterways were just outside Armitan and as well as providing natural water drainage systems for the extensive farmland around the village, they were also a natural hiding and recreation playground for the village children who learned to swim in the larger brook and who showed off their acrobatics by jumping off a bridge into the water below. A boy broke his neck and died, after having been challenged by others to dive into the water below, too shallow, and his dive too steep.

He climbed on the railing of the bridge and Anna watched as he stood there, a skinny boy her own age, around eight years old. He lived at the corner of their street, the child of a house painter and decorator, whose wife, the boy's mother, sold cans and jars of paint, brushes and turpentine, wallpaper and pots of glue from the shop which was the extended front of their house, and still had the appearance of a converted front room. The boy was with a group of boys and a few girls that went to the public heathen school in the village. They never went to church on Sundays, or maybe only once a day, and then to the Lutheran church and Anna knew that you might as well be a heathen if you went there. They would go to Hell all the same, whether they went to that church or not, because God wouldn't listen to their prayers, partly because they acted sinfully. They danced, listened to the wrong non-church music, read forbidden books, and they did other heathen things but Anna was never quite sure what that was. She just knew that Lutherans and heathens, as well as Roman Catholics, got it all wrong; that much was clear from the way her father and mother forbade them to make friends with these children. That's why groups of children fought and taunted each other when they met in the street. Even here when swimming in the brook, Anna's group of friends kept to themselves and Anna stayed close to them, to her brothers and cousins.

At night in her bed she sometimes shivered when she thought about all the things she did not understand, like dying and going to Hell. It was better not to let your thoughts wander that way; she knew that Hell was fearful and painful and nobody in their right mind would want to end up there because you would be suffering into all eternity, whatever that was. Much more painful than falling off your bike, that's for sure.

The boys on the bridge screamed and egged on their friend, "Go for it Hans — bet you daren't!"

They formed a circle of skinny jumping boys behind him where he stood on the bridge, their swimming trunks either too small or too large and sagging, their bare feet grimy with the mud from the side of the brook where they'd been playing and jumping about and from where they'd suddenly surged towards the bridge, laughing and shouting. Their naked, thin and white bodies were bent as they laughed, and they bashed their knees with their hands and then clapped as if enacting some kind of ritual before making their offer to the Devil.

Hans looked puny and scared and then suddenly he arched forward, his two arms sticking above his head and he lowered them in front of him, as if he was going to grab something, a tree, his mother, anything at all to hold onto, but there was nothing there and he went down, head first. The gang of boys ran to the side to help him out when he surfaced, to scream and shout at his bravery. Only Hans didn't come up and as they edged closer to the water he still didn't surface. "Come on Hans!" "Where is he?"

Suddenly there was a farmer, coming past on a tractor on the way to his field beyond or perhaps on his way home. Someone screamed at him and pointed to the middle of the brook.

"What on earth…" he shouted, as he stopped in the middle of that bridge, leaving the motor of his tractor idling, the noise of it silencing the boys. He got off his high seat, ran to the side of the stream, shook off his clogs and stepped into the muddy water. He pulled his jacket off, sucked air into his nose and then disappeared completely from sight under the green and black surface.

Quietness descended on the world around, except for the sound of the tractor motor. The wind stopped together with the shouting and there was only the buzzing of a few flies as the farmer came back up holding the lifeless body of Hans, very white, his small swimming trunk too big now and dripping.

"Is he dead?" someone whispered and another boy said almost triumphantly, "He's broken his neck."

The farmer shouted at one of the boys to run up the road to the house and get a doctor, the police, a car. The other boys that were still left there on the bridge were told to go away, go home. "Go! Don't stand there and stare. Go home! Be safe!"

From that day on their parents warned that they must not jump off that bridge, and definitely no more diving, not from that bridge nor from any bridge over any brook, for that matter.

"You see what happens when you disobey. It's dangerous."

But some time later they forgot and they did it again, daring each other. A few of them even dived off the edge of the railings again, scared and aiming for the middle of the brook, the deepest part and making sure that they hit the surface of the water with their bellies, hard and painful. Anna shivered every time somebody jumped, and then she jumped herself and nothing happened, just her toes touching the muddy bottom of the brook, and perhaps her father was right and they were special, protected, chosen by God until He saw fit to collect them.

Hans hadn't been special. Was that because his family didn't go to church on Sundays? She wondered about this, his parents were such gentle people, never loud, never shouting at their children, and now they had a permanently sad look on their faces; both had gone grey and old very rapidly. An older brother left the village, had gone to stay with family far away, the winds whispered. How could the parents live with the thought that their Hans was now in Hell, Anna wondered? Did they know? She certainly couldn't imagine what that would be like for them, or for Hans, and she decided not to think about it.

As the summer went by the children once more acquisitioned their spaces along the brook, it's where they belonged, where they played, where they sat in groups or gathered, lying on their skimpy towels spread on a patch of grass or jumping around, and when summer turned into autumn and then into winter, they found other hide-outs in the village. There were plenty of them, the woods and the fields full of dark secrets, cow dung and molehills, empty barns at the back of farmyards that creaked and whispered and where no one ever seemed to come except for birds and creepy crawlers, the disused railway track gone brown and overgrown with weed. They would play their games on their way home from school, skipping, shooting marbles, conkers, hide and seek and tagging. Their parents were far too busy to watch them. They worked hard in that village, the shopkeepers, farmers, small artisans, office and factory workers and cleaners and they didn't have the luxury of time to worry about what their children did all day long. It was paradise, only God was watching over his smaller creatures for as long as they believed what their parents told them.

*

At the end of the afternoon the children went home for their evening meals and if they were late they were punished and grounded for a few days, or a week at most. Sometimes, when disobedience was too flagrant and too worrying, they might get a beating from their fathers when he came home at the end of the day, showing them who was boss and they'd better listen

71

and behave. Johannes seemed to distinguish between his sons and daughters in that the boys received beatings on their backside whereas the girls might be slapped across their face or simply be threatened with a proper beating.

They would play in their groups that were split into the Lutheran or reformed church school, the Calvinist church school, and the heathen or public school, and from the minute they could talk and definitely from their first day at school, they knew which clan they belonged to.

Anna was part of the Calvinist school group and for a while she knew that they would all go to heaven and that they had God on their side. Their group would mock the others for being unbelievers who would rot in Hell whereas they would have a place in Paradise. They were never quite sure what this meant, and sometimes Paradise was as worrying as Hell because of this not knowing, but it would be much better and lighter in Paradise and they would walk with all other believers and not suffer pain. It gave them courage when they were still small and at primary school. Once they were past that age their certainty corroded. They began to realise that these other children they had taunted before, and who had taunted them, weren't that different from them. They would meet each other again in secondary schools in other villages or in Gelen as some of these schools admitted children from different denominations, and they'd sit next to each other and cycle back and forth together. As no Devils waylaid them, as books opened up different worlds, as friendships were forged, previous certainties became less so, black and white convictions greyed and frayed and their parents seemed less all-knowing. They realised there was a different world outside the village and that this world contained many different things they had not known about before. Their parents didn't know it all, fathers appeared less powerful and mothers more pitiful, and God never came down in the promised fury of killings and maiming and thunder when they shouted "no" at their parents, or when they stamped their feet or when they were found out having been smoking, or having kissed a boy or a girl, or having read forbidden books, or listened to the wrong music, pop songs, songs about kissing and even cuddling and the unmentionable. '*Je t'aime mon amour*' appeared to be about the unmentionable act and even then no one was struck dead.

There were nine siblings in the Dent family. Anna was the fifth child, with an older sister and three older brothers, two of them twins, and then there were two younger sisters and two younger brothers. She was always the middle one, never old enough to participate neither young enough to be protected, neither too old nor too young, always neither. After primary school, Anna's older brother Bert and sister Liesbet attended a secondary school in the next village up the road, whilst the twins Stephan and Gerard went to a technical college in a village to the south of Armitan. The twins were two years older than Anna and as children they always stuck together, one island within that muddled and confused world of children, with their needs and their wants. The twins always behaved in tandem. When Gerard was ill, so was Stephan and when Stephan wanted to become a car mechanic and later a doctor, so did Gerard. Outside the house, they barely acknowledged Anna or Liesbet for that matter. Girls were beneath them, that much was clear.

When Anna's older brothers and sister went to secondary school they started to raise their eyebrows and they would huff and bristle at their parents' decisions; they were found with banned books or music magazines that showed girls in low cut dresses and boys with strange haircuts, or they'd whistle songs that definitely weren't psalms. They'd claim that friends were allowed to come back home late at night, even see a film or go to parties where they danced and what was so wrong with that? Johannes would grumble. "What is this world coming to?" and forbade them, whereas their mother would sometimes smile her kind smile and then carry on doing whatever it was she was busy with, noncommittal, avoiding trouble.

Johannes and Greta didn't want change. They wanted God's safety and the security of worshipping the only true God, a way of life they'd defended during the war, they said. Hadn't Johannes worn the uniform of the Dutch army and hadn't he had to hide from the Germans? Hadn't they been brave when helping to hide Jews from the harm that would otherwise be inflicted on them by the godless Germans, the Nazis? This needed to be continued, this watchfulness, this denial of further godless interference by the world outside, which would inevitably be destroyed by God's wrath, if not immediately then later, when the end of the world came. All these new and rebellious ideas were no less than God's challenge to His true believers.

Armitan wasn't only a secluded village but also a very old one that went back in history some way. Previously it existed in much smaller manifestations as a neighbourhood that was known under different names, Armsfield, and even Armstown, until it became Armitan in one of the documents found in a local cloister in the fifteenth century. Just a hamlet it was then, without proper connections and paths to nearby towns and villages. The French occupied it at one point but they were driven out again, and soon after there was the beginning of some schooling for the children and the first factory was built, still there, just up the road from where Anna lived. The factory needed a canal for the processing of paper, and then

74

improvements in the road and connections were forged to the surrounding villages and to Gezel, the provincial main town. The small community of Armitan always were god-fearing folk and they built their church, and so this little hamlet acquired official village status. A railway line was built which went through the village, but then it closed again before Anna was born and only the station and the station road remained as a reminder of what once was there. The rails were dug up leaving behind only a few stretches of rusted tracks.

Now, a large family of seven children and their parents lived in the former station master's house, the father an important looking man who wore a suit and a tie most of the time, not often witnessed in the village, and with brown hair that was cut sharply short until he became bald. The mother was hardly ever seen, rarely venturing out of the house except to go to church on Sundays. Either her husband or one of the older children would be sent out on a regular basis to the local greengrocer, bakery and butcher for food, which they'd carry back in bags hanging from their bicycle handlebars. The parents didn't mix much with others. However their children went to the Calvinist church school and they became friends of Anna's and of her older brothers. There was a girl the same age as Anna, and although they went to the same primary school in the village, the parents took them to a different church on Sundays.

"Synods," Gerard said and sucked air hard up his nose followed by "pffftt" between clenched lips. "Synods are toads, just like us," Stephan said. Johannes clipped him around the ears and said he must not say things like that. Nevertheless, they all noticed a vague smile around his lips so perhaps calling them toads wasn't so bad.

The Dent house and shop stood in the middle of the main village road with the house an extension at the back of the shop, which was built when Anna was little, to replace the smallholding at the other end of the village, in which her grandfather now lived alone after their grandmother's death, well before Anna was born. The Dent shop sold everything village women might need for their kitchens, bedrooms, corridors and best front rooms; from crockery and saucepans to curtains, bedding tables and chairs, from toys for the village children to books for all ages even if the selection was quite small, from hot water bottles to storage jars and tins and vases, to postcards for the odd tourist in summer and New Year cards. Later they would also have Christmas cards, although Johannes disapproved of these except for the ones that sent God's blessing. The tourist trade would grow over the years, with more and more visitors coming to camping sites that mushroomed around the villages in this beauty spot. With the tourists there would be an influx of new ideas, people who would cycle around noisily on Sundays and who'd come into the shop in shorts and low cut tee shirts. Some of the tourists were Germans and Johannes would grumble that they were thieves and that you couldn't trust them. He refused to accommodate them and professed not to understand German, so that they wouldn't come back but rather drive or cycle to the next village, where a more accommodating shopkeeper would make sure they got what they wanted.

As Anna grew up, the shop interior was modified several times and an upstairs floor was added, but the layout always remained a muddle of gangways, display shelves high and low, cupboards and wall hangings, and a paradise for playing hide and seek in after closing time when Johannes wasn't around, at the end of the day; it was a playground of dark and mystifying objects and tools, of racks full of gadgets and shelves full of grown up mysteries, many of them breakable, and therefore to be treated with care; toys that you would never get for your birthday or for St Nicholas because they were too expensive and books that Anna would take away secretly to read and then put back again without anyone noticing, as long as she didn't tear or smudge the pages.

During the day this shop would claim their mother Greta and the children would roam the house or the yard or the village roads unsupervised, except perhaps when an older child was told to watch the younger ones.

All day long Johannes muttered to himself, and to Greta, and sometimes to the children when they bumped into him, in and out of the shop through the connecting door of the tiny office between the house and the shop. They tried to avoid him, as it was never quite clear whether they'd be punished for an imagined misdemeanour or a real one, or whether he'd be in a good or a bad mood. At lunchtime, Johannes would slump into his chair in the front room and twiddle with the knobs of the radio, a large black square box that had a rattan looking cover for the speakers, while Greta would then hurry through to the kitchen, potatoes boiling, vegetables steaming and she would warm up some meatballs prepared at the beginning of the week or boil up some sausages and cook a pudding that more often than not ended up burnt because her mind was on other things, and she looked confused when the burning smell pervaded the house. Once Liesbet was considered old enough, and when she was at home during the holidays, she would be tasked to keep an eye on the food and burnt pudding would be a less frequent dessert than it was during the school year. At the weekends, and on days off school, the boys would set the table with the cracked plates and the miscellaneous assortment of knives and forks. It was difficult to keep a full set of eleven and some disappeared mysteriously, to be replaced by a mismatch of others, usually cast offs from the shop.

Anna couldn't bear to eat burnt pudding, even though everyone insisted that it was perfectly all right with enough of the sweet red sauce over it to drown out the taste. Anna felt sick and refused to eat it. She sat at the table alone after everyone else had gone, even baby Rienske had been put into her cot upstairs to sleep, and Johannes had read a short bible piece and they'd all thanked the Lord for their meal. Anna saw the hand of the clock on the mantelpiece move forward, closer and closer to half past one, when school would start. She'd be late and be sent to the headmaster who would punish her. Johannes had settled himself in his chair in the front room, next to the radio. He'd insisted that she eat the pudding as *'there was often nothing to eat during the war and even now, swathes of children across the world go hungry and she should be grateful that she didn't have to go hungry.'*

Greta was tidying away the dishes, washing them and leaving them to drip dry in the rack on the side, which was filling up. She'd quickly dry them and put them away before going back into the shop for the afternoon until Rienske would wake. She stood with her back to Anna who pushed half of the pudding into the bin that stood next to the divider between sink and cupboards and the table in the day room, and then again made sure her mother wasn't looking as she pushed in the rest.

"It's gone," she said. "Finished."

Greta looked back, smiled and said, "You'd better hurry then. You'll be late for school." Anna realised that her mother knew perfectly well what she'd done.

*

78

Anna immersed herself in the games they played in the schoolyard and on the way home. She loved chucking the colourful marbles, to touch and win, so accumulating bags full of the glassy beads with the blue waves, the whites, greens, yellows and reds, the smaller ones with their clear see-through glass and the larger ones, they called the shooters. She considered herself to be a master of this game, where winner took all, and she flicked the marbles into the holes, fired and bombed precisely and effectively. Yes, she would show all of them, the other children, even if at home no one cared or noticed.

She had a grubby little bag, sewn together by Greta from a left over piece of material, probably a curtain she had been sewing for customers. She would tie the bag's elastic cord firmly around her wrist and at the end of the afternoon it would be bulging. Her hands would be dirty with the black soil and her nails black-rimmed. She'd be covered with smears across her face where she had wiped her short blond hair back with a handful of marbles.

When she won a round, her sense of victory was almost physical, a twitch in her stomach, a loud grin on her face, her hand wiping her face once more before dropping the handful of dirty glass marbles into her bag. Other girls and boys often pushed her but she always pushed them back, and wiped the glass beads on her skirt, which was now also smeared and hung poorly over her grubby knees, knee socks fallen down her long thin legs to her ankles, the brown shoes scuffed to white at the front. She walked away and when she got home she showed them off to her younger siblings to admire. Not to Bert, Liesbet, Stephan or Gerard, they would only look at her with their condescending smiles; they were far beyond playing this game and she knew that soon she would be too. But not yet.

"I won," she said to Henry. He was still small, even though he was only less than two years younger than she was. He cried easily and didn't want to get involved in the jumble and tumble as opposed to her own constant noisiness, her laughter and shouts. This younger brother was withdrawn and thoughtful. He would come straight home from school and rarely dilly-dallied on the way, as she did. He'd sit inside the house, waiting for Greta to come out of the shop. He smiled at Anna and he liked it when she involved him in her games, which she rarely did. She never felt the urge to fight him, as she did with her older brothers and sisters. He'd never put her down. But most of the time she simply ignored him as well as her other younger siblings.

"Oh well, what do you know. Do you want to have this nice one?"

He accepted her offer and put the blue and red marble away in his trouser pocket, underneath the big and dirty handkerchief that was in there. He beamed at her, a lovely smile as if there was suddenly sun on water, lighting it up, making sparkles that resembled the fairy tale colours of her marbles.

Then she was away, out of the backdoor into the small yard, where she entered the bicycle shed to hide the bag of marbles on a shelf behind some tins. She returned to the kitchen and washed her hands under the cold-water tap, wiped her face with a damp soiled flannel and picked up her library book that was amongst the heaps of books, papers and folders on the side.

She went to the front room, which was quiet and empty of people. Where was everyone? It was a long rectangular room divided into a dining area that was only used on Sundays, and a sitting area. A big black organ stood in the corner of the room at the back next to the patio doors that opened up to the small tiled patio in the backyard, and which was bordered by a large brick flower container that had no flowers, only some weeds and grass.

The large organ dominated the dining area that had a table with eight chairs around it, and when used on Sundays would be opened up and extended to twelve seats. There was a single glass fronted cabinet on the side, placed on top of a long row of locked wooden cabinets alongside the outside wall. Behind the glass were two rows of books, thick and old, and sometimes Johannes would unlock one of the cabinets and take out a book to show his children.

There was a book that had a cloth cover, all dull brown and grey and which had black and white photos of survivors of concentration camps. Only recently, Johannes had taken it out to show Anna and the twins and he said, "We should never forget this, what the Germans did." She shivered every time she revisited in her head the pictures of the naked men and women, thin as rakes, and of the children with big black eyes and bodies that seemed to consist only of bones covered by some skin, eye sockets that stared at her from a grey and black background as if accusing her.

The front part of the room held her father's comfortable chair next to the radio and the small gas heater. There was a large sagging sofa and her mother's chair where she would sit on Sundays after church services to drink her tea or coffee; there were a further two mismatched chairs lined up next to each other, with barely enough space to walk behind them. The seating was arranged around a low glass coffee table. There were two empty dirty cups on matching saucers and an ashtray holding a brown cigar stub and several cigarette ends. Her father must have been here with a visiting wholesaler.

Anna considered that it might be dangerous that no one else was around. Her mother might come in and tell her to get the table ready for the evening meal or ask her to do something else, a quick run to one of the shops, or tidy up the kitchen, or… anything. She decided to go back to the bicycle shed. It wasn't very cold and she could sit there without being disturbed, read her library book about an only child whose mother and father let her go on a camping holiday with a friend and where they had a real adventure when they were cut off by the sea water when looking for shells. God was with them though and He got them right back, and the parents were so happy to have them back that rather than punishing them, they actually gave them a present and they thanked God on their knees for his help.

Anna wondered about that girl and that family and their relationship with God. It seemed so much kinder than her own, which was one of punishment and anger, with God always watching in a bad way, out to punish and distribute *wraak*, revenge, to the wicked, which she didn't quite understand. She wondered about Him being so vengeful in their everyday life. It must be something to do with them, something they, His very own creatures, had done unwittingly.

Chapter Six: 1960-1962

The Netherlands

In the early sixties, a year after Anna started secondary school in the provincial town of Gezel, the Berlin wall was built, separating East Germans from their West German compatriots, and often from their family and friends. Johannes shook his head, muttered at the wanton communists and the waywardness of the world in general. More and more, it seemed as if the world was hurtling towards self-destruction, even though the war had been won. At what cost! God's will and design were unfathomable though, and all that his children could do was to be constant in their belief in Him and that everything was for the best. Daily prayers now included the plea for protection from communists as well as all other evil.

Anna had been to Gezel before; after all it was the nearest largest town. Sometimes her mother took her on a shopping trip and sometimes she went with her father in the back of his Volkswagen minibus that he used for delivering carpets and curtains and chairs to customers, and for picking up goods from wholesalers in Gezel. It was also practical because he could take his whole family, with Greta in the front and the children on specially fashioned benches in the back. When he went to Gezel, however, he usually went on his own, but sometimes he'd take one or two of the children. Anna loved these trips to Gezel, as Johannes would drop her off in the bookshop in the centre of the town, where the owner would allow her to sit in the children's book corner to flip through the books on the twins, *Saskia and Jeroen* and the various *adventures of Jip en Janneke*. Later, she picked up *Siske the Rat*, or a *Godfried Bomans*, but those she wouldn't show her father as he had made it quite clear that these writers were not God-fearing and would, if let, imbue his children with wrong ideas and expectations. Anna would therefore keep the less controversial authors within reach, to show him when he returned to pick her up for the drive home.

Initially, she was captivated by the stories of children and their families so unlike hers, where a mother had the time to read stories, where the food on the table was never burnt, where children talked with their fathers and mothers and were given answers that made some sense. Not at all like what happened in the real world, where the only reading was from the Bible and parents didn't have time. Books opened up worlds that were very unlike their village life and the people who lived there. Books made you believe that life could be different, and that it did not have to be this frantic, fear-instilled and noisy capsule, surrounded by a scary God and an even scarier Devil. In Anna's world, God was so powerful that he could make you die and drop you straight into Hell in one fell swoop. Just like what happened to Hans, who'd died when he jumped from the bridge into the water below and who, she feared, was now in Hell, even if she couldn't really understand why that was so.

When she read about Siske de Rat, Anna realised that some people were less preoccupied with God. If anything, Siske's life was a mystery to her; a boy growing up in Amsterdam ... how far was that? ... whose father was away and whose parents then wanted to divorce. It was for the first time that she came across the word 'divorce' and it made her wish her own parents would separate so that her father would no longer scold her mother, or even hit her.

And the two shall become one flesh. What therefore God has joined together let no man put asunder.

She shivered when she read that Siske eventually killed his mother.

Walking along the bookshelves in that shop in Gezel, she came across many books and writers she'd never heard of before; books that were forbidden, even though the shop owner was a professed Christian. And when she no longer went to the bookshop with Johannes, she found the books in the village library, took them out and hid them under the mattress. She'd just have to be careful that she didn't pick up books that were way beyond her, as the librarian would then look her up and down, take the book, read out the name of the author aloud, and sometimes the title and say, "not suitable. You cannot have that yet. Do your parents know that you want to get this out?" And then she would put it on a pile of books behind her and Anna would look down and mumble that she hadn't known and that she would look for another one.

*

"It's a better school," her father said when she asked why she couldn't go to the same secondary school that everyone else attended, the one in the next village up the road. Why couldn't she go with her best friend Gemma?

"It's a new school in Gezel and these schools are part of our Church," her father said. Johannes had done his homework, had talked about this with the teachers at the primary school and with the elders and the vicar. He'd read about it in the Church newspaper. He lectured Anna and her siblings on the history of their church, talked about the reformation, about separations of believers in the nineteenth century and Anna's

85

head spun, trying to work out what the difference was and why this should affect her. Why was she the one to be singled out for this new experiment, a school of their own?

*

Johannes though was determined. Even if he wanted his children to have an education, after all God did encourage the use of talents, he had become worried about the books that his older children were reading, the comments they made, the questioning of whether it was necessary to go to church at all. Bert even had the temerity to say that he, Johannes, was old fashioned, that people were beginning to think differently and that everything was not as black and white as he made it out to be. Worst of all, Johannes had found evidence that Bert had been reading Jan Wolkers and his story about his childhood in Oegstgeest, highlighting the author's rebelliousness against his father who'd been a staunch Calvinist believer.

Anna sighed. Perhaps the new school would all work out; going somewhere completely different, where no one else from the village would be. This might just help her to discover a larger world, beyond Armitan and church. After all, there were bookshops in Gezel and fashion shops of sorts; there was a large ice cream parlour, some cafes and the fast food outlets at the railway station.

When in September, she started at her new school, she was immediately disappointed with the ordinariness of it. Although the building was newly refurbished, the girls and boys in the class were so much the same as the ones she'd known in the village; they came from different villages around the town, as well as from the town itself. Like Anna, these boys and girls were curious and self-conscious about going to this very new school that they were told was just for them, God's chosen children. They started and ended each school day with prayers and often there'd be a brief reading from 'God's Word'. All the teachers were male and, Anna thought, imitated both the village vicar and the church elders with being strict and self-important, even if the elderlings were mere farmers and peasants, whereas these teachers were young, and pretended to be knowledgeable about the subjects they taught. They wore dark suits and ties, even though some of them had only just qualified and looked not much older than Bert. She had to laugh when she imagined Bert in front of a class.

One Saturday, when cycling back from school alone, Anna felt down and depressed. Her legs were like tubes of lead and she pushed them down and round on the pedals, her face and body catching the slight breeze that began to feel more and more like a wind turbine, determined to stop her going forward. She felt exhausted and decided that she was no longer able to fight everything and everyone. She knew that her life would never change and she was caught in the trap of her parent's life and religion. She'd never be able to escape the monotony and she'd never find out more about a wider world around her. They would always prevent it, the teachers, the church, and her parents. She bent her body forward to avoid catching the breeze, but the wind teased her more and blew her hair into her eyes and she wanted to stop cycling, sit down and cry. A car horn beeped loudly as she crossed the road halfway home to join the cycle path on the other side. The car's brakes screeched as it came to a stop just a meter or so away from her.

"*Godverdomme*, Goddammit." The driver's face was red behind the front screen; she could see the outline of the swearword on his lips and the shape of his mouth behind the screen.

"*Godverdomme to you,*" she muttered as she cycled away on the path, not looking back. She imagined that God had heard both of them swear and despite the driver's obvious anger she felt a certain comradeship with him. They'd defied God together, and she was equal to him. The driver pushed his horn again and balled his hand in a fist before starting up and driving away.

Her body ached and she was sure that she was going to be ill, perhaps she had an incurable illness. Perhaps this was God's punishment even before she'd uttered the swear word, just because He could see in her heart and knew that she was going to swear?

She tried to think about the wall in Berlin; the teacher had talked about it during a history class that morning and then at the end of the day in prayer. "May God look after all these people imprisoned in a godless country."

She only vaguely understood what was going on in Germany, she wasn't that interested, and it was too far away. Johannes said it was an omen that the world was going to pieces. He'd been going around the house, shaking his head, the way he did when he disagreed with what happened in the news or with a local event, muttering about the world falling apart and how wrong it all was, people buying televisions and watching all kinds of sinful programmes, and now the communists were making the world an even more dangerous place than it already was, and all these events foreshadowed an oncoming doomsday; the sins of mankind were coming home to roost. Anna thought that perhaps he was especially distraught because, after all, despite the fighting everyone had done in the war to resist the Germans and their evil plans, the world still was not a good and reformed place. Bits of the world were still falling apart and then they would hear him constantly mutter, "What is this world coming to?"

Anna learned from Johannes that the Russians should never have been allowed to march up to Berlin. The Allies, by which he meant the Americans and the English, should never have retreated from the parts of Germany they'd occupied at the end of the war. They should never have given in to the dastardly Stalin, who after all, everyone knew could not be trusted. Churchill had been right that they should not have given in to Truman, who'd simply been too worried about the Russians.

"How," he'd sigh, "Could these leaders have let the world slip into this nightmare, and after they had, at such a high cost, won the war against Hitler?"

He'd ponder out loud as if beseeching them, addressing his children, to understand and agree, even if these events seemed to them to be happening in a different part of the world, one that was far removed from their day to day life, and none of them affected Anna as directly as her current malaise.

"I'm feeling sick," she said to her mother, when she entered the kitchen by the backdoor.

Her mother was in a hurry. It was Saturday again and past lunchtime and this was a very busy time for shops in the village when the next day, Sunday, everything of course would be well closed and shuttered. Customers were already queuing at the till, and there was only one shop assistant, a young girl just out of school, not nearly enough for a busy Saturday and she definitely couldn't be trusted on her own.

On Saturdays, the village people came out for their weekly shopping thrills and the Dent shop was one of the largest in the village. It offered a collection of household goods: carpets, curtains, tablecloths, sheets, pillows and other bedding requirements, pots and pans, cutlery and china, ashtrays and flower vases. The Dent shop provided a true collection of the necessary and the idiosyncratic, with separate sections for toys and bicycles, including spare parts, as well as garden furniture.

Greta looked at Anna and sensed some of her distress, but she was already turning away, indicating that she couldn't deal with anything more at that time. Her face had the beseeching look of someone very put upon.

"What's the matter with you? How ill?"

Anna's face was now red and she glinted at her mother with nearly closed eyes, an animal in distress ready to attack, but she swallowed and said, "I'm bleeding. I don't know what's the matter with me, my tummy's aching badly."

She blinked away her tears, sure that some terrible disease had just struck her. God had caught her out. He was bound to, as He must know by now that she didn't want to know about Him. He was punishing her. He had heard her swear, not just today, and as they were told over and over again, He could look deep into your heart, and so He knew more likely than not that she would like to do nothing more than run away from Him and the claustrophobia and that she wanted to belong to a world that had nothing to do with Him.

Liesbet came into the kitchen, her eyebrows raised, half smiling. "Rienske's asleep," she said. "What's up here?"

Greta turned towards her when she spoke to Anna,

"Already. You're only eleven." It was clear that she wasn't talking to Liesbet or about Rienske. She spoke as if whatever was happening to Anna was her fault and it should not be because she wasn't old enough.

"Can you help her Liesbet? Give her some pads of yours? She's got her period …"

She was bleeding to death. Some unmentionable disease had taken hold, the aches were clear, and then all that bloody mess, unnatural in view of where it came from, a part of the body that should never be mentioned, and her mother could only smile in an embarrassed way and ask her sister to deal with it. Anna felt the warm wet mucus well up in her nose and into her forehead, she snorted it up loudly, as her eyes were brimming and she could barely see her mother. She wanted to be told that she wasn't the cause of some unmentionable disaster that would strike her dead; she didn't want to be brushed aside. Not this time.

Her sister said, "*Oh?*" then joined Greta in a soft laugh, but quickly put her hand over her mouth and became serious again, embarrassed now as their mother was, and then she shrugged her shoulders.

"Oh yes, that's fine. Come with me, Anna."

One after the other they walked up the steep narrow stairs, with a carpet that had faded with the numerous steps taken by children going up and down, up to their bedrooms to sleep in the evening and down again in the morning for breakfast, and sometimes they went down in the middle of the night in search of their parents because they couldn't sleep.

"You've got your period. Don't worry, you're not ill, we all get it sooner or later. Girls I mean," Liesbet said, handing her some grey flannelly strips from a shelf in their joint cupboard. "I'm sure Mother will explain later. It has to do with getting babies, you can't have babies if you don't have periods."

Now Anna was even more confused, and at the same time felt stupid that she hadn't put two and two together, that she didn't know something that obviously everyone else knew all about. She felt stupid that she'd never paid enough attention to the half-sentences, the giggles and the allusions by other girls, cousins, and her own sister.

Not me. I don't want any of it; this is utter and total rubbish. I haven't got the time for this. It'll make me one of them and I'll become like them. I don't want to be a woman and have babies.

*

The Berlin Wall was being built and people were locked in. "All Truman's fault," her father said. "Truman should have realised the wickedness of Stalin, that godless Communist, worse than the Nazis."

Johannes added that the Nazis at least were German and there were Germans who still belonged to some kind of Lutheran Christian bond. Lutherans were related to Calvinists, even though they'd relapsed. Russians and Communists were pure heathens. That much Anna understood from what he said.

It had been a long summer and now in the autumn, the world was divided up once more between the good and the evil. This war would be a long and cold one, but to Anna it seemed that she was being forced behind a different wall, one that kept her inside so that she couldn't see what was outside around her in her own country; she wasn't allowed to see any of it.

Only now she wanted to sleep and she didn't want to have to deal with this mess, the embarrassment of it. Her thoughts were like those little, white puffs of cloud in the sky, pushed along in a hurry by a strong wind, never able to form properly, but always dissipating before settling into something more permanent. After Liesbet had gone back down the stairs again, Anna walked into her parents' bedroom, locked the door and sat down on the double bed that took up most of the room and wondered what to do. She kicked a black shoe that peeped out from under the bed, one of her father's, and then kicked it again so it slithered right to the middle under the bed. He'd shout at her mother for not having put his shoes away properly. The clouds in her head continued to pester her, formed and reformed, never remaining still long enough for her to work out the detail of what she was and who she was. Her mind was a broken up puzzle even to herself.

The school, the religious Calvinistic Reformed Church, parents and siblings, all lined up and then suddenly crumpling. New friends, Jana, Christa, Leanne, are they really friends? The world so small and at the same time beyond my reach, sometimes I can barely breathe and outside this small world of ours there is a scary and unknown space. Grownups and parents are always right; they are merciless and hard, they insist they have the best in mind for you, even if they destroy all your hope; they know everything. They have the true belief. God will reward you, but only once you die. Living is about serving God, everything and everyone is Calvinist, the shopkeepers, the headmaster, the teachers, the books, the trees, the water, my marbles, my toys, and my skates. They will all go to heaven, but I may not, because God is merciless. Everyone will sing in Paradise, which is like church, and I must not doubt that. Theirs is the only safe way of life; girls will marry and have children, but one of her aunts doesn't, and they will all believe and come to heaven afterwards, although Hell is the next-door neighbour. You must never doubt any of this. God will hold you to account, He created a world in Calvin's image; Calvin is a man who is nearly as great as God; so was Colijn, but he went wrong when he didn't condemn Hitler: he was a coward and everyone knows that Hell burns for cowards, even if they once were believers, just alongside Paradise; and then there's someone called Kuypers, and there were e so are many others.

She couldn't stop the formation of the clouds. They just carried on and on, grammarless and like unfurling balls and then dissipated with a 'puff'.

All great men are good, but only true believers are. Where is the fit? To be a wife a mother a good sister, a good cook, a good knitter, a good cleaner, a good support. Girl to become woman is helpmeet to man-boy.

The woman-cloud in her mind became larger and larger but it was empty, and then streaky puffs appeared in her brain-sky: *A helpmeet, the wife of … maybe you'll be a teacher but only teach the Word of God. God who? God what? Why God? I don't want it.*

Where was the fun in any of this? Surely, it couldn't be all there was to living? She wanted to have fun, she wanted to see films, she wanted to go out to parties with boys and girls and dance and listen to loud music, and she wanted to be listened to by grown-ups who would explain what the real world was about. She wanted to read the books that would tell her things she didn't know, didn't understand. She wanted to be away from it all.

Anna groaned, grabbed the pads Liesbet had given her, and wanted nothing more than to scrub herself clean, scrub all the messiness away for good. She hated herself and her body, hated the not understanding, the not knowing, sensing that she was being lied to. She hated the trap in which she found herself.

East Germans were trapped. But she was too. Puff.

*

A year later, Anna's periods stopped. Her mother took her to a gynaecologist in a darkened consultation room with heavy green velvet curtains that half covered the windows. Outside was a large tree whose branches and leaves formed patterns across the window, so that only small dots of white sky were visible and the shadows cast further gloom across the wall at the other side of the room. The doctor behind a large wooden desk intimated that Anna's symptoms presented a puzzling

94

phenomenon, although she never learned what it was that he told Greta, who was dressed in her meek, submissive look with best Sunday frock, and she clutched her handbag on her lap almost as if in prayer, as if asking for forgiveness for something Anna had done.

Greta didn't really want to deal with this awkwardness, this embarrassment of a daughter who refused to function normally. Greta didn't know how to deal with this in front of this male superior wisdom. That much was clear to Anna. After examining her, the doctor asked Anna to leave the room and to sit in the waiting room for a while, which was empty except for the girl behind her desk who answered the telephone and who was bent over a large black typewriter with a single sheet of white paper. The girl banged the large keys to chase away the eerie silence and the potential demons that occupied the empty chairs.

Anna wondered whether the doctor didn't want her to hear what he told Greta because he would talk about unmentionable parts of her body. Perhaps he thought she didn't know that she had these or whether this was simply because doctors didn't talk to children, even if she was now a fully menstruating woman, at least she had been for a year.

She was called back into the consultation room after fifteen minutes. The doctor was a large and heavyset man in a grey suit, with an immaculately ironed white shirt and a dark blue striped tie. He had a pair of glasses pinned on the tip of his nose, through which he peered when he scribbled something on a notepad. Looking over the top of his glasses at the room beyond her, he handed Greta the piece of paper that he tore off the pad while he addressed Anna.

"Here is a prescription. There is not much else I can do, as I said to your mother. Gymnasts and other girls often stop having their periods, it's because they are underweight and engage in intense physical activity. It will rectify itself in due course, not to worry. These are tablets that will induce a period every month. You must take one, every day, for three weeks and then not for a week."

He turned from the empty expanse of the room to Greta as if she, Anna, was no longer there, and she fiddled with a clump of dusty dirt that had lodged itself in her coat pocket, stopped herself from taking it out to see what it was. Her mother smiled her stupid servile smile, Anna thought. She seemed embarrassed at taking up time, and then she worried, *but why?* Why this shyness and servility? When Greta had fumbled with the prescription and managed to push it into her handbag and closed the clasp, Anna got up and left the room first. Greta followed after shaking hands with the doctor and mumbling, "Thank you, thank you very much."

The tablets were green and large, and on the cardboard to which they were fixed were written the first two letters of the days of the week for three weeks, and for the first three weeks she took one every day and a few days later a period followed, a drib drab of brownish menstruation that made her feel even more angry and messy. Why take these pills anyway? Life was in fact so much more pleasant without periods and if she didn't take them she'd be fancy free; no mess, no worries, she could take part in ball games and swimming lessons at school, whereas other girls sat in the changing room, with a note from their mother, asking the teacher if they could be excused that week. If she didn't take the pills she'd never again have to own up or be embarrassed at the publicity of it all, this having your period, this escape of blood and mucus from your body leaving a mess in your underwear and a cramp in your tummy. Well, why would she put up with it?

She was fine, Anna told her mother, who was too busy to notice anyway. After six months she visited their local GP, who wrote out another prescription, and six months later again. No one seemed any the wiser and then the GP said that it was all right to do without tablets because this kind of thing 'will have to sort itself anyway.'

"It will be fine," he said. "By the time you get married God will take care, don't worry."

*

Neshnafad, 1977

I stretch and fold my fingers that have become stiff with the continuous writing. It would be good if I could get hold of a typewriter. I'll ask Mike where to get one, perhaps shopping for one in Tehran will be better.

I get up and walk from the kitchen table to the sitting room, stare out over the small front yard and the empty street beyond. It's hot and the air forms a silent wrap around the houses and the street, as if I'm back in my dream that still lingers somewhere in a corner of my brain.

It's almost lunchtime and Mike will be home soon. I'll do some more writing tomorrow, the memories of the village keep flooding back in the moment I put my pen on paper, and Anna takes on a life of her own, taunting me with the way she asserts herself and she changes what I had intended to write. Already, she has upset some of my own memories and replaced them with her own.

I walk back to the kitchen, close my notebook and take it to the bedroom where I put it under a pile of tee-shirts at the back of my drawer.

Chapter Seven: 1977

Iran

Mike walks quickly to his car. It's a quarter to nine and if anything happens on the way and he's held up he'll be late for his lecture. At eight-thirty in the morning, it's hot already and he throws his jacket on the back seat with his briefcase and quickly reverses out of his space in front of the house. He nods a *hello* to his neighbour who also appears to be in a hurry, and who is out of the street even before Mike is. It's only a short ten-minute drive for Mike if he crosses the main road and takes the route across the campus, where all is quiet this time of the morning.

His students are waiting for him when he enters the lecture hall. He likes the way they immediately stop talking to each other when he comes in, with their keenness to learn, and he feels confident in their presence, so unlike his experience of the last few years in England. He feels at home here, respected and recognised for who he is. England was fine for a while and for as long as he'd been a postgrad, however, he's very glad this opportunity came up, to become a lecturer, a professor as his official title is, at the University of Neshnafad.

After his lecture, and having answered a couple of questions by students who stay behind to chat with him, he speed walks to the cafeteria to get his caffeine. Despite the hot weather, he has got used to his morning coffee when in England and sticks to the routine, although he'll have tea later on and he'll drink lots of water in between. The coffee tastes foul, even worse than in England, but it gives him the kick he needs. He should get his own jar of instant coffee, some decent brand, but he never remembers to ask Katie to get some when she goes shopping and never thinks of it himself when they're out. He'll have to get it from Kourosh as they cater for foreign tastes as well as Iranian.

One of his colleagues comes up to him and asks if he'll be at the meeting in the afternoon. Of course he will, it's part of who he is now, a professor, a member of the staff team, one of the bright young men who will help this country come together, *inshallah*. They talk for a while and then it's time for his next lecture, and before he knows it the morning is over and it's time to go home for lunch. After lunch, he'll come back and work in the lab with one or two of his Master students and then he'll attend the meeting. Days just fly by, especially with this lunch break they all take in the summer when they go to their air-conditioned homes to avoid the midday heat. Katie will have cooked something, and then they can make love in the afternoon and have a snooze before he takes off again. Life is good. Even Katie is enjoying this new routine, he's sure, as she rips off her clothes and then his and he'll turn her on top of him as she bends over to kiss him.

Such a difference with living in London, he tells himself again. No need to cross half a town to get home, to take tubes, to run for a bus, and to be stuck in traffic jams. Here he can enjoy his work. He has colleagues who also are friends, they live in a closed community, they have accommodation that is more than adequate and quite modern compared to some of the houses some people live in, and also compared to the desolate flats they used to have in London. Moreover, it's all subsidised and the rent is cheap. The pay is more than adequate. He's happy here, so much happier than he's ever been before.

He frowns when he remembers that Katie has said something about feeling cooped up and wanting a job. Of course it's bound to be harder for her, moving here from the busy life she had in London, studying and then working and having a large group of friends, more than he had he thinks. Katie has never realized how fed up he'd been with the feeling of alienation he had in London, she never realized that he had felt a stranger in the England that she loved so much, that it could never be his home. He remembers the day they went on a trip to Canterbury, to wander around the Cathedral and to get a feel of the town. It was his idea and he has regretted it ever since. They should have checked the opening times, but they went on a whim and when they got there the Cathedral was closed, but they admired it from the outside and then wandered around the grounds and the town. It was a chilly day and they huddled close together on a park bench to have a look at the guidebook they'd bought. "Long live Enoch Powell," someone suddenly said behind them. Katie looked bewildered, stared at the man who stood there smirking. Mike pulled her up sharply. "Let's go. We can do without this."

Katie objected, and he could see she wanted to say something back but he wouldn't let her. He pulled her away as fast as he could. He didn't want to get into an argument, didn't want their day together spoiled, he was afraid perhaps that she might see him in a different light, in the light of someone who didn't belong because his skin had a different hue. He wasn't sure. "This happens," he said. "It happens a lot here in England. Let's just get away. It's not important."

Katie didn't understand at all. He saw it in her face, which was one of disbelief with her mouth half-open to say something sharp, and he pulled her with him towards the small café outside the park, where they had a tea and some cake. He said, "This is England for you, you hadn't realized? It's not so bad in London because we're usually with friends and we live in reasonable areas. Also, it's different there when you're with me."

"But…" she said. She didn't finish her sentence; just screwed up her eyes the way she used to, still does, when she was trying to get her head around something.

Later, she seemed to have forgotten, but he'd been even more resolved to leave that country as soon as he could, to go back to a place where he would not be stared at because he had black, curly hair and a dark skin, where he would not be asked by all and sundry where he came from because he was not obviously Jamaican or black, or … He wanted to be at home. He wanted to be recognised and accepted, unquestionably.

When she asks, he agrees with Katie that life in London had been good to a certain extent. They had fun, they had lots of friends, they went out together, saw films, and did all the things you did when you were young and a university student, when you were in love and when you lived with your girlfriend. He wondered if she'd ever noticed that all his friends in London were foreigners who came from Bolivia, from Spain, from Italy or they had parents who had lived the colonial life abroad. Perhaps she'd never really noticed that he had very few English friends, unlike Katie. They don't talk about this much. He knew at the time that English people didn't take to him easily, that they were suspicious, that they couldn't quite place him; an Iranian from a country that was up and coming with the Shah and the oil. They were never sure whether he was alright or not, whether they should accept him with open arms or be careful about his motives for being in England, or that he might take something away from them. Underneath it all, most of them looked down on him; someone from what they considered to be a developing country. Yes, he liked English culture, he loved the language and their books and their concert halls and the performance of classical music across London, and perhaps in that sense he was westernized, whatever that meant, but he had always known deep in his heart that he wouldn't stay, that he couldn't stay. He'd always known that he couldn't live with that sense of being an outsider, of being like Camus' *'l'étranger'*. He wanted to belong, and be part of his own country's promise of success. He wanted to live his life off-guard and be relaxed about himself.

Katie is different and sometimes a bit naïve, but at least she's completely honest and open and she's smart and attractive and he still feels so lucky that they met. At the time when they met, he'd been at a bit of a low ebb. Strangely enough, his half-girlfriend then had been Dutch as well and he'd been to The Netherlands to see her family, but their relationship had cooled when her parents appeared unhappy about their daughter being in a relationship with someone from Iran. Teresa had decided she wanted to stay in The Netherlands after a year of working as an au pair in London. She would never come to London for him, let alone to Iran, and he of course was unwilling, as well as unable, to move to The Netherlands.

Katie doesn't know about this, as he has never told her. At first, when they had just met, he simply didn't want to tell her that he was disentangling himself from a relationship, and it seemed odd, somehow, that this should have been another Dutch girl, but then later he decided it wasn't worth bringing up. After his experience with Teresa's parents, he was not at all keen anyway to try and meet Katie's Dutch relatives. Katie was hardly effusive about her relations and he had quickly realized that she didn't want to talk much about her childhood, or about her parents, or the religious background and the fights and disagreements. She mentioned a boyfriend once but that seemed to have been a platonic relationship as far as he could make out, and she'd broken up with him before it became really serious. Mike suspects that her family would have frowned upon any pre-marital relationships, and that this was probably the reason for not having jumped into bed with this Paul, the boyfriend, or for Paul not having tried it on even. He hasn't really thought about it much, because she dismissed it all in a few sentences, and now it all is so distant from their life here, and so irrelevant.

Her parents of course had not reacted very different from the way Iranian parents would, he thinks, from the way his parents would react if either of his two sisters had tried to engage in a pre-marital relationship. He's glad though that neither he nor Katie have ever had any inhibitions about what they want from each other and he still wonders sometimes whether she'd been a virgin or not, that first time. She hadn't seemed very experienced, but then he'd been fumbling too and she'd seemed quite matter of fact and had said she was on the pill 'for medical reasons.' He wasn't sure he believed her but doesn't think about it. He is sure she's faithful to him and that's enough as far as he's concerned. He wouldn't, he thinks, try anything behind her back either, wouldn't dream of it. Not that there is much opportunity here in Neshnafad. He smiles as he turns the car into their street.

Katie is outside the house, she's talking to the neighbour's wife and he waves to them as he gets out of the car. She's such an attractive woman, his wife now, and his smile turns into a broad grin as he walks up to them.

Chapter Eight: 1963

The Netherlands

Quarrels followed by punishments emerged and flared up out of nothing. They had a way of erupting like unexpected storms, the kind of thunderstorms that came with gusts of wind that shook the trees outside, blasted the air around the house and darkened the sky with clouds in the image of an army of gods and devils, intending to come down to earth to fight it out with their underlings. The trees were threatening on days like that. They groaned and bent and then suddenly they stood still, as if saying all this had nothing to do with them and nothing would make them break or submit. After the storm, they shook out their leaves, let the water drip off and down the branches, and once the sun came out the leaves glistened again and were happy once more.

"I'm never going back there! I want my own life. They don't care about me anyway."

Anna's grey blue eyes had gone dark, nearly black, and they glistened like the leaves of the trees after a rainstorm; her mouth was set but her cheeks quivered. Her face was red and her breathing sharp and loud. She even stamped her foot on the floor as if she was a small child and not the grown-up she wanted to be.

"Well, you can stay here as far as I'm concerned. I'll check with my mum but I'm sure she'll be fine with that," Gemma said.

Gemma was her best friend, the one she ran to when it all got too much, the one she confided in, the one who was always there. They had been best friends since the first grade of primary school, when they sat next to each other in one little bench.

Gemma's hand extended and she vaguely pointed to the room with her little finger, as if she was politely drinking a cup of tea with Anna, whilst leaning on the table with her other hand. They were in the schoolroom, which was the meeting room for the headmaster, Gemma's father, and his teachers, or sometimes for a parents' meeting or a meeting of church elders. The room was on the first floor of the low school building, and you reached it by a flight of wide stone stairs that sounded hollow when someone walked on them. It was the only room on this floor, and it was above the largest classroom at the front of the building. The rest of the school was single storied and with a flat roof. The classrooms ran along an extended corridor with a cold granite floor that echoed with the noise of the children when they came in and hung up their coats and jackets on the coat pegs attached to the walls. The classrooms were square rooms with walls covered in drawings and posters, mainly about church and bible meetings, but some had drawings of trees and houses and people, and the rooms had brown wooden desks for two, each with an inkwell with a sliding black cover in the middle. Blue ink stains covered the dirty wood and small drawers held a pen, a pencil and whatever books and notebooks the class used at the time. Each classroom held three rows of seven of these desks, and behind the teacher's table in front was a blackboard, with a packet of white chalk on the ledge. High windows looked out on the tall trees that bordered the school building, and further away, beyond the headmaster's garden, were fields interspersed with country lanes, detached and isolated stone houses, farms with wooden sheds and barns behind hedges and gates. Beyond, if you followed the country lanes far enough out, you could just find yourself in another even more isolated village or perhaps a main road connecting the villages to a town further afield.

The primary Calvinist church school was at the edge of Armitage, a kilometre or so up the canal road, well away from the one main road that passed the other side of the village edging along woods, and this road was their connection to Gezel, where Anna attended her secondary school.

Anna had cycled to this primary school every day from the day she started in the first grade until she left after having completed the sixth grade. To begin with, she would go with her elder siblings; later she would take charge of younger siblings in the same way. When she was still small, the road along the canal would be a challenge, stretching out endlessly in her mind, but now she realised it was only a short and less than ten minutes cycling distance from her home, compared to the hour-long trip each way to her secondary school in Gezel.

Next to the school building was the small Calvinist church with the vicar's house attached at the side. The church had been built a long time ago when a small group of people decided to remove themselves from the Dutch Reformed Church, with their imposing building including a church tower and clock, and founded the Calvinist religious community in the village. Church and school belonged inextricably together; parents who attended the Calvinist church sent their children to this Calvinist school. After the pastor, the headmaster was an important man, although Anna's father once thought loudly that the master and his wife were 'pretentious' and 'not any better than we are, whatever they thought.'

Gemma stood at the top end of the long, rectangular, dark wooden table with ten wooden high-back chairs, four on each side and one at each end. The surface of the table was covered with deep crags and scratches, as if men, God's followers, Anna thought, had angrily put a knife into it whenever they wanted to make their point about the devilishness of non-Calvinists. She sat at the opposite end from where Gemma stood, and she had her elbows on the table, her head resting on her hands like a sullen giraffe as she looked up at Gemma. Anna's blond-brown hair was cut short and square and looked untidy giving her a boyish appearance, whereas Gemma's thick and full dark-brown nearly black hair was carefully and neatly combed into two pigtails, one on each side of her face, with small red ribbons at the end. Gemma's high cheekbones, thick eyebrows and her glowing, lightly tanned skin gave her a more mature appearance, like that of the girl who'd take charge of the little dwarfs in the fairy tale book. Gemma knew what she wanted and usually got it too. She observed Anna coolly whilst picking up two wet and freshly washed and wrung jumpers that she'd put on the table in front of her, as well as a large white towel which was dry.

Gemma's mother used the school meeting room to dry her family's knitwear and other delicate items on towels spread out on the floor. A number of garments were already so arranged around the table, and the chairs had been pushed under the table to make more space. Gemma held the two wet jumpers in her arms like babies waiting to be suckled, and then started to arrange them on the dry towel that she spread out on the floor. She had washed these garments in a large sink downstairs in a workroom. She was her mother's little helper, smug in what she considered to be her territory, in the knowledge that she was the headmaster's daughter, which in their small village community imparted on her an importance that other girls could only envy. Anna was fond of Gemma and unquestioningly trusted her best friend, although lately they had seen much less of each other than they used to … all the fault of Johannes who'd decided that Anna should go to the Calvinist school in Gezel, whilst Gemma's father appeared to be much less perturbed about heathen influences and had allowed Gemma to attend the same school as their older siblings.

Amongst their friends and former school friends, Anna again was the odd one out and at times she hated her father for it. It seemed that he insisted that she would be different. At other times, she thought that this was perhaps not so bad after all. She wanted to be different, didn't she? She didn't really want to be stuck in the village and this way she was no longer part of a group that had started its life in primary school.

Unfortunately, after a year at her new school, nothing much had changed and her life simply continued in the same routine, and the rules were if anything even stricter than she had known before. She envied Gemma who would never get herself into the kind of quarrels she got herself into with her father and school authority. The suffocating rules. She sighed. Nothing had moved on much in the lives of their parents, not since the War or even before, she thought, and going to this strictly Calvinist school further away than any of her peers had not changed a thing. Her father never stopped talking about the War and instilling on them the necessity that they should stay firm in the fight against an encroaching sinfulness of a wider world. And that included guarding the dress code of his daughters and his wife. Her mother would never even wear as much as a pair of trousers. Moreover, Johannes considered with distaste and alarm the disturbing and growing unease around them, across the country and further afield in other countries, the encroaching godlessness, the increasing terrors of a cold war between super powers with atomic bombs, the sinful fashions and rebelliousness of young people, and he made it clear that he would do his utmost to keep all of that at bay.

Anna wondered how it was possible that Calvin still ruled their lives as much as he had done when she and Gemma sat in the benches in the classrooms below, along that spooky and now empty corridor. It was as if Prince William of Orange and his stand against the Duke Alba and the Spanish king in the sixteenth century, and the hard won religious freedom for reformists and Calvinists, were still as much part of their lives as Churchill, Hitler and Roosevelt were, the way Johannes talked.

Calvin's followers were still writing books on what they considered to be the true faith and they were still quarrelling about obscure texts, thundering their sermons from pulpits and university debating societies, admonishing their sons to follow the scripture, keeping their wives and daughters in check, making sure that they couldn't do any harm to others or harm themselves, because they had no say in it. They were girls, future mothers and wives, respected so that they could be the helpmeets to their men folk who had also learned to live in accordance with the biblical precepts. Even if some of the girls were clever, they would always be Eves born out of Adams, never really quite equal, and they were certainly not expected to voice any opinion that differed from their menfolk.

Anna sighed again. She had once more managed to upset her father and had run out of the house slamming the door behind her and shouting that she would not come back, ever.

"Do you think it's a good idea?" Gemma asked. "I mean, you know, perhaps it's easier if you just changed your skirt. It is ridiculous, I agree. It's not that short. Mine is shorter and my mom doesn't seem to mind. And if my mom doesn't then my father wouldn't say anything anyway."

There seemed to be a different rapport between Gemma's parents. "She's got the trousers on," Liesbet said once, and Anna wished her mother would put on trousers too.

Anna stood up and looked down at the offending garment, a short black skirt coming halfway up her thighs but worn over a pair of thick black tights. Johannes had made it clear that the skirt was offensive and 'indecent', and that she was forbidden to wear such clothing. Anna pulled up her nose and snorted. "No, I'm not taking it off. I've had enough of him telling me all the time what I can and cannot do."

She sat down again and resumed her posture with her chin on her open hands and elbows firmly on the table. She stared at Gemma.

"Well, what *are* you going to do? You won't be able to stay here forever I suppose and you'll need to eat," Gemma said.

Anna was well aware of the hopelessness of her situation. If only she could break out of this prison. If only she had friends or family who could help her, who would want to help her. She sighed again, louder this time. If only she had parents who would stop interfering with her life and let her be, who would stop telling her what clothes she could or couldn't wear, or telling her what time she had to be home. And if only she was not so frightened, deep inside, of what would happen if she simply disappeared from this village and from its God altogether. But where to? "Well, I'm staying here for now. I'll think about it. I've got some apples," she added.

She hadn't brought any clothes of course, not brought anything for that matter. She'd just slammed the door behind her and got on her bike before anyone could hold her back. She might get bored; surely she couldn't just stay in this room forever, she knew that. She wanted to win this battle, wanted to pierce through her father's iron rules, God's rules. *Gods and Fathers.* She must have it out with them; she must try it out and see if she was going to be struck dead when she told Him to go away. Her stomach turned but she wouldn't even let Gemma notice that.

Sometimes she couldn't breathe with all the anger and questions in her head. She didn't even know anymore whether or not she believed in God. He had always been there, for as long as she could remember, He had always dictated what she could and couldn't do; they had always bowed their heads before and after each meal. "Please God bless this food, amen." They had always sat on their knees as little children before going to bed, hands folded and eyes firmly shut, "Please God look after me and wake me up in the morning, thank you, Amen," as if they might die otherwise. Even now, Johannes assumed that they still said their evening prayer before getting into bed, only he was too tired to check up on them and her mother had given up long ago, what with all the little ones that still needed her attention.

Anna was scared not to believe and afraid that she would go to Hell if she doubted God and she would much rather just ignore Him altogether. But at least she would know, wouldn't she? It was the not knowing that she found most upsetting. It was as if a little demon drove her to go further and then still further in her rebelliousness, to test her father and God and see what would come out of it.

She wondered if He did exist, if He really would mind if she wore a short skirt. Surely there must be other things He was worried about? If you thought about it, all those biblical Israelites really wore silly long clothes after all, well the men did anyway and yet no one seemed to mind that. They could wear long dresses if they wanted to, whereas a woman couldn't wear trousers, or short skirts.

Gemma got up. "I'll get us some tea," she said and left the room. When she came back, she said that her mother was all right with it if Anna slept in the schoolroom for one night; she would let Anna's parents know she was staying over.

To Gemma her mother had expressed amusement. "She'll forget all about wanting to run away. She'll be too scared to sleep and will run home at first light." But Gemma wasn't going to pass that on to Anna.

There were some cushions and an old blanket in a cupboard, and Gemma brought some sandwiches and a glass so that she could fill it up with water from the small toilet tap downstairs.

Gemma's mother didn't have a high regard for Anna's parents or for anyone in the village for that matter and she would be happy to stick the needle in wherever she could.

That night, Anna tossed and turned on the hard floor. The blackness of the night was like the Devil himself and he seemed to be out to strangulate her, wanting to take her away. Once she cried out loud and woke herself up. She was afraid to die, afraid of the heat of Hell and afraid of being alone in this deserted room. She shivered under the blanket and tried to push back the blackness inside her skull, but couldn't think of anything with which to replace her dismal thoughts. She lay with her eyes wide open. How could she rid herself of this fear?

The next morning she quietly left the schoolroom, cycled home and slipped in by the backdoor. She went to her room and took off the offending skirt and shoved it to the back of the cupboard she shared with Liesbet. She found her library book and hid in the bicycle shed at the back of the house. At lunchtime her mother prepared the food in the kitchen and put out the plates, knives and forks for nine, including the baby chair for Rienske. Bert and Liesbet would not be back, they were staying with friends. Her mother came to the shed and said, "Give me a hand, will you? Put the glasses on the table, will you?"

When her father came into the kitchen, he said, "So you're back then. I see you've come to your senses."

Anna shrugged her shoulders. *Just wait. You may have won this time but that's because I'm dependent on you. It's because I'm afraid, so afraid. It won't be like that forever.* She was smouldering fury and helpless.

*

In Germany, there were East Berliners who escaped from their side of the wall through a tunnel underneath to the west and Adolf Eichmann was hanged. Anna's father made a few scathing remarks followed by, "What is the world coming to?" He knew about these events, they were part of the world he contemplated in his newspaper, and he shook his head every time he listened to the news. These Russians and in fact all of the communist regimes including China and other countries were from the Devil, and he nodded approval at Eichmann's execution.

"This," Johannes said, "is what you must know about; the badness of the wider human race. We should always be mindful about our own place in the world."

He never actually said that they were the chosen ones, the ones that carried out God's wish on earth in the way He had always intended it to be, but he seemed afraid to consider the alternative, not belonging to the chosen ones. This world they lived in now, he implied, was only a temporary existence that would prepare them for the afterlife. That was the most important part of their existence - death and what came after that. Death was the big bogeyman, and at the same time the pulpits told you that it was the gateway to heaven.

Johannes assured his children and his wife that Communists and the German Nazis were inherently untrustworthy and that together, these two groups of people and the countries full of them, were to blame for many things that had so badly gone wrong in their own lives during the War not so long ago, never to be forgotten or forgiven.

Johannes would talk about all the things that were wrong in the world. He would relate, in short sentences almost as if he was shy to mention it, what happened during the War, the gassing of the Jews, the execution of freedom fighters, the overrunning of their own country as well as many others, Belgium, Poland and France. He had his picture album, the one he shared with Anna and her older siblings and that he kept behind lock and key in the glass-fronted cupboard in the front room. The pictures still haunted her and she wondered whether Hell would be just like that.

Even though she tried, Anna couldn't really imagine what Johannes might have been like as a child. No one talked about it, not his sisters or their husbands, not her grandfather, not her mother, whose childhood similarly was a big mystery, except that Greta's brothers and sisters seemed to enjoy each other's company whereas Johannes' sisters always looked askance at him.

His children tired him out, Johannes often said. They gave him headaches, they were too demanding and not at all like they should be. He had little patience with Greta also and was often angry with her.

"Mother," he would say. "You're of little help. Why do you always indulge them? Why do I always have to tell them what's right and wrong?"

Greta didn't answer when he said that, she seemed to be afraid of him sometimes.

"Because you're soft on them and too easy going, I have to always punish them," he'd say. "Just see what happened with Anna. If it had been up to you, you would've just let her wear that skirt, well above her knees, looking ridiculous and indecent." He sighed, "Not only that, but then it's up to me. And you know that it's wrong!"

At other times Johannes appeared forgiving and was friendly and pleasant. Anna knew that he liked it that she was a keen reader and that she was clever and consistently got high marks in school. He liked it when she jollied about, laughed out loud and was helpful and when she resolved complicated crossword puzzles in the newspaper or told an anecdote about school. He liked it when she was polite and did as she was told, got herself ready without a murmur to go to school, to go to church, or to help her mother. Then he would talk to her as if she was a grown up and could be trusted, as someone who would understand that all his chastising and temper was only for her own good.

*

Anna sat down with the others at the table and Johannes said the prayer before lunch, adapting the words by thanking God that they had all gathered together to eat this bread that He had provided to them even though they didn't deserve it. In particular, he was glad that they had Anna again within their midst. Anna looked through the slits of her eyes around the

115

table. Her parents and siblings had their eyes closed, and at the end of their father's prayer they all rattled off their prayer in turn, starting with Stephan who was the older of the twins and finishing with her youngest sister Rienske who was five now and already proficient in saying out loud the prayer, "*lord please bless this food, amen*", before they started to eat.

Chapter Nine: 1963

The Netherlands

There was no escape. However hard you tried, it would always catch up with you. Sin was everywhere. Somehow or other you breathed it in along with the clean and crisp country air, and then you breathed it out again, polluting everything and everyone around you. Sin wrapped itself around your head and body and limbs and was part of you whether you liked it or not; you ate it and it ate you, sometimes you choked on it. As you grew up and understood more, sin became your companion; it was your identical twin, your best friend but it was the wrong friend, you couldn't shake it off, you would never be clean because of it and sin would in the end be your downfall. Sin must be male. It is a '*he*,' oh yes of course the Bible is full of '*he's*', so why should sin all of a sudden be a female serpent? But Eve was female, and sin seemed to cling to girls and women more than it did to boys and men. Girls developed breasts, they menstruated, both were sinful weren't they? Breasts should never be mentioned and menstruation was a curse. Simply by showing too much bare skin, women seduced men and females became pregnant; even if girls were weaker they were also more responsible for the sin in the world. That was understood.

Anna and Gemma were lying on their towels in the verge of the patch of land next to the brook. Surreptitiously, Anna looked at Gemma as she lay there with her head turned to the sun and her eyes closed, and she envied her. She couldn't quite put her finger on it yet, why this was so, but she did envy Gemma. She would not really like to be Gemma and didn't really want to have Gemma's parents, especially her brothers or that boring sister of hers, none of that, but when she looked at Gemma that summer's day, when they were just the two of them, sin reared its head up. She was full of envy.

Gemma was beautiful, she thought, and Anna wanted Gemma's breasts that were developing so nicely compared to her own flat chest. She wanted Gemma's skin and the shape of her head, her beautiful thick hair, but most of all she wanted Gemma's self-assurance and the way she would simply assume her place in the world, never questioning. Anna was envious and that was sinful, even more so because she actually thought of Gemma's breasts, saw them even, and weren't you supposed to pretend that they didn't exist?

Gemma was lying on a skimpy towel in her old bathing suit, stretched to a faded off blue white and hanging loose around her frame because it was far too big. It was obvious that someone else had stretched it before Gemma got to wear it. The bathing suit was a hand-me-down from that big sister of hers, and her sister was twice Gemma's size, always had been as far back as Anna could remember. Nevertheless, Anna thought, the shapelessness and the looseness of the swimsuit didn't seem to matter, it didn't at all detract from Gemma's attractiveness. Gemma got away with it, as she got away with whatever she wore. She wondered what it was like to have breasts like Gemma, to be whistled at by boys and even grown up men, who all appeared to think she was at least five years older, ready for their flirts. She'd heard them, and Gemma would just giggle when a man whistled after her and she would keep her head up high, provocative in her childish way. Gemma knew her worth, was hugely self-confident and nothing seemed to touch her, no Devil or God haunted her as they haunted Anna. Gemma shrugged and shook her head when Anna tried to talk about her own fear and restlessness.

"What are you talking about? We're fine, we haven't done anything bad in our lives?" she would say. "Besides, I don't think at all that God is bad. There is Jesus, remember." And then Anna didn't persevere. She would laugh with Gemma but deep inside the questions continued to gnaw.

Envy was bad and Anna rubbed her towel through her hair as she stood there, drying herself after the swim in the murky water of the brook. They were in their favourite hide out on this summer afternoon after school, away from the rest of the boys and girls, with books in their bags to read. They would sun themselves until their arms were red, and they imagined they'd be beautiful and tanned and glow all over. Anna dropped her wet towel on the grass and spread it out, sat down with her arms around her knees and looked over the meadows stretching into the distance where the green met the blue of the sky.

In early spring, this countryside was still bleak, flushed with the rain that came down in sudden lashes, straight from the low grey skies. The wind chased the clouds and bent the trees, hit the hedges, rattled the gates, and the first sheep out there stood huddled, heads down into the grass that was only just beginning to grow again after the cold of the winter.

That early in the year, every chilly raindrop was full of God and the Devil, and the wind elaborated their fight for power and possession of this land, where farmers grew corn and beets and wheat from the clumps of clay and tufts of grass, and the farmers were as silent and deliberate as their fields whilst they

119

prayed that God's will would be done, but only let there be just enough rain, not too much and not too little and yes, Our Father who art in Heaven, just make sure that the land is fertile and we are able to pay our bills, that our cows give enough milk and our sheep drop lambs that are healthy, and that our grain will grow so that we can buy the necessities for our families, our ever increasing broods of children that you send us in your mercy because you know what is good for us.

And so God and the Devil lived there all around them almost in a convivial way, the one couldn't do without the other, keeping guard on that land and its people. And Anna and Gemma knew this and understood. Even, if in June, the milder weather had won out over the callousness of March and April, and the sheep had dropped their lambs, and the sun had won through over the rain and the clouds and the wind for the time being, then behind this deceptive calm, God and the Devil were both equally present as conjoined twins, fighting it out over ownership, not just of the land but of all the people who lived there, including Anna and Gemma, watching them and overhearing their thoughts and everything they said.

Cows were grazing peacefully, far away from them behind the sandy path and the wire fencing that reduced to small specks on the horizon. It was late afternoon and the sun was low in the sky. There was the hum of bees and the distracting cow flies that Anna slapped away with her book or a piece of clothing, whatever was at hand, and they were the only sounds in this deserted patch on the land outside the village in the middle of July. They had settled behind the bank of the brook, far away from the bridge where Hans had died all those years ago, but which, once more, was filled with kids who were again daring each other and running around. Anna pulled at her swimsuit with her thumb and forefinger to stretch it down over her leg. It was too tight for her, and like Gemma's it was also worn and faded, and she wondered whether she would be able to convince her mother to give her the money to buy a new one this time, and not be given the next second hand one that her sister had worn out already. Once before, she'd had a new one that her mother had bought for her, when she was eight or nine, from the small village shop that also sold ribbons, buttons in different sizes and colours, needles and elastic and baby things, as well as children's swim wear in the summer. Two elderly sisters were the owners of that shop. They were considered quite posh and a bit strange because everyone knew they voted for the Liberal Party and not the Reformed Church Party or another religious party that everyone else in the village voted for. They were different from the rest of them, were more regal, as if not having a male as part of their living arrangements gave them a solidity that other women lacked, an independence that made evident their self-sufficiency, even if Anna could not, at the time, understand how that was possible. They had their grey hair in large buns at the back of their heads, wore blouses that buttoned up to the neck and that had long sleeves in summer and in winter, and they wore pleated woollen skirts with flat shoes, solid and sensible. The two women had always been there, for as long as Anna could remember, and her mother used to send Anna or one of her siblings to their shop for buttons or a reel of cotton or pins and needles. Even if they did not have the right size of bathing suit, they would order one for you and then it would come a week or so later.

This time, however, she didn't want to go to that shop. She shivered at the thought; the earlier imagined glamour had gone. She had come to realise the dowdiness of what was on offer there, and what she really wanted was a new and modern swimsuit in her size, or even a bikini. She should try and convince her mother to give her the money and she could then go to one of the shops in town instead, a real fashion shop, where they stocked all kinds, even bikinis like Brigitte Bardot wore, and which she would very much like to have. She'd seen the pictures in the music and film magazines that her brothers hid under their mattress, and that were on show in the paper shops in town. Although she might convince her mother, and Greta might just let her buy whatever she wanted if only to be rid of her nagging, Johannes should never find out. But then neither of them ever went swimming anyway.

Gemma was lazy and not very talkative and she kept her eyes closed, now lying on her tummy with her head resting on her forearms, face sideways. Her back was reddish brown after a week of sunshine. She slapped at a fly that was trying to land on her shoulder and grunted. Anna wanted to look like that and to have that back and that waist. She suppressed a sigh as she rolled over on her wet towel with the grass prickly on her legs. She wanted to stroke her, but Gemma would think she was crazy if she did. You never touched anyone except for a handshake or a goodnight kiss on the cheek, and even that was something her father seemed to be uncomfortable with. Her parents were not naturally tactile, no one in their family was, someone might pat your hand or arm but there was no demonstrative kissing or stroking, ever, and so it was difficult to carry off touching someone without coming across as strange. Her awareness of Gemma next to her was overwhelming. She pulled a comb out of her bag, four teeth missing, and furiously hacked through her wet and tangled hair, to rid herself of the suffocating thoughts. She stuffed the comb back into her bag and closed her eyes to let the sun caress her skin, the heat of it slowly burning all thoughts out of her until she dozed off.

Sin was in every step you took, it caught you out, ran with you and took the lead. It was like death in that poem they had learned and commented on in one of their Dutch language classes, the poem about the gardener of a Persian nobleman, who ran up to his master in some beautiful place or other in Persia. That was a country far away as Anna knew, where they had a Shah (or was it an Emperor?) who had a beautiful wife called Soraja. Anna had seen pictures of her in a magazine in the hairdresser's, which was her uncle's hairdressing shop, and she had wondered if her uncle realised these pictures were there. Johannes would have torn them out.

In the poem, the gardener was frightened because he had just met Death with a capital D, grinning at him, and the gardener told his master that he would have to go far away, to a place called Isfahan, because he must at all costs avoid Death. He didn't want to die. And then that same evening the master had a conversation with Death and asked him why he had scared off his gardener, and Death said 'but I was not trying to scare him off at all, I was simply surprised that I saw your gardener here as I was supposed to take him from Isfahan in the evening.' Even Greta had known this poem when she had mentioned it to her. Anna was surprised, but then the inevitability of death, no matter where you were, added to the mixture of dread that was building up inside her.

The inevitability of this appointment with Death, to Anna, was like the inevitability of Sin. You just couldn't get away from either, and behind Sin was God who would punish you and you would die and be in pain for all eternity. She couldn't quite imagine what that meant but it would not leave her, that sense of dread, it was always there with her. The two went hand in hand, God and Sin, Sin and God, inevitable companions because only God had a key to all of this, somehow.

She inhaled a deep breath of air and spat it out at the sky. She wondered why Gemma was not bothered by these thoughts in the way that they invaded her, inevitably and obsessively, sooner or later. She was wide-awake again, sat up and pulled a small bottle of oil out of her bag wrapped up in a sticky, plastic covering. She poured some on her hand and rubbed her arms and then her legs.

"You want me to rub your back with oil?" she asked Gemma.

"No, I'm okay, have just done it," Gemma said, not bothering to open her eyes, her face turned away from Anna to the sun.

Anna looked at her own legs, with knees that were all scarred, even though her legs were nice and shapely and better than Gemma's. Anna was much taller than Gemma. Gemma had fairly short legs that were round and muscular with heavy thighs, not slim like hers, but so what? Breasts were much more important because they made you feminine and attractive, and Gemma definitely had got breasts, visible and daring, already.

How had she, Anna, managed to get so many different blemishes and scars on her body, especially across her legs and knees, as well as odd scars on her arm, as if she had been punctured and painted on with a blunt pencil? Why, as a child, and even now sometimes, did she always have to be the daredevil and show off by cycling faster, running faster, jumping furthest and inevitably falling over, stumbling over rocks, grazing her knees, arms, elbows, fingers and even once or twice her back and shoulders?

She turned round on her tummy with her head resting on her folded arms in front of her and closed her eyes, but couldn't rid herself of the picture of Gemma lying next to her and she wanted to touch her, feel her breasts, kiss her and hold her and have Gemma's arms around her. Gemma could be her mother, her sister, her best friend, could be everything that she yearned for and couldn't have. Gemma could provide her with a hiding place. But she wouldn't, Anna knew. Gemma had no idea.

Chapter Ten: 1977

Iran

"Let's spend some of the summer holiday travelling around Iran," Mike says that first year when we live in Neshnafad. "We could go to Tehran for a couple of weeks and stay with my parents, then spend some time on the Caspian at my aunt's villa. Remember she offered?"

We can't afford to go travelling around Europe and see our friends in London, I know that.

"We can always go next year, to London I mean," Mike says. "Why don't you ask Tessa if she'd like to come over here and visit us in the autumn?"

Tessa's got a new boyfriend and she's written that they're getting married next year. I'll write to her, find out if they'd like to come together perhaps although I doubt whether she will. She's already let me know that she doesn't like what's happening in Iran and says she wouldn't feel comfortable.

We lock the flat and drive the journey back from Neshnafad to Tehran, the same long, dusty road full of potholes winding its way through desert and mountains, the same road that we took when we came down to Neshnafad from Tehran last year. I remember my excitement during that first trip, the unfamiliarity of it. I remember the long stretches of road, without another car or living being in sight for miles until we'd come across another small hamlet or a signpost to towns off the road, signposts that I couldn't read.

The dust and the heat are overwhelming and I have never seen or experienced anything like it, not in Europe, not even in Spain on that road with Tessa, although that was hot. I would love it if Tessa comes to Neshnafad and visits us, but when I mentioned it before in one of my letters she was not very keen. Tessa said that she and Ben, her new boyfriend, were busy, and besides there were too many uncertainties about Iran, although I don't understand what she's talking about. I think newspaper stories always paint the worst pictures and the reality is that we are having a very comfortable life here.

We take pit stops at the few roadside cafes where coaches unload weary travellers, people from Tehran and local people on their way to Qom, to Natanz, Isfahan and Neshnafad or to Shiraz or even Bandar Abbas. I haven't been to any of these places, although Mike has promised that we will visit some of them if I want to. He doesn't seem keen about anything along this route and says that they are just so many places with lots and lots of mullahs and religious people and he can do without them. Some of the wives we know, our friends, have relatives in these places, but I can only try to imagine what they are like by putting a picture together from the stories they tell me, about visits to relatives living in small houses, where women are covered in chadors and men attend the local mosques and pray a lot for the Shah to fall.

The roadside cafes are large square halls with white washed walls, and with rows and rows of wooden chairs and tables. They have fairly basic facilities, toilets where I haul up my trousers, fold them up to just under the knees and balance myself, squatting on the two grimy tiled supports at each side of the hole in the ground, hoping that I will not wet my clothes. I remember the public facilities in London and other places and think that perhaps it's just as well you can do your business without needing to touch anything, as long as you manage to keep your balance of course. I am glad, however, that our house has all the modern conveniences, which includes a western toilet and washbasin and a modern bathroom with another toilet, bath and shower.

"What will we do all these weeks in Tehran?" I ask. I can see the fun of the Caspian but Tehran in the middle of the summer will be hot.

Mike shrugs his shoulders. "There's not that much to do in Neshnafad either," he says.

He's right. Tehran has bookshops, restaurants, and clubs and there's a private swimming pool near his parents house that we can use, and his sister Susan and her new husband will be back from their holiday in London. Then there are his cousins, Parvaneh and her brother Habib and younger sister Mariam, who enjoy partying and who will organise trips to clubs and restaurants. Besides, I may have time to get some serious writing done.

I have not made as much progress as I would have liked with my notes on Anna; I've been too busy getting to know my new friends in Neshnafad. One of these has asked me to take over some of her teaching hours at the infant school whilst she's away in England for six months to look after her mother. The infant school is linked to the university and is for ambitious Iranian parents who want their small children to learn the English words for trees and flowers and birds. I like the children that I'm teaching, the four and five year olds. They're so very polite, and want nothing more than to hold my hand while they walk through the corridors or outside on the playground, or they come up to me and give me a hug as they enter the classroom where I will sit and wait for them. Their Iranian mothers tell them to behave and to be so very nice to me, and to my amazement they are.

The school will be closed over the summer as will everything else, the university departments, the primary and secondary campus schools, and also the local British Council compound where I sometimes go to get books from the library and meet with some of the English teachers. Betty and Rosa will be going 'home' for a month, to visit their parents and friends and family. Mike is right, there won't be much to do in Neshnafad, as we would be on our own.

"It's probably going to be uneasy wherever we go," Mike says.

"What do you mean, uneasy?"

"Well, the thing Tessa was talking about in her letter to you. I'm sure that foreign newspapers and news are a lot more transparent about what is happening here. All those rumours …"

Suddenly I know what he's talking about. I haven't wanted to recognise it and have clung to the belief that everything is fine. In reality, there is unease about, even where we live, an unease that's spreading from the town to outlying villages, the university and our compound. We hear more and more rumours and whispered accounts of what is supposedly happening in Neshnafad, Tehran, Qom, Tabriz and other places. Rumours enter our secluded lives, whispers crawl up the hill from the town below and they insert themselves into our day-to-day conversations, up on our hill from where we overlook Neshnafad. Apparently, there was another American woman who shouted at Ali, our grocer, who didn't understand her, or perhaps he refused to serve her because she was wearing shorts. Different versions of the same story circulate. Perhaps it is even a story about the same woman that Betty and I came across at Ali's store. Stories differ depending on who tells them.

"Ali," someone told us, "Pointed at the door and the woman shouted at him and came back later with her husband who threatened Ali. But then Ali refused to budge and she had to go elsewhere to get her shopping."

More and more Americans, the consultants and the advisers, as well as other nationalities are sending wives and families back home. In their Friday prayers, Mullahs make reference to their leader in exile, someone called Khomeini, but few in our compound speak openly about this opposition to the Shah's government. Listening to the stories, it is as if I'm entering another unknown and hostile world within the one I am trying to come to grips with. This world of ours seems to be under attack, from within and without, and I understand very little of it.

"Who are these mullah's? How come they're so against the Shah and modernisation?" I ask Mike. "Why are the *bazaaris* and others in cahoots with them?"

"Big questions and lots of different answers," Mike says. "The Shah hasn't exactly made himself popular with the common people here, especially not with the mullahs and the *bazaaris*. They hate him and you cannot blame them. The Savak, the Iranian secret service, has a lot to answer for." He stops as if to think and then adds, "There's more unrest in Qom, that's where it all started." He says that the government expelled Khomeini because of his anti-Shah lectures and that the Savak put him on a plane to Turkey. Later, however, Khomeini moved to Iraq from where he's stirring up unrest by sending messages back to Qom and Iran.

I am amazed at how little I know about any of this. "You're right," I say to Mike. "However much I enjoy living in

Neshnafad and amongst our friends, it's probably better not to be there for a full two months without much to do. I'd just stick out like a sore thumb, a foreign wife, a *farangi*, wouldn't I?"

"You mean there's safety in numbers, once everyone's back?" Mike grins. "I wouldn't bet on it!" and when he sees my face he quickly adds, "Just joking — it'll probably all blow over. Tehran is more anonymous anyway. Neshnafad is a backwater in comparison."

When we return to our car after one of our pit stops, I hook my arm through Mike's, then pull his head down and whisper, "Perhaps it's time to try for that baby, what do you think?"

He puts his arm round my shoulder and pulls me close quickly, hugs me before anyone can see us, and I wonder for just a second whether I should tell him now, whether I should have told him before, but I don't. I just won't let the past come back into our life here; he doesn't need to know. He wouldn't want to know.

I'm Katie and I am what I am today, wife of Mike, a foreign wife living in Neshnafad; that is what I am, that is what we are together, a couple, happy. I have made new friends here and we will start a family and everything is as it should be. The future is ours. There's no need to rake up the past.

*

This time I like Tehran. I like staying in Mike's parents house, more so than I did previously when we were in such a hurry to move on to Neshnafad, to start our new life there. The house is large and comfortable, with a separate television room and a large sitting room downstairs. This is the drawing room and it has beautifully kept furniture, a large sofa and comfortable chairs around a low antique coffee table. Against the wall is a gleaming dark wooden sideboard with glass doors that reveal shelves full of dainty tea glasses, silverware, bowls and cake dishes. An enormous chandelier hangs from the ceiling over the coffee table. The drawing room has large windows that look out on the small courtyard in front of the house and to the side where some shrubs have been planted against a dividing wall. It's always cool in this room, even in August, because of the air-conditioning that is left on to preserve the furniture, but the room is only used when people come and visit and for special occasions such as Nou Ruz. When I'm in Tehran, I like to just sit there in one of the comfortable chairs and read. No one seems to mind as long as I don't leave any noticeable traces behind. Next to this imposing room on the side of the house is the large dining room that has a table for twelve, but the room is always dark and a bit gloomy because the only side window looks out on the wall and the thick ornate net curtains are drawn shut, day and night.

During the day, the summer heat is an all enveloping heaviness that wraps itself around everything inside and outside the house, a heat that slows down the brain functions of the living, human or animal, and even the plants and vegetation, so that movements and shape become slow and fuzzy, and as the day moves forward from its early morning clarity and promise, into the heavy jelly-like air of the afternoon, the chill breeze of air conditioners is almost uncomfortable in contrast when I rest spread-eagled on the bed in the guest room, reading Dostoyevsky, Tolstoy, Graham Greene, Iris Murdoch, in fact anything I can get my hands on in the small English bookshops in town. I observe myself from outside my own body, observe my body sinking into an eternal, heavy and warm presence, a body that has neither past nor future, the body of a goddess without human baggage or restrictions. With Dostoyevsky, I judge guilt and punishment in Russia, and then with Murdoch I become one of Iris's women, clever and in charge, never to be

132

beaten, always searching for my own place in the world around me.

When Mike comes into the room, he joins me on the bed. We make love at every opportunity, in the morning when we wake up, in the afternoon when we claim the need of a siesta and in the evening before we fall asleep exhausted and entangled, and I cannot get enough of him and I seem unable to satisfy his hunger for more. I pin him down, sit on top of him and then he turns me over and holds me and enters me all over again, always wanting more. I imagine that we have only just met, that we are discovering each other for the very first time during these weeks, without a care in the world, and we unlock nooks and crannies of ourselves that we did not know we had.

Mike goes out during the day leaving me behind in our room. He says he's meeting up with a few old school friends or he's sorting out some of our residence papers. He doesn't need me for these visits and I don't want to go with him. Although I've met one or two of his former school friends, they like to speak in Farsi and I'm happier with my book or I write for a couple of hours.

Tehran, as the setting for our secluded life, is like a film set that has been put together just so that I can live my present story and discover who I am. Tehran is as old as it is new to me. It is so different from anything I have ever known and at times I pinch myself. I imagine that it has only just come into being so that I can discover it, see how the women live in it and shape it, despite men taking up all front line positions in banks, shops and agencies. There are the many beautiful women and the not so handsome ones, the young and the old, girls, mothers, wives and companions and there are the very old. I have never been so obsessed with women and how they look, dress, and behave in ways that I am unable to decode, as if I'm constantly looking at them through thick, distorting glass frames and their world is as alien to me as my own past.

The variety in the dress code is astonishing, and chador and latest western fashion rub shoulders in the shopping streets and the down town bazaar. How can I not notice them, all these women, and not be one of them?

I want to be part of this life and long to fit myself into the mosaic, I want to feel a kinship with these women, this new me who will be this future self as mother and wife, and who is lover now and a teacher and a writer. Here I am without history, I am a woman creating my own present and future, I am in charge and will no longer be haunted by an irrelevant past that sometimes rears its head to condemn me for sins that have long since been buried.

In Tehran, much more so than in Neshnafad, fashionably dressed women mingle in the streets with the black chadors and the colourful tribal dresses of the Kurds, the Tajiks, the Pashtuns, the Baluchistan and others that no one seems to be able to explain to me where they come from exactly, and I am impatient with the disjointed bits of information that come my way. Always, the in-laws are concerned that I become entangled in unnecessary knowledge and information, impressing on me that what other people do, how they behave, who they are, is not important as long as we stay away from them. Perhaps they are wary of trusting anyone, even their own daughter-in-law. They have managed to survive upheavals for centuries in this country, where rulers come and go, and they will not let their hard won security be endangered by a temporary intruder. Am I still considered to be that, an intruder, someone who is looked at with suspicion? Mike says, "Don't be silly."

On Fridays, pretty little girls and boys play in the parks with their parents and siblings, they sit on blankets spread out across the grass under the trees, and the blankets are laden with boxes and bags of food and people. On the surface, there is carelessness and a self-assurance that fits me like a glove. I snuggle into it, I play deaf and dumb to whispers and undercurrents in conversations, I absorb the smells of jasmine, saffron, turmeric, parsley, cinnamon and limes and taste the lamb and chicken kebabs put in front of me, spoon up the rice and khorests, delight in the lubia polo and the ghorme sabzi, take bites out of the quince, plums, pomegranates and prunes, and defy the heat on my skin with the blissful coldness of the coolers whirring full blast over me and over Mike's naked body in the guestroom, with cool cotton sheets wrapped around us. When spent, we lie back and smoke a cigarette, speechless, watching the smoke curl into the breeze of the artificial air whirling upwards to the ceiling.

I draw lines over Mike's body with my finger tips, follow his bones and muscles, feel his fleshiness and his solidity which yields easily to my touch, and I am hungry for the next embrace, the forgetfulness as he grows hard again against my hip when I put my hand on it and stroke it. I trace my fingers through his inside thigh and then back up again, as he slowly opens my legs and touches me again and again, never enough, always we want more of each other.

On weekdays I sometimes go out with my mother-in-law, who tells me to call her 'mummy,' just as Mike does, but I feel uneasy about that. "Of course," I say.

She takes me to the bazaar, shows me where to buy the best materials for curtains, takes me to her dressmaker for a new dress, skirts and a blouse, and to her butcher to buy the best meat there is in town. In Tehran, Parry wears well-cut skirts of a dark hue with long sleeved crisply ironed cotton blouses, and here also she carefully puts one of her scarves over her hair which is dyed black, and ties a big knot under her chin before she gets into her husband's Mercedes. She drives this big cream-coloured coffin like any Tehran taxi driver, never giving an inch to the hooting and the pushing and bullying of other drivers who push their cars forward into every available space on the busy down town roads.

I sit up straight in the car in the front seat next to her when she swears like a trooper as someone is trying to cut her off. "Bastard thinks he can push me." Parry doesn't quite put the two fingers up, but her look says enough and I wonder about the woman I met in London, who seemed so terribly frigid then. There's none of that here. Here she will rule and not let male drivers get the better of her.

On our return from shopping trips, she parks the car outside the garage door in the quiet side street and lets the motor run, gets out and opens the front gate to the house and shouts for Hassan to open the garage door and he comes running. After she has manoeuvred the car into the garage and Hassan has closed the street door for her with a bang and much puffing, he unloads our shopping, takes the meat to the kitchen and puts it in the fridge, drops the bags of herbs and other dried stuff on the floor in the storage room off the kitchen, deposits the bags with tablecloths, napkins, dresses that the dressmaker has finished and knick-knacks that will find their place somewhere in the house, next to her on the floor in the pleasant and large sitting room where she sits back, to wipe her forehead with a small clean handkerchief. She will then take her shopping out of the bags and spread them across her lap and on the small table and floor in front of her, and all of us in the house must come and check and confirm how nice it all is. Hassan will bring us tea and glasses of cold water, to recover from our efforts.

On her way into the house, Parry will grab a cigarette out of one of the packets lying around, on the hall table, on a side table in the television room, or in the kitchen and when she sits down, far back into her chair to admire what she's bought, she inhales deeply as if she has just completed a successful rescue mission and saved the nation.

"*Xanoom berfama-eed,*" Hassan says. "Please mistress, here you are." He puts the tray of tea and glasses of water in front of her on a small table and goes back to the kitchen.

We will sit there and chat for a while drinking our tea before she shouts once more for Hassan to give him instructions for lunch and what to do with the meat, the vegetables and the herbs, so that a little later the delicate fragrance of his cooking spreads through the house and food will be ready before her husband comes in from his practice, for him to eat and then go back for his afternoon surgeries in the hospital. Often he doesn't come back till very late at night, and so the lunchtime hour may be the only communal meal they have.

With Parry, or on Fridays as a family, I visit aunts and cousins whose names I forget as soon as we leave again and who press on me their teas and sweets, until Mike tells me that I should leave something on the plate and that only then will they stop urging me to have more, *another one, your plate is empty, please,* and from then on, rather than dutifully emptying my plate as I was brought up to do, I adopt the opposite strategy to make clear that I am no longer hungry. I drink the tea from the small dainty glasses in the holders with their silver handles, set on tiny saucers with small silver spoons and with a lump of sugar from a silver bowl. The halva is thick and unyielding to my bite as I try to nibble at it; the sweet cakes come in an endless supply, with pink, light blue and yellow toppings. The aunts always look as if they have just had their hair done, and are dressed in smart skirts and blouses or wear long sleeved dresses with matching shoes. They laugh and talk, their powdered faces and bright red lips frozen in a continuous smile to show me how pleased they are to have me in their house, to meet with me, their nephew's foreign wife. Their hair is perfectly coiffed, thick and lustrous, and I can only wonder which God decided that they must have it all, all the hair in the world, thick and shiny and full of bounce, whereas my own hair is straight and flat and I keep it cut as short as possible in the heat, when the sweat makes it damp and unmanageable.

Sometimes Sharrokh comes back from the hospital early in the evening, and if there are no guests and they haven't arranged to go out for dinner or to visit relatives, they make themselves comfortable in the television room, collect a plate of food from the kitchen prepared by Hassan, and talk while watching television on the large black and white set that sits on a low table in the corner of the room. Sharrokh talks about rumours and whispers he's picked up, although he always leaves a lot unsaid, as if we can guess what he intends to convey. "It's not good," he'll say. "Better not to talk about it." He turns to me. "You see, better not to talk about politics in this country. You get caught out. Can be very dangerous."

An old suspicion flares up in his eyes; he smiles at me. "You think you can trust people, but don't. Never trust anyone outside this house, never talk about what we talk about with anyone."

Now that they have accepted me as their son's wife, he is committed to my safety, as well as that of his own children, and I need to be brought up to speed with everything there is to know about the complications of being a non-Muslim in this society, about the difficulties that you may encounter and how you can avoid them.

"Muslims are relative newcomers," he says and he tells me about the minority religions in this country, the Zoroastrians and the Baha'is. Parry may chip in and she'll say that this is something Muslims can learn from them; how to wash and keep yourself clean and tidy, and how, when you've been away, you want the cleanliness of fire to purify you before you go back into the house and that's why you jump over a fire when you return or come home.

Susan, who's staying for a few weeks as her new husband is on a tour of oil inspections in the south of the country, chuckles at something she sees on television and laughs out loud at jokes that I don't understand, whilst she applies a new layer of bright orange varnish to her toes, spliced apart with rolled up tissues.

"All nonsense," Parry says, looking at the TV. "This country is going to the dogs completely if you let them, these people."

Parry has black and white opinions about the people that live in this country, and in particular about the Muslims. She says that none of them wash properly.

"Look at Hassan and look at the house he lives in with his family, it is never clean in the way we keep our houses clean. Always dust and full of children."

Her thoughts on other non-Muslims are similarly condemnatory. There are the English, the Americans and other Europeans, none of whom are as clever and well behaved as they think they are and all are part of dirty treachery that has been a never-ending burden of their country, Iran. The world is full of people, who should be kept in their place, and meanwhile Iran and its people suffer and they are unable to live the free life that they should be living in this country that is so rich and so badly managed by all these quirky groups of nationalities and races.

She takes a deep breath after this monologue, as if she needs all her concentration and energy to say this. Her husband nods as if in agreement with most of what she says, only he tends to be somewhat milder and reflects that there are very good middle class Muslims, who will have no truck with what is happening now. He has colleagues, as Parry well knows, who have very similar values to their own. Moreover, he says, not all of Americans and English and Germans are bad. Haven't they lived in America and in England and enjoyed the lifestyle?"

I am bewildered at the vehemence of some of Parry's prejudices and wonder if, in her view, anyone is any good at all. Mike just laughs, and says she doesn't mean it, she's just frustrated at all the things that keep going wrong in this country and the constant worries about what might happen.

He says that with the rumours flaring up in the streets, the bazaars, the newspapers and with the reports of increasing Savak cruelty and savagery, people are at a loss and worry about what might happen, how all this increasing unrest might turn out badly for them and their family.

"We will be free," Mike will say when he joins in the conversation. "Mark my words, it will all get better, the Americans won't let this country go to the dogs. We are too valuable and Iranians have a long history of civilisation, we are not an Arab country, we are different and we are civilised and will westernise in good time. Also, we've got oil. The Shah will come to his senses, and even if he does not, there are a large majority of intellectuals whatever their religion who will help keep the Ayatollah and his clergy in their place."

His father shakes his head and gets up to take some dirty plates to the kitchen. He mutters his prayers, his lips moving ceaselessly. Once in a while he chants out loud, but no one takes any notice until he comes back into the room, picks up his plate and puts some pistachios on them from a bowl in the middle of the table.

Later Mike asks, "How's the writing going? Are you actually writing as you wanted to? I haven't seen you at it here, not when I'm around anyway. Nor for that matter have you let me read anything." He smiles.

The truth is that I write when Mike is not around, in the afternoons when everyone else in the house has their afternoon nap, and whenever the mood takes me. Sometimes I write early in the morning before I go down for breakfast and before Parry will ask me to join her on one of her trips for the day. Sometimes I write in the morning, and I pull up a chair at the dressing room table and stare at myself in the mirror before I carefully put pen to paper. Sometimes the words come and sometimes I just sit and look at the woman in the mirror. I see her large grey-blue eyes against the white, the clear skin of my face that has acquired a perpetual slight tan. I know I am not exactly beautiful but I am attractive enough. My lips are straight and determined, not too thick and not too thin, unless I smile at myself or purse them together to make myself look angry. I look at the straight light-brown, and now almost sunburned blond hair that's cut in a bob and will stick out in all directions early in the morning when still uncombed. When I stand up, the mirror shows a slim girl with long arms and legs, which also are slightly tanned below the knees and up my arms. I don't have the dark complexion of my Iranian family and my features easily give me away as non-Iranian, a *farangi*, when I walk around in Tehran or Neshnafad.

I dress well on the days when I'm out and about in town with Parry, if somewhat more conservatively now than I used to in London. When we go out to a party or a club or a family gathering, I wear brightly coloured dresses or tight trousers, fancy shirts and tops and fashionable shoes and sandals.

"I'm writing," I say, turning to Mike. "It's about a Dutch girl who wants to break free. The girl has to make choices about staying with her family. But it's not easy, you know, writing about a cold and damp country with such a different culture when you live in a hot and mystifying and sometimes alien country, where people and the environment are so different. Sometimes I can hardly remember what it was like in London, let alone what Holland was like all those years back."

"Can I read it? Will you let me read it?" Mike asks. "It's about you, of course, isn't it?"

"No, no, not yet, it's all very tentative, I'm not quite sure where I'm going with it," I say. "The girl's called Anna by the way and she is not me. I'm making her up as I go along."

"Your brother called you Anna I seem to remember," Mike says.

"Mmm ... that was just a tease, I told you," I say. "Our grandmother was called Anna. He probably thinks I'm like her; she wasn't a very pleasant woman though. She was very hard on our mother. Mind you, she had twelve children so it couldn't have been easy."

Mike raises his eyebrows and shakes his head. "I think you're kidding me," he says. "If it's about Anna, it must be about you, whatever you say."

I ask. "When are we going back to Neshnafad? I had a letter from Betty, she and Rosa will be back any day now. She's actually very unhappy about coming back and says she wants to stay in America. She also says that her family in the States insist there's something brewing here in Iran and they advise her that she shouldn't go back. Something about the Shah and the oil and who owns it. Perhaps even a change of government in favour of the mullahs. Are they right?"

"Nothing to worry about," Mike says. "This country has a great future. We're rich and we're sitting on a fortune. The Shah will realise soon enough that he has to tone down a bit, and give the mullah's some leeway; he's not stupid. Perhaps we can get rid of him and have a real democracy here. As long as the mullah's don't get too uptight. We're not there yet, but we will. Is she not coming back then, Betty?"

"Yes of course she is, she wouldn't leave Behmand, would she? And his work is in Neshnafad. He doesn't want to be anywhere else. She loves him. He wants to do something back for his country, living here, paying back the investment in his studies and all that."

*

Early September, we go to the Caspian Sea for a week, but the weather has changed and we spend most of the time sitting wrapped in blankets looking out of the window at a grey sea and deserted beach. We drive back to Tehran to stay for a couple more nights, and in the middle of September we pack our suitcases and bags and fill up our little blue Volkswagen to drive back to Neshnafad.

Mike's mother fusses about who will drive and insists that only Mike should be seen behind the wheel. She says it's better if I don't drive, not without a scarf anyway, through those backward villages, and where will we eat on our way from Tehran to Neshnafad?

"*Don't go to Qom,*" she says. "*Stop somewhere else on the way. Don't touch the toilets wherever you are and don't eat food that is made at the side of the road. You'll be ill.*"

She continues to expound on the dirtiness of the indigenous people, their disregard for cleanliness and the hopelessness of

143

public toilets, holes in the ground, shit all over the place, muddy, never cleaned properly. If she had her way she would march in an army of cleaners on a daily basis and have them scrub the whole country clean, teach the natives how to keep their houses free from dirt and grime and dust, using bottles and bottles of cleaning liquid and disinfectants that they probably don't even know exist. Mike shakes his head and winks at me. He hugs his mother and reassures her that we will be absolutely fine and she has nothing to worry about.

Over the summer, I have learned to drive our car in Tehran, copying the way Mike's mother drives, ignoring the shouts of the taxi drivers and pushing my way forward, amid the battered and bruised Keyvans. I can't wait to be back in Neshnafad, to be independent again from taxi drivers and Mike's mother, or Mike himself for that matter.

On our last Friday in Tehran, I tell Mike that I think I'm pregnant. I know it's early but I missed a period and I haven't missed a single one these last six months. Mike beams and hugs me and wants to make love again there and then but I stop him.

"Your mother is just outside, she says she wants to show me some of her tablecloths and we can take one of them."

"She can wait," he says. "We've got something to celebrate, and if not I'll make sure we do."

Very early the next morning, we set off for Neshnafad, the car laden with clothes and books as well as with essentials that Parry insists we take: herbs, dried fruit, tablecloths, some more cutlery, a few pieces of materials, *you must find a dressmaker to make you some new clothes*. We don't tell them our secret, not yet, and before we get in the car we once more jump over the fire in the courtyard, lit by Mike's father, to make sure we have a good journey and peace and happiness without bad spirits,

144

and then we wave goodbye and Hassan closes the gate behind us.

Chapter Eleven: 1977

Iran

In Neshnafad the heat lingers on well into the autumn. I continue to teach at the infant school on the campus; the children profess to like their 'nice English teacher.' They cling to my skirts and bring gifts that their mothers have wrapped for them, in gold and silver paper and tied with dainty strings, boxes of chocolates, trays of halva and other sweets, a small miniature, some embroidered serviettes. I ask Mrs Talebani, the headteacher, whether I can accept them, whether this is custom.

"Of course," Mrs Talebani says. "You must accept them; they will be very offended if you don't. They are happy with you and want to show you they like you and that their children like you."

Mrs Talebani is a brisk and self assured woman in her mid-forties, who wears immaculately tailored and ironed dresses, with collars and short sleeves, belts around her middle to set off her well-kept curved figure. Her hair is pitch black and shiny and cut short. She wears large white button-shaped earrings that set off her dark skin and that match her necklace and white-heeled shoes.

Mrs Talebani runs the school like an army major and is respected by her staff and the parents for her business-like charm and reassuring smiles. The children troop around her

146

when she comes into the schoolyard in the morning and she receives them as if they are, each and everyone, a gift from their parents. Sometimes, when she and I walk together or have a meeting in her office, a sparsely furnished room with a large desk and meeting table, she tells me about her life as the youngest daughter of a local bazaari, who wanted to improve his daughters' lives from that of his own wife and sisters, who all had very little education, and were married off before they were sixteen.

"He was a wonderful father," she says. "Unfortunately he died of a heart condition, a hard life you know, and now I make sure my mother and her sisters are proud of me and I support them." She wears a wedding ring but it is not clear that she is actually married, or who her husband might be. She never refers to him, we never see him, nor does she have a picture on her desk in her office.

We make an appointment with one of the university gynaecologists, who takes me on as one of his private patients, and we attend his office in town, which is one of the few smart buildings in one of the better parts, with a reception desk and a cool whitewashed waiting room where a hushed silence reigns except for the whirring of the air conditioner. The room looks as if it has been directly copied from a photo of one of the smarter Harley Street practices. The specialist is an affable little man, sharply dressed in a grey striped suit with an impeccable white shirt with golden cufflinks that just peep out from his jacket sleeves. His consultation room has the coolness of a humming refrigerator, and a nurse hovers around, picking up on his nods and brief comments to her that I don't understand, handing him his gloves, showing me the curtain behind which the examination table is laid out like an exquisite gleaming spaceship with the equipment to tie me down so as not to be lost in space. He is, he says, American educated and will do a test first as well as making sure that I am in good health and can I please leave a urine sample with his nurse and they will have the outcome when it comes back from the university lab in a week's time or so.

"No hurry, is there?" He smiles. "You'll have months of waiting if it is positive."

After my examination, during which the nurse continues to smile and hover wordlessly, but nodding and pointing out to me what to do, how to lie down and strapping me in. He tells me to get dressed.

"Have you been pregnant before?" he asks when I come out from behind the screen and Mike has been invited back in.

"No," I say and he looks at me as if he's going to say something but then bends his head and starts writing his notes.

"That's all right then," he says. "You appear to be in good health, let's just wait for the tests."

Mike picks up the results a week later, an important looking green-blue envelope with my name on it in curly ink written in Farsi and then underneath it in smaller writing in English, Katie Rastrakie, wife of Mike Rastrakie, and hands it to me. It's positive, as I expected, and Mike hugs me and wipes away a tear in his excitement.

"You are silly," I say, "Let's have a party, tell everyone."

"But first, let's tell my parents," he says. "They'll be delighted; this grandchild will carry their name after all. Unlike my sister's children ..."

I will never understand the importance attached to the father's name and this obsession with continuing the lineage so that the unexpressed expectation is that your first child will be a boy. I'm not sure I want this child to be a boy and tell Mike that I hope for a girl. In the end it doesn't matter, we agree.

I wonder whether I should continue to write the notes on Anna, whether I really want to catch up with Anna now. Do I want to elaborate on what happened to Anna however much I fictionalise it? I'm very uncertain of the outcome, and how I will work the plot of Anna's story. But for a few more months, every morning when it's still cool and before Mike gets up and we have breakfast and he gets ready for work, I sit and write my notes and let Anna tell her own story, whilst I whisper to myself that I will have a child, whisper it while I'm writing, despite the sickness that starts almost immediately and every morning, so that Anna's sickness and my own heaving stomach seem to blend into one.

As the heat of the summer abates into the warmth and windiness of autumn, a golden glow hangs over the dust and dryness of the landscape, to be blown away by the relentless winds that will suddenly flare up, as if angry and as if gods have decided to chastise the earth, to chase people back indoors, and then as suddenly as the winds have started they calm down again. The river is dry and waiting for the rains to fall. To ration electricity and water, power cuts have started so that for lengthy parts of the day there is no light, and we cannot take showers or flush toilets, nor can we find a reprieve from the heat under the coolness of the air-conditioner. There are electricity cuts everywhere up here, in the flats and houses in our compound and beyond, that have been built on hills and higher plateaus, well above the town. The men fill up buckets and bowls of water, when suddenly and at unexpected times the electricity comes back on, and the water splutters out of taps that we have left open to make sure that we hear the brown water beginning to trickle through, followed by a more certain stream of clear water, and in the middle of the night, I will stand under the shower and let the water gush over my swelling body. Then the air conditioner will whir and blow cold air across the bed, and remove the lingering and stifling heat from the rooms.

The weather cools down further and the frequency of the power cuts reduces, and we are able to settle into a calmer routine in which my body slowly begins to fill out and sickness makes place for a lazy contentedness and expectation of something portentous. The rains start.

First Rosa and then Betty returns, and we drive to the local grocery shop in one of the side streets. We're happy to have our freedom and we use our husbands' cars whenever we can. Sometimes Betty drives, or Rosa takes her husband's car when he has no need of transport, or we drop our husbands off in the morning before we drive to the shops or the town, on the days that I don't teach. Mrs Talebani has agreed to limit my teaching load to three mornings a week.

Betty says she and Behmand have decided to try for babies, and that she will go to America once she's pregnant as she refuses to have a child here in Iran. She wants to make sure a child will have American nationality. Betty is visibly unhappy after her visit to the States; she is restless and frequently sulks, as if she has lost something special and she admits to being homesick.

"Behmand has become obsessed with wanting to spend the rest of his life in Iran and I have never considered this seriously," she says. "I really had not understood what that would mean, and how much I would miss my country. I'm just not cut out for all of this, this kind of life. And I'm worried about what's going to happen here …"

Betty has let her short hair grow into a tail, low in her neck. She looks plain with her hair pulled back and without make up, and she acquires a habit of looking at her friends with an urgent and eager expression, as if she's waiting for them, Rosa, and myself and anyone else around, to provide a solution to her dilemma. Whenever we meet up at night, husbands and wives in someone's apartment or on a terrace or a balcony, Betty hovers around Behmand as if she is making sure he is comfortable. Behmand is lazy but handsome in that Iranian way with his regular features, a small mouth set in a fleshy round face, a slightly crooked but small nose which makes him look sexy, and with deep brown eyes that bore straight through you and give the impression of deep and important secrets. He always appears to be asking for something, his face a perennial question mark with raised eyebrows, but we never know what it is and he doesn't explain.

He clearly loves Betty, and will say so out loud, "God I love that woman," to us, his friends, as an aside when we hang around, but I think that he takes her for granted, her constant care, her being there for him as a matter of fact.

"He's so goddamn quiet sometimes," Betty says. "He always acts as if there's just nothing else to talk about or to ask for. As if this is it! I want him to tell me what he thinks. I want him to talk to me. Like he used to. It's as if I no longer know him."

She doesn't say what she wants him to tell her, but Rosa and I guess. She wants to put him in her pocket and take him back to America, where she can be sure to possess him. Behmand never looks at other women, or makes comments as some of the men do, when they think their wives aren't listening. He hasn't got it in him, we think. He's too laid-back. Betty doesn't trust this quietness and his reluctance to talk to her about perhaps returning to America. In this country and because of her own insecurity, Betty needs him to tell her all the time that he loves her, or that he finds her pretty or that she's special. Like the other men here, Behmand envelopes himself in a cocoon of male self-sufficiency that rebuffs the women around them, that takes the women for granted. I think sometimes that even Mike is doing this. It's a side of him that I don't recognise from our London days. We used to be equal there. Here I'm not so sure.

I imagine that his mother, who, Betty says, adores him, spoilt Behmand. His mother is tremendously proud of what her son has achieved, that he has become a doctor who has made it in a world that, until he left for America, consisted only of the local village, with his father selling odds and ends, saving and saving to give his son a better future.

"And, of course, I helped him too," Betty says. "After we got married in the States I worked all the way through his studies and paid the rent and for most of the food."

It looks as if Betty has taken over the baton from his mother and he comfortably adjusts to this constant caring and adoration from his wife. Betty hovers, puts one leg in front of the other, stands next to his chair, pouts at him and makes sure that the rest of them in the room realise that he is hers. She puts her arms akimbo, pushes her body forward as if to make sure that he knows she is there. I watch her and silently tell her to take care, don't do this I want to say, you will get hurt.

When I look up I notice that Mike is watching me, following my look and my thoughts and he smiles at me. Perhaps our understanding is still intact and I've simply been imagining things. Mike is very relaxed and very happy.

"I hope I'll get pregnant soon," Betty says. "At least Behmand won't be unhappy about my going to the States and leaving him here on his own. We've agreed that I should have the baby in America, if I get pregnant that is." She looks at me and I sense her envy.

"I don't know why I'm not pregnant yet, you seem to have done alright, haven't you? We've tried for a long time."

"Just relax," I say. "You'll be fine."

I'm a liar. I have no idea whether she'll be fine or not. I don't know why I got pregnant so quickly; by rights I should not be. I push the thought away, and I feel sick again and run to the bathroom where I heave and clutch the rim of the toilet as if I'm ready to pull it up from its fixtures, and then my fingers relax. I look at myself in the little mirror above the sink, which has a lovely ornate frame with Persian female figures, dancing and whirling in floating dresses and nearly bare bosoms, with diaphanous veils draped behind them.

"This is what I am now, the wife of Mike and about to give birth to a little princess or prince," I whisper. *"I have no past."*

My eyes look very grey and large in their whites after I splash my face with the cold water, and I stare at myself for a steady long five minutes before I turn round and go back to the room, where Betty looks up as I enter, looking forlorn.

"I'm sorry," I say. "I just felt really sick. Not your fault. I'm okay now."

"I'd like to be as sick as you are," Betty says and I give her a hug.

*

Autumn turns into winter, which is a pleasant ten degrees above zero.

"God keeps the waters under the earth warm even in winter so that the roots don't freeze in this country," Mike says. "That is an old Persian belief. Mind you, it can get very cold in Tehran. I used to do a lot of skiing up in the Alborz Mountains when I was a boy, before going to England to study."

Recently, he has started to tell me about his childhood, as if living in Iran and now becoming a father has created an irresistible urge to let me know what this country means to him. This is his birthplace, and he is as rooted as Behmand and the other men are, even if his story relies on different myths from those of our Muslim friends.

Fire and water, purification, good and bad, light and dark, they are all part of his psyche and upbringing, and as my bulge becomes larger and visible, I try to make sure the baby listens as well, after all this country is going to be its home. I have no intention of giving birth in England or in The Netherlands, alone. I will stay here, where I belong now.

"I used to skate," I say. "I was a really good skater, got medals for completing long distance tours. I once skated eighty kilometres over frozen canals and lakes; the coldness of it and the exhilaration. Strange really, how you can enjoy these things, just because you're going over ice, which is like a moon landscape sometimes, and skating is much faster than walking, sometimes even faster than cycling. It was marvellous, those long stretches, no cars, no bikes, just the cold wind and the grey sky and the flat expanse around you, of ice and frozen fields, everything frosted over. There was a peacefulness that you don't find anywhere else in Holland."

Mike looks at me and raises his eyebrows in surprise and then nods.

"So we have something in common, a love of cold weather and being out and about in it," he says, and grins.

It's nice to share memories and feel this empathy with the man I love and I wonder how much we really want to share, whether it's necessary to know the truth in all instances or whether it's better to be ignorant of some of the things that happened in our past. Do I really need or want to know whether Mike had previous relationships before me, whether he was hurt or what he promised? He clearly doesn't want to talk about any of it. Isn't it enough to know that we love each other now and that we share a life, soon with a baby as well, and be a family? Would it be better for him to know all of my past, all of the painful truth even when I don't know how to deal with it? Why am I writing about Anna and what do I hope to achieve with writing down her story, when at the same time I'm unwilling to share the truth with Mike, about who I was and what I did?

In Neshnafad, during that autumn and then the winter, rumours and whispers do the rounds between the residents on the campus and our residential area across the road. Rumours come our way about unrest, student rallies, and mullahs who will no longer tolerate barbarities done in the name of the Shah, about the secret police and American and western culture in general. People are hurt, we read about it and hear about it, but nothing of what happens affects any of us directly. At night, we're safe under the protection of guards around the compound who will stop intruders, so we are told. It's as if we've become our own separate tribe, Mike, Behmand, Parviz, Rose's husband, Firuz, Kombis, Kurosh and Khyan, all married to 'foreign' wives; Rita who is English, Tina, who is German but speaks English because she has spent most of her teenage life in America with a father who is in banking, Jennifer who is from London and who is a full-time teacher at the British Council in Neshnafad and who has two teenage sons at boarding school in England, and of course Betty and Rosa.

The men will sit and talk during get-togethers that we, their wives, arrange, a lunch on a Friday or an evening birthday party for one of the children. Sometimes, they stroll around the campus or the residence after they come back from their afternoon lectures, seminars, consultancies and meetings and we, Betty, Rosa and I, go on walks with Rosa's children, or we meet up with other wives and children before we go back and have our evening meals, once it becomes dark. Sometimes, we'll sit together on the balcony of one of the flats or the houses, looking over railings into the dark and towards the lights of Neshnafad in the distance. Sometimes, Mike and I will sit together on our small secluded patio in the back yard and Mike will tell me about what he's heard, what he has read in the Farsi papers. He will tell me that people in the town, the mullahs and *bazaaris* in particular, are becoming angry with foreigners who seem to think they own this country, only because they're pumping the oil. He will talk about the religious fundamentalists who are beginning to mutter out loud against the Shah's seeming surrender of the country, their country, to the West and in particular to America.

"These ordinary folks, they don't want their wives uncovered. They're angry that their daughters have to take off the hijab in schools and universities, by decree, even if the daughters and their fathers in particular are fine about it. The Shah's forcing a lifestyle on them that is alien to them. They don't want pop music and western dress to replace their own way of life. And in a way I'm sympathetic to that. We have a rich culture and we don't need to simply ape everything that is coming in from the West. I just hope that they, the Muslims, are not going to dictate how we non-Muslims and non-believers, have to live and what we can and cannot do or say." Mike says.

He adds. "But if we can get real democracy in this country and be rid of the Savak and all that, I will vote for whoever brings us that."

Occasionally, I stumble across a quarrel or disagreement when out shopping, when wives of American advisers shout at Ali again, when he doesn't understand what it is that they want. I can see Ali's eyes flicker, I see the sullenness in the way he pulls down his lips as he points at his goods and says, "*Xanoom, Berfama-eed, xeili motshakker am*. Thank you very much," and then he silently wraps up their meat from the freezer, puts the potatoes in plastic bags followed by the butter, milk, the deep red tomatoes and the aubergines, and carries it all to their cars outside, nodding his head all the while and putting his hand on his chest as they drive away.

"Perhaps they have had enough of it all?" I ask Mike.

"Who?" he says. "Who's had enough? The Neshnafadis or the Americans?"

By January, when my baby bulge has become quite visible and undeniable and the sickness has receded, there is a restlessness amongst our group of friends, and whereas previously everyone had been careful not to criticise openly either Shah or mullahs, we now talk more openly about our expectations and what we think is right or wrong with the system, even if the men will remain cautious and look around them, do a lot of nodding and fall into deep silences as if they need to weigh up what they can and cannot say. Afterwards, there is the laughter of relief when someone makes a joke about it and it all washes away.

Allah-oh-Akbar, people whisper and shout, as if expecting a coming of something new, something that they know only their God can deliver and will deliver.

As my baby grows and moves inside me, I sit down again to try and write my notes about Anna, but I am stuck. I find it too hard to think about what happens next, what happens to Anna and what happens to Gemma, even though the story is taking me there. I'd like to push it away, in the same way that Iranians never want to talk openly about what bothers them most. Why am I pushing myself to do this, this writing?

My child grows inside me and the world is changing around me, again, without asking me, and there is nothing I can do about it. I have no control over what is going to happen in this country and it makes me feel uneasy.

I haven't even begun Anna's real story. All I have done is skirt around the edges, made a story of where Anna lived, talked about the imaginary village. I am avoiding the real story that I need to tell, if only to myself. I have messed around, pretended that I know what I am writing about.

Of course, Anna's is only a story with a plot and with characters, some of whom are maybe too close for comfort, but nevertheless it's fiction, I must remind myself. I'm waiting for my child to be born, but the world and my environment are not the way they are supposed to be. They are not comforting, and they no longer promise the certainty that I long for.

Where am I going now with Anna's story? What will happen to me and to my child, our child? Will I be able to look after it, protect it, here in this country? I'm almost certain it's a girl, my little girl, who will have loving parents who must love, protect and support her.

I pick up my pen and start writing again. I will finish this story before my child is born.

Chapter Twelve: 1963-1965

The Netherlands

It was a Saturday and the November cold swept in with Anna as she entered the kitchen through the backdoor. It was well past lunchtime and the table in the extended kitchen area had been cleared. She was hungry after her bike ride back from school, her morning lessons now over. At the same time that she opened the back door, Johannes came into the kitchen from the opposite end through the dividing door between the front room and the dining area, and the gust of cold wind slammed the door shut behind him even though he tried to grab hold of the handle.

Johannes shook his head, "Can't you close that door?" He was upset more with the news of the night before than with the slamming of the door. He had just listened to the latest update on the radio, the shock, even twelve hours after the event, still audible in the announcer's voice.

"President Kennedy shot dead. Shot dead!" Johannes said. "What's the world coming to? Shot, just like that! What does it mean? This is terrible, totally unbelievable." He took a short sharp breath and then coughed a rattling noise from his chest, talking at the same time, so that Anna could barely hear what he said. "I just can't believe it."

Anna threw down her brown leather school bag, which landed with a heavy thud on one of the chairs and took off her gloves. Her face was red from the wind and the exertion of cycling. The kitchen was part of this muddled room that no one knew what to call. Was it in fact a kitchen? Was it a breakfast/dining room? Was it the backroom? It had an old fashioned water pump in the corner that would deliver glassy, clear drinking water as long as you swung the pump handle up and down with force, as well as a tap for hot and cold water connected to a small gas burner on the wall. At the other end of the worktop that extended from the basin along the wall was a gas stove with four rings. Yellow painted kitchen cupboards underneath the worktop held a mishmash of saucepans with their ill-fitting lids and some baking tins. Another set of cupboards acted as a room divider between the dining area and the kitchen area. These cupboards were stacked full of non-matching plates, cups and saucers, beakers and glasses, chipped serving dishes and bowls. Wooden chairs, in different colours, were placed around the large, dark, old mahogany table. Some were cushioned, and others were just plain wooden kitchen chairs painted yellow. The room always looked untidy and cluttered with pots and pans on the kitchen board at the end. This time of the year there was an assortment of different coats, jackets and winter scarves and gloves over a chair in the corner. Notes were pinned on the side of the dividing cupboards and a sideboard held a collection of small vases, saucers, a wallet, a few loose coins, little glass jars and tins with buttons, curtain rail hooks, a notepad and sticky tape. Everything would be tidied away once a week by the home-help, but would reappear surreptitiously during the following days until it was tidied away again, in drawers and cupboards.

Anna took off her thick, long coat and knitted, woollen scarf and threw them on top of the pile of coats in the corner of the room. She slung her gloves on top of the coat and sat down to pull off her shoes. "My feet are frozen," she said, ignoring Johannes. "I really need some warmer socks."

Her mother stood behind the sink with her back to Anna and Johannes, tidying up the cups and glasses left dripping in a drying rack. The tiny kitchen area was far too small for their large family, and like the rest of the room was in a perpetually dishevelled state, always full with the kettle, a small saucepan, crockery and chipped broken cups and saucers, and always in need of clearing just like the rest of the room.

Greta turned round at the noise of the slamming door and the voice of her husband and looked from him to her daughter, as if she was not sure what either of them was doing there. The other children had disappeared, and her mind was already on the next thing that needed to be done. The shop would open again after lunch and it was a Saturday, which meant a busy day in the shop. She would be needed to serve the customers, to find them household equipment, birthday cards, paper to write on or for wrapping, perhaps some curtain material or bedding, all items that the villagers would come to buy, as they were always in need of an endless supply of basic and not so basic goods. Greta's mind could not focus on a president's death or a daughter just back from school with cold feet and in need of socks. All that would have to wait.

Greta didn't have time for politics or world affairs. She left that to her husband who knew of everything that mattered. He'd made that quite clear from the start of their marriage and when the first children began to arrive. He knew about politics and the wider world, he knew what was right and wrong in God's eyes, he had a clear grasp of the rules and regulations on how to keep their children on the straight and narrow, what was good and what was bad and he knew about church requirements and programmes. He always knew best, and it was wise to keep your own thoughts to yourself, if you had any that differed from his. Even if it became more and more difficult as the children became increasingly rebellious against his iron rule, she avoided saying anything that might be controversial in his eyes, as it would only set off her husband into one of his angry polemics. Greta focused on the basic comforts of husband and children, the food, the cleaning with the help of a weekly, and on the customers in their shop. If one of her children asked her to make a decision on whether or not they could stay with friends, whether they could have a new coat or why they couldn't stay out late, her response was the inevitable, "Go and ask your father."

Anna pulled off one of her shoes with a sigh and grimaced, puzzled by her father's dismay at this death of an American president. Why did he get so worked up about these world events when he forbade his children to have anything to do with anyone who was not a member of their church? He surely seemed concerned about things in the wider world of politics as if they were connected to their own lives. There was a yearning in him for something beyond the smallness of his existence, a yearning to belong to something larger and this was puzzling. Anna just couldn't square this wider political interest with the imposed narrowness of their own lives, the drudgery and hardness of the rules that he imposed on them. America was so far away, so disconnected from this village, so utterly irrelevant. When once she looked it up it in her atlas, it might as well have been on the moon, The Netherlands, a small dot within Europe, and far beyond that America, Asia and other places, and she did not expect ever to get to any of them, given how stuck they were here. Besides, even if she tried to get away, she'd need money, opportunity, and all she had now was the certainty that Johannes would stop her from going away. She hadn't even been to Amsterdam or to any of the countries around, like Germany, France or England. America was just too far away to be taken seriously.

Sometimes, when newspapers were left on the coffee table in the front room, she looked at the grainy black and white photos of a president, a minister, the leader of one of the many political parties in The Netherlands, but she rarely read the reports, fearing that they would be no more than confirmation of everything Johannes said about the world, second-hand from whatever their church preached. She was reluctant to listen to opinions expressed by church leaders. She doubted the truth of anything they said. There were other newspapers that Johannes would not allow in the house and she was curious about these and what they had to say, *De Groene Amsterdammer* or *Vrij Nederland*. Sometimes they received a bundle of magazines and papers in a hard cover, a week or so after publication, a shared subscription. Johannes always insisted on seeing them before anyone else did. There were women's weeklies and he did not approve of these as they had too many advertisements for fashion, Moreover, there would be articles about worldly people, who had completely perverse opinions and who led despicable lifestyles. Once, Anna caught Johannes tearing out the pages of a magazine that had advertisements of bras, big white bras that covered completely the breasts of a beautifully tanned lady, and he crumpled the page and threw it in the bin. Liesbet, who also noticed, pulled up her nose audibly and said "Huh?"

"You should not be exposed to this kind of thing," he said.

They weren't allowed to read the pop music magazines that were emerging everywhere, with photographs of singers, film stars and other heathens. In particular female stars such as Brigitte Bardot, with her very short skirts, her bare arms and legs and waist and her big breasts, were abhorrent to God and to Johannes. There seemed to be something inherently degrading about the skin and flesh of a woman, something sinful and appalling, and perhaps that explained why men were so suspicious of women, Anna thought. Johannes forbade them to listen to the new rock and roll, Elvis Presley, the Beatles, and later the Rolling Stones. They did anyway, and his was a losing battle.

The Dutch performers that Anna loved for a while, Boudewijn de Groot, Liesbeth List and Ramses Shaffe, who sang of rebellion, love and friendship, not of heaven and hell, were also strictly forbidden. She listened to them with Gemma or some of her brothers' friends, who always found ways and means to get hold of anything that was banned from their house. She learned the words of the songs, printed in full in the tatty black and white magazines, to encourage herself in her plan to move away and never come back. When angry, she'd hum to herself the song of the butterfly that died on the water after having kissed flowers and after having learned to recognise all of the smells. She would like to be a butterfly and to fly away, but she didn't particularly want to die too soon, like butterflies.

They, the twins and Anna, hid the music magazines, which circulated amongst their friends. Bert and Liesbet considered themselves well beyond sharing anything with Anna or the twins, and she was grateful that Gerard and Stephan sometimes allowed her to share their secret collections, hidden under their mattress, in the bicycle shed or simply left in a box underneath their bed. They'd realised that Greta rarely had time to look at everything that was in the house, nor did she seem particularly interested, and the help-girl cleaning their rooms would not tell on them. The twins had threatened her, Anna didn't know with what.

The more Johannes forbade them, the more they disobeyed. It was as if he put bars of chocolate just out of their reach and told them that they were bad and shouldn't be touched. They wanted every bar they could get hold of, and the more they became aware of forbidden fruit, the more they wanted it. Anna joined Stephan and Gerard when they listened to pop music on the jukeboxes that appeared everywhere in the town and even in the village. There was a new one in the ice cream salon at the end of the street, and the twins befriended the son of the owner so they would meet in the salon after closing time and listen to every single in the box, stacking them up and then pressing the play button, and they learned to rock and roll when the blinds were down.

Johannes was upset when he found out and threatened everyone with punishment. He would destroy their chocolate, whatever it was, and he would hide it so it became invisible. Only he didn't know how. First Bert, followed by Liesbet and the twins and then Anna, they would be grounded. Their pocket money was withdrawn, although, as they pointed out, they barely got any, or they had to help out on Saturdays, delivering parcels wrapped in brown paper to farmers out in the countryside, on their bikes, or they had to do the shopping for their mother, vacuum the kitchen floor, anything that he could think of. It became clear that the more he forbade and threatened, the more they found ways and means to do whatever they wanted to, to avoid him, to go underground. Their only fear was that God would punish them, but He never did.

Johannes was fighting a losing battle, and he knew it. Not only was rebellion and disobedience and godlessness rife in

Johannes' very own family, it was rampant across the country, where first the Provo's and then the *Nozems* — provocative young rebels taking their cue from Teddy boys and greasers abroad, wearing jeans and leather jackets, and listening to this new-fangled noise that was supposedly music — gathered in Amsterdam on their bikes and mopeds and ignored all limits of what was allowed and acceptable. They defied all authority and challenged the Dutch government as well as church authority, so that Johannes would sigh, helpless, "What is the world coming to?"

Anna looked up from her struggle with her shoes and saw that Johannes' face trembled and that he pushed against the table with his hands shaking. She saw that he was very upset at the death of this Kennedy person. Was he afraid? Of what? Why would he be afraid if the worst that could happen to you was being struck dead by God? And why would God strike him, Johannes, dead?

Years later, Anna would wonder how it was that Johannes and his generation of dour men were so afraid of what might happen to them and their children, so that they punished and threatened all these children with Hell in the name of an almighty God.

Johannes was not a very tall man, in fact he was slightly shorter than Greta, and as he grew older he developed a bit of a paunch like most men of his age, and this made him appear even shorter, diminished somehow. He smoked big cigars, no longer just at the end of a Saturday as he used to, when work was done for the week and he could look forward to a day of rest on Sunday. Every day, a few puffs of smoke would be blown across the sitting room, and the ashtrays would have stumps of cigars that would shorten a bit. The smell of the cigar smoke lingered, and Greta had to wash the white net curtains regularly in order to get rid of the stench and the grey sheen that settled on them as the weeks passed.

Johannes frequently sighed and he would stop and stand still, behind breath, as if another step would finish him, wheezing like a tractor out of fuel. Anna wondered if he might just come to a halt one day wherever he happened to be, in the middle of the road, in the middle of a room, sitting in his chair or talking to customers in the shop. He was nearly bald and he looked a bit like one of the ministers, she couldn't remember his name, only he was less well groomed. His sparse hair around the base of his head, just above the collar of his shirt, was straggly and grey now and there often were little white flecks of dandruff on his dark and shiny suits, worn out but good enough for weekdays. He had a new suit and a new white shirt for Sundays, for going to church and also wore those on special occasions, a funeral, a wedding, a birthday and a visit to a doctor or to a wholesale merchant in town.

*

Johannes was the only son and eldest child in a family with three younger sisters. He didn't talk much about his youth, and neither did his father, Anna's grandfather Bart, who would sometimes visit but was clearly uncomfortable with the comings and goings in this house of his son, and after half an hour of being ignored in the front room, he would get up from his chair and say to whoever was around, "Time to go again. Will see myself out." He'd mumble that he had promised to have lunch with his daughter Mena or would have a coffee with his other daughter Hennie. Greta would suddenly come in with a cup of coffee, put it in front of him, apologetic, and she would urge him to stay, he was always very welcome. But no, he had to go; he didn't want to be a burden. And then he was gone again and they heard his little moped puff-puffing away along the road, until he disappeared round the corner. His wife, Anna's grandmother, had been dead a long time.

"Dropped dead, just like that," Stephan said. "Aunt Hennie says so."

He didn't know why however and they forgot to ask. They didn't miss a grandmother who had been dead for such a long time. They assumed she'd be in heaven with all other Calvinists who were dead, and so there was nothing to be sad about. She'd have a much better existence than she could hope for here with them.

Anna was named after Greta's mother, but she couldn't remember much of this grandmother. When still small, Greta took her once or twice to visit an elderly lady in a front room crammed full with dark and imposing furniture. The lady was dressed in black; black stockings, black shoes and a black dress with a white collar around a thin neck. Anna and the twins had to take off their shoes and not touch anything with their sticky fingers. The younger children had been left at home in the care of Liesbet. Greta sat upright and looked uncomfortable, almost as if she was visiting the doctor, asking him for advice. Grandmother Anna had small black stones for eyes, in a face that was wrinkled like one of the potatoes that their father stored in big wooden crates in the cellar, alongside the apples that were always just as wrinkled, and her thin grey hair was drawn back in a bun low behind her head, resting on the white collar. She never once smiled and didn't talk to them, only to their mother. When she died, Anna was not allowed to go to the funeral, not even to the church service but had to go to school. Bert and Liesbet went however, in their best Sunday clothes, but afterwards they wouldn't say anything about it to Anna. Curious about where her grandmother had gone, she found the grave in the graveyard, and shivered when she imagined her lying there underneath that stone, as cold as she was before and probably wearing the same black dress and white collar. She wondered whether she'd risen up to heaven in the middle of the night. She imagined her grandmother going up like a witch, and being sat right next to Jesus and God. Perhaps she was happy though, there in heaven where she no longer had to suffer all her children and grandchildren.

In the same way that she feared her grandmother when she was little, Anna for a while was very afraid of Johannes. He seemed all-powerful and clearly could do with them whatever he wanted, punish them, hit them, tell them to go to bed, in the assurance that God would even punish them worse if he didn't chastise them. They addressed him '*Father*', a title he owned like a medal obtained for bravery in the War. Bert, Liesbet, Stephan and Gerard became more and more reluctant, however, to accept this authority. They first objected to his commands, and then they said that Johannes was wrong. They said he was old-fashioned and he bristled at their comments, but in the end he couldn't stop them.

In the kitchen, with Anna impatient for food and complaining about the cold, and looking at his wife and daughter with this devastating news of the death of Kennedy, Johannes was disappointed when he saw both Greta's and Anna's blank and indifferent expressions, and he realised that neither of them would react in the way he expected them to, neither of them would understand the godlessness of this act of violence perpetrated against a president.

He turned to Anna. "Your mother is not interested in these things, she does not understand."

As if her mother was not there right with them, was not listening with a half-smile of apology on her face. Why was she so apologetic, all the time?

169

"Well," Anna said. "It's terrible of course. What's going to happen to us now?"

Perhaps there would be the dreaded atom bombs flying towards them, annihilating them and causing the end of the world that everyone talked about all the time? Would this be the end and the beginning of the real cold war? Perhaps the Russians would come now that Kennedy was out of the way, or perhaps it was the Germans who were to blame for all of this. Johannes and God were in agreement that the Russians and the Germans were untrustworthy, ever since the end of the War when the Russians cheated the Americans out of Berlin. But then her father himself had said that the Americans hadn't minded much, had they.

She couldn't remember exactly who this Kennedy was, didn't really know enough about him or what he stood for politically to make a reply to Johannes that would satisfy him. She had seen photos of this President Kennedy and his glamorous wife Jackie. They lived in a world so utterly removed from hers that they might as well have been living on the moon. She assumed that they lived in a loving family environment, you only had to look at the pictures of them in the papers, so well dressed and the way they held their children, a real family, as it should be. Not like theirs, messy and sprawling, with a mother who ran from one thing to another, without ever stopping, and a father who would forever remind them how hard it was to make ends meet without them being obnoxious as well.

There were no photo's in their family photo albums of them all dressed up like the Kennedy family, except for some early ones when Bert and Liesbet were still little and Gerhard and Stephan were babies, dressed in their old fashioned little jumpers and Liesbet in a cute dress with a white collar and her mother still looking so very young compared to now. She looked like a nurse in a uniform dress, with a white collar wearing her gold necklace. In the photograph, she smiled as she looked at the twins. She looked happy. Anna hadn't even been born when that photo was taken, although she realised that her mother must have been pregnant with her, so somewhere she was in that photo as well. What had happened? Had God been too generous with his allocation of children? It was as if the more of them there were, the more disillusioned they'd become, Johannes and Greta.

They were a noisy bunch, all nine and too many of them. They often fought and quarrelled until Johannes would tell them to be quiet. They vied for space, for attention, and were told to behave or else. Then there was the certainty that if they didn't show respect to either God or Johannes, they would be punished, by God and Johannes.

The Kennedys perhaps had an advantage in that God wasn't watching them in the way He watched their village and family and each single person that belonged to their church, from all extended family members out to the farmers and the farm workers, as well as the teachers and all the boys and girls in the village school and those that went to secondary school outside the village, all their cousins and all the families, however many children there were. God simply couldn't have the time to concern himself with non-believers such as the Kennedy's. Although the Kennedy's were Catholic of course, but that was as good as being a non-believer. No, God was too busy with them here in the village.

Unlike the life of the Kennedy's and people in America, their life in the village was strictly church regulated through codes and catechisms, interpreted by Calvin and Luther and Zwingli, a few centuries ago, but especially by Calvin. There were so many rules. They couldn't travel on Sundays, to begin with they weren't even allowed to cycle on Sundays, but later that rule was relinquished and even Johannes would use his car to go to church; they had to attend church twice on Sundays; they weren't allowed to read any of the books that Anna would like to get her hands on and sometimes managed to hide under the mattress; girls weren't allowed to wear short skirts or even trousers, but that rule was done away with as well, after a while. There were just so many rules, for everything. Ignoring any of those rules might condemn you to eternal Hellfire, for example, because God did not like girls in miniskirts.

How come that the Kennedy's were so admired by her father? For what? *"The right man for the western world - a bulwark against communism."* Kennedy had a glamorous wife who could wear whatever she liked, even trousers, and she could leave her shoulders bare and wear shorts when she sat in the sun. On top of all this they were Catholic, the Kennedy's. How come that they were not all damned? Or perhaps they were? Were they just not aware of it, this damnation hanging over them, and did Johannes know this?

"I've still got to do some homework," Anna said. "And I haven't eaten yet. I'm hungry."

Johannes opened his mouth to say something but closed it again, then turned his back and walked out of the room. A shame about Anna, she was becoming a real disappointment, she was such a clever girl and so sullen at times. He liked to boast about her cleverness to whoever wanted to listen, including the wholesale representatives that came and sold their goods to him, sitting in his front room, spreading out their samples of curtains and bedding materials, pictures of toys and household goods. He would even show her school reports to them, "*look at how well she does, her marks, she is really clever that one.*"

He told them that even if he was only a shopkeeper in a small village in The Netherlands, his children were as bright as those of politicians and others. He, Johannes, would make sure that they achieved whatever God wanted them to achieve. They had talents, every single one of them, and so he would allow them to multiply their talents, as it said in the Bible. "*Don't hide your talents under a bushel.*"

Only, times were changing. Johannes worried about Bert who was becoming so rebellious, who was scathing about them, his own family, who would tell him, his own father, that he wouldn't obey his silly rules. Johannes worried about Liesbet, who had a boyfriend now, needed careful monitoring so that nothing untoward would happen to her. Although the boy she dated was acceptable, from a good church background, young people nowadays wanted to do all kinds of things … they stayed out late if let and he hated to think what might happen. There were Stephan and Gerard and although they appeared less rebellious and less inclined to be contrary or raise their voices, nevertheless they simply went their own way, and he needed to make sure that they continued to follow the path of God and church.

Then there was Anna. She was becoming a real worry to Johannes, "*too clever by half.*" He would need to keep a tight watch over that one, make sure that she didn't stray; he couldn't work her out sometimes. Greta never seemed to notice, she was far too lenient, she let their children get away with all kinds of things and then didn't tell him, like that time she let Anna wear that ridiculously short skirt.

The vicar had told him that Anna claimed she was unable to learn the Catechism by heart because she had too much homework and her brain was full. Imagine that! Where did she get these ideas? He had to watch Anna. Then there were the younger children. Of course they were still much more malleable, but nevertheless they were demanding of so much attention and with the shop wearing them out, him and Greta, it was hard to keep an eye on everyone. Sometimes, he felt like just giving in, just like Greta did. He could feel very tired.

On his way out of the kitchen, Johannes picked up the keys for the shop from the table. He would ponder this huge event, this killing, as he mulled over so many other things. There were so few people around in this village that you could talk to. His family were the burden that God had given him in this life. He would have to deal with them somehow. His children would secretly laugh, well they thought he didn't notice, when they read reports in the newspaper or heard on the radio news that there had been demonstrations in Amsterdam. They'd call each other names using the term *"you're a Nozem"* as if they knew all about what it was, as if it was all a big joke. He was really and truly wary of so many things nowadays, and was very disappointed, always so disappointed. They should know better and realise that these rebellious young people in Amsterdam and other cities were just troublemakers, who were without any belief, the result of godless parenting.

Johannes shook his head and fumbled with the bunch of keys to unlock the big front door of the shop. He pulled up the blinds from across the glass panelling and opened the door wide to a woman with a shopping bag already waiting. She smiled broadly at him and nodded, "Good afternoon, Johannes. Everything all right?"

She went straight for the saucepans and the crockery and picked up a few things and put them down again. Greta, who had followed him into the shop, was busy unlocking the large till on the counter in the middle of the shop. They were ready for the Saturday afternoon.

Once in a while Greta would go back into the house to make sure that the smaller children were being taken care of by the older ones, or were safe with friends playing outside. Sometimes, one of the children would come running into the shop, crying or shouting, and she hurriedly shoved them back out of the shop, half listening to what they said, so preoccupied was she with the shoppers and keeping an eye that no one walked out with anything they had not paid for.

*

After her parents had disappeared into the shop, Anna walked to the kitchen cupboard to pull out some bread and cheese. Liesbet came in and looked all cheerful at her.

"I'll make you something special. I've learned how to do this recipe at school," she said.

"Where is everyone?" Anna asked, looking around.

Liesbet shrugged her shoulders. "Dunno. There's a shopping list here for the greengrocer. Can you go and get that? I'll just tidy this stuff up when you've finished and I've got to make sure that the washing is taken in from the line outside before it starts to rain again."

Anna looked outside the kitchen window where sheets and towels flapped in the November wind. Ever since Greta had become the proud owner of a real washing machine, she put washing in the machine any odd day of the week, not just on Mondays.

"Okay, but then I'm going out. I'm seeing Gemma this afternoon."

Liesbet looked up. "Oh? You're still seeing her then? I thought you'd fallen out or simply ignored each other now that you're in different schools. What are you two up to, still chasing those boys from the Institution? Has she taken one of them under her wings?"

"How do you know? What do you know? It's none of your business. They're fine, just boys like all boys. We're friends."

"Well, don't let your father find out. He'll be really very angry if he discovers that you hang out with them. They're trouble. There's a good reason why they're there, they're thieves and liars mainly. You wouldn't understand!"

There it was again, *you don't understand*, even her sister was at it, everyone always implying that she would not understand, when what they really meant was that she was getting herself into forbidden territory, and this made her even more determined to get into it and find out what it was that was so bad.

"What do you know anyway?" she said and pushed her empty plate across the kitchen table towards Liesbet. "That was really nice. Have you got some more?"

"Just a bit."

Liesbet looked pleased and spooned the leftover bread, tomato and egg from the frying pan and added a couple of cucumber slices.

She made it look really classy, Anna thought.

"How did you meet them anyway?"

Liesbet wouldn't give up, would she?

"You should be careful."

Liesbet didn't take risks, and tried to instil caution on Anna, being the big sister. Anna tried to remember, sure that Gemma came across the boys somewhere and of course they, like all the boys, would befriend Gemma, given a chance. She was one of the prettiest girls in the village. Teake and Jasper were fun though, different from the other boys they knew. They seemed so grown up, even if they were only a couple of years older than

Gemma and Anna; they claimed they were seventeen. They were so totally indifferent to what people said about them, they were not afraid of anything or anyone. They laughed about being in the Institution, the big house in the woods just up the road to Hazen. It was really a large mansion and was well hidden behind old large trees, just behind the entrance gate and the trees lining the drive to the front door. There was a large garden all around the mansion with flower beds and more trees and lawns, so that the building itself seemed to rest in the perpetual gloom of shadows that made the large windows look black and threatening. Beyond the garden, at the back and on its two sides, were the woods. The gate at the front was locked at night with a big padlock. Only boys lived in this Institution, certainly no girls, and sometimes the older boys were allowed outside and were free to wander into the village, although not many did, preferring to take a bus in the direction of Hazen which had a few more shops and where they could whistle from the terrace of a café at the girls passing by. They had to be careful though. If someone complained about their behaviour they would lose their 'freedom ticket,' Jasper said.

"We just met," Anna said to Liesbet. "We got talking. They're fine, not big bad guys as you seem to imagine."

Jasper had told them that he and Teake were in their last year of their stay; they'd be out once they were eighteen. In preparation, they were allowed to spend some days visiting the village or go shopping even as far as Gezel, whatever they liked. So why were they still there? Anna knew better than to ask. She didn't want to come across as stupid and so she nodded in agreement with whatever Jasper said. Anna enjoyed their banter and the unusual conversations they had, although she sometimes pulled up her shoulders or sighed when Teake sucked up to Gemma, who clearly enjoyed his flirtations, and who would strut about like a peacock. They talked knowingly about Amsterdam - how Anna wished she could go there once — and about what it was like to live there and how they'd go out in the evenings and visit bars.

"It's not like this, living in this backwater," Teake said. "You can have real fun in Amsterdam if you want to. There's always something to do, if you can get away."

"Yeah," Jasper sighed and balled his fist and stretched out his arms high above him, wriggled his hips and then sang, "I'm gonna be a DJ when I'm out of here. Yeah, Yeah, Yeah."

"Whatever," Teake said. He sucked up the air in his nose in derision and snorted loudly. "Maybe I'll just get a well-paid job somewhere so that I can come and listen to you sitting at a bar with a couple of nice girls." He winked at Gemma, who looked shocked.

"Just kidding," he added. "I'm definitely not going to be a DJ, I'm going to earn lots of money and become rich and then I'll buy a boat and travel across the world. But before I do all that I wanna meet with your family so that you can come with me to Amsterdam and then sail with me all over the world, once we're married."

"Serious?" Gemma said. "You want to meet my family? Well. Why not." She looked at Teake and when he didn't blink or look away, she said, "I'll talk to my father. I'm sure he'll be fine with it and then my mother will agree."

"You kidding?" Teake asked and shook his head. "Well, I bet your father won't have me in his house."

"You bet!" Gemma said.

Liesbet's comments that Jasper and Teake were trouble confirmed Anna's doubt about Gemma's success in her potential mission. How on earth was she going to convince her father that Teake was okay to have as a friend?

And what to do about Jasper? Anna wasn't that interested in Jasper. He once made a half-hearted attempt at putting his arm around her shoulder, the way Teake did with Gemma. "And how about us?" He'd smiled what she considered to be his sneaky smile and when she shook him off almost immediately, by pretending she had a stone in her shoe, he didn't even try again, that's how interested he really had been.

Jasper didn't talk much when they were with the four of them but Anna suspected that this had nothing to do with being shy. He was, she thought, just playing a game with them, and playing it on behalf of Teake who was his best friend.

After her lunch, Anna ran out to the greengrocer and impatiently waited until it was her turn. Everyone seemed to have all the time in the world in this village on this Saturday afternoon, and before you knew it she'd have to be home again for her evening meal. Every single person ahead of her in the queue chatted to the greengrocer and they asked after his son and his newlywed wife and whether she was in the family way yet, not directly, but joking.

"And? Going to be grandparents?"

At long last it was her turn and she followed the slowness of the greengrocer, weighing a kilo of apples, the beans for Sunday, picking up a large cucumber, a lettuce and did they have any bananas? She walked back quickly, ignoring people who called hello and who wanted to stop and chat, and she slung the bag with the shopping in the kitchen, which was once more deserted. Outside the kitchen window, in the yard, she saw her younger brothers and she could hear Liesbet's voice somewhere in the back. She grabbed her bike, which stood against the kitchen wall and cycled away to Gemma's who was impatiently waiting for her outside her house, her foot on one of the pedals of her bike, ready to go.

"Where have you been? It's nearly three o'clock! We said we'd meet them at three!" Gemma shouted at her, her eyes ablaze and her mouth angry. "I've talked to my dad. He says I can ask them over for a cup of tea this afternoon and my mum has agreed. My dad wants to talk to them. Isn't that good?"

Anna stopped her bike abruptly and raised her eyebrows. The headmaster was going to meet with Teake and Jasper and would actually talk to them? The next thing would be that Teake would come on a Sunday and she'd take him to church, while the whole congregation would be sitting backwards in the pews to stare at Gemma, with Teake just behind her, and then he'd be converted and she'd have Teake as her boyfriend. Gemma would see to that. She'd got it all worked out. She really had got some guts, Gemma, and when she had something in her head she would have things done just so, in her own way. She was lucky to have parents who didn't just shove her out of the way but who listened to her and talked to her, however crazy her ideas were. She'd always get what she wanted because she was so utterly sure that she deserved it and that she was right.

"I was held up by my sister. She wouldn't let me go and then I had to go to the greengrocer's. You don't have to shout!"

Gemma was already on her bike and cycling. "Come on, let's go, before it's really too late. I told Teake I would see him at the corner of the main road, next to that garage."

They pushed their pedals, bent over their handlebars and chased the road and defied the wind that hit them hard, but when they arrived at ten past three there was no one waiting for them. Gemma looked reproachfully at Anna. *Your fault*, her look said, but she didn't actually say it and Anna looked away. When they turned to look along the road once more, they saw Jasper. He was walking fast towards them and waved both his arms when they saw him. They looked at him expectantly. His breathing was rapid and shallow as if he'd been running.

"Where's Teake?" Gemma demanded.

"Well, something's happened, Teake can't come," Jasper said. "He's grounded, the supervisor is a real bastard, knew that he wanted to get away and made him angry last night, said something about the mess in his room and that he didn't think Teake would be allowed to leave the Institution as soon as he expected, not this year. There was also a letter from Teake's father …"

He trailed and stopped talking then fumbled in his pocket and got out a scrap of paper, handed it to Gemma. "He wrote this without our supervisor seeing it, and gave it to me. They had a real bust up last night. Teake hit him …"

Again Jasper hesitated, as if he expected them to say something, to tell him that it was all right, or maybe he didn't actually want to be there, didn't want to be the messenger, as he had never quite believed in this mission anyway, knew it was doomed from the start.

Gemma looked at him and then frowned, and her expression changed to anger. "But it was all set up," she said. "My dad agreed for you two to come and have tea with us. What am I going to tell him?"

"I don't think Teake wanted to come to your house to meet your parents anyway," Jasper replied cruelly. "He hates fathers and he hates families. His father beat up his mother."

What's new, Anna thought, and looked at Gemma. "What are you going to do?"

Gemma turned to Jasper, who had once more adopted his casual posture, hands in pockets, grinning. "When will Teake be able to come out again?"

He took one hand out of his pocket and swept back his long blond hair from his forehead. He showed his large white teeth, encased in pale red thick lips, and suddenly he looked much older than seventeen. He was at least twenty, Anna thought, he's older than Bert. He lied when he said he was seventeen. His eyes looked dull and there was a curious agedness about him that she couldn't comprehend, as if he knew things, as if he had experienced a life far beyond what they could only begin to imagine. She shivered and at the same time wished he would put his arm around her shoulders, as he had done before. Jasper, being older, made him more attractive. "Mmm …" Anna said, in echo of Gemma. "What to do now?"

He was handsome with his regular white teeth and straight nose, although his thick lips and his eyes had a hint of cruelty. He squinted slightly without looking directly at Anna when he turned to her. It was as if the light was too much for him so that he needed to half close his eyes and protect them from what they saw. He had a pleasant voice that belied his demeanour. Anna was not sure whether he actually winked at her first before he turned to Gemma.

"Not sure. He probably won't be allowed out for a fortnight. His dad will come and visit next week and I don't know what will come out of that."

He was quiet then as if waiting for another response from Gemma. When neither of them responded, he added, "You don't seem to be a bit worried about me. Aren't you going to invite me to your nice tea party?" He grinned mockingly.

He turned to Anna and his grin widened. "From what you've told me about *your* dad, I know he wouldn't want to invite *me* for tea."

Neither Gemma nor Anna said anything.

"Oh no, I can see it," he said finally. "I'd better go now, you've probably had enough. We're too much for you, aren't we?" He sauntered away and swaggered defiantly.

"Wait," Gemma said. "Can you tell Teake that I'll be here in a fortnight, same time?"

"Okay, can't promise anything though." He waved and carried on walking.

The chilly November wind picked up some of the leaves and blew them across the road. They swirled backwards and forwards before they landed on a heap against the hedge at the side, which was bare of leaves and pruned short, ready for winter.

What would Gemma do? Would she give up this project as a lost cause? Surely, she must see that the whole thing was hopeless and that they were wasting their time? Of course, Teake was attractive. Not as handsome as Jasper was, but he had an easy smile in that angular face with large brown eyes set in clear white. His high forehead and his wide-open eyes combined with the direct attention he gave to whomever he talked to, gave the impression of someone who was thoroughly honest, and belied the casualness with which he told them, only a few weeks ago, that he had belted his father so badly that he had to stay in hospital for a week. But then, his father had hit his mother, not for the first time either.

It was very obvious that Teake was attracted to Gemma and Anna realised that Gemma wasn't going to take this setback lightly; her mission was not accomplished. She had a stubborn look on her face as she kicked the leaves further under the hedge. Anna recognised that look. Gemma was unwilling to give up what she has started. Teake had become a rescue mission and Anna wondered if she herself perhaps had once been a similar project in Gemma's world, back when they first became best friends, when they used to spend afternoons together and when she took her, Anna, under her wing at primary school as if she had realised the dark thoughts in Anna's head and would do her utmost to make life better for her.

It was becoming dark, the light fading rapidly now as the days shortened at a pace, catapulting them into the winter gloom.

"Shall I come with you?" Anna asked Gemma, hopefully, not wanting to go back home yet and not in the mood to sit down and do her homework or be given another chore to do.

"Can do. You want to stay for dinner? I'll ask my mum. My brothers are all home, might be fun," Gemma said. "Will have to explain to my dad why Teake isn't coming though." She frowned.

"Perhaps not to eat," Anna said. "I'll just come for an hour or so and then go home for the evening meal. I've still got some homework to do."

She didn't like Gemma's brothers much, they were noisy and rowdy and she'd simply exchange one large dinner table with rowdy people, bible reading and prayers, for another. The difference would be that Gemma's mother would read at length from the Bible. Anna didn't know of any other mother or wife who did that, and Gemma's mother seemed to become even more pompous when she lorded it over all her brood, including the older boys, as well as Gemma and her two sisters, one younger and one older. There surely wasn't another man in the whole of this village, or in the country for that matter, like the headmaster who would simply sit back and let them all get on with it without saying much, and when they'd finished and had said their prayers, he would get up from the table and mumble that he needed to do something urgently, for school, for the church, for parents, for one of his children.

They locked themselves in the school meeting room upstairs, having told Gemma's younger sister to go away. Anna commiserated with Gemma although she was not the least bit worried about Teake or Jasper. In a way she was relieved, hoping that this would be the end of their friendship and that she'd have Gemma back to herself again. Neither Teake nor Jasper were going to provide her with a way out, they were just extra trouble to work around. Liesbet was right.

The streetlights were on and the village had closed down when she cycled back home along the dark road, now nearly deserted. Shops were lowering their shutters and drawing their blinds and a sole late shopper hurried back home to prepare for Sunday. Nearly all the shopkeepers in Armitan were related to Anna and all of them would be in church tomorrow. She passed the bakery. Her aunt was about to lock the door and waved at Anna when she passed.

"You're alright?"

When she was small, her uncle had allowed Anna into his bakery once or twice, accompanied by her nephew, his youngest son, and they watched how he and his eldest son rolled and slapped the dough, covered it in white flour and then opened the big iron oven with a stick and the heat jumped out with the flames at the back. She had looked in awe at the big black baking trays on which they placed the tins with the dough for the loaves. Sometimes, there would be cakes, and the sweet, yeasty and doughy smell in the bakery would be overwhelming. On the wide wooden worktop in the middle there would be more baking tins, filled with dough to be baked next, all waiting in line like so many soldiers going on parade or into battle. When the men pulled out the large baking trays, her uncle would shout at her and his young son to move out of the way, to move quickly, and then they piled the ready loaves on carts standing at the ready to be wheeled through the corridor, through the backroom into the shop at the front of the house, where customers would already be waiting, eager for a warm loaf straight from the oven. Some of the loaves disappeared into a delivery van waiting outside, the motor running, with another son behind the wheel.

Her aunt, who now smiled and waved at her as she passed, would stand in the bakery shop behind the counter and sell the loaves and the cakes. She was a large woman and she wore an apron over a short-sleeved flowery cotton dress no matter what the season, because it was always hot in their house and in the little shop, and also noisy; as noisy and boisterous as in Anna's house, because here also were children of all ages and sizes, all boys except for the second child, her cousin Mary, who was much older than Anna and married, living in her own newly built house at the edge of the village. The boys who lived at home helped their parents in the bakery or in the shop or in the house.

Theirs was a real family business, Anna thought, unlike the shop of her parents. None of her own siblings wanted anything to do with the shop, and sometimes she thought that her father didn't want them to anyway and that he was pushing them out to go to school, to learn and become qualified for something different.

She passed the village hairdresser, another uncle whose wife was her father's sister. Their shop and salon were already closed. The windows were dark. Her uncle and aunt both worked in the salon, just like all parents in the village jointly shared the work in shops and on farms, except for the factory workers or the labourers and the odd office worker. Her uncle was the hairdresser, and he seemed eager to apply a perm to all the village women over a certain age and give them grey fine curls that would not be blown out of place even by the fiercest storms. These curls would remain solid, on top of and around the women's heads and faces for a week at least, perhaps even a fortnight, and then he would wash-wave them perfectly back into place once more. Sometimes, he rinsed the grey hair with a blue tint, which the women considered to be smart. He also cut hair, and women and girls in the village all had the same short layers so that they looked like identical porcupines. More recently, he had begun to experiment and cut hair in bobs, straight around the head and straight over the forehead. Before he started cutting, and after inviting the girl or the woman to sit on a high chair, he swished a wide white cover around the shoulders as if preparing her for an operation. Anna's aunt would sweep up all the hairs from the floor and make everything look neat and tidy again after another head had been trimmed into neatness and obedience. Their salon also smelled, but this was a smell which was heavy and impenetrable, and which had a whiff of sweetness mixed with charcoal, unlike the yeasty sweetness of the bakery.

Anna's hairdresser uncle was different from most men in the family and in the village. Like other men in her family, he didn't talk much, even to his customers, but unlike most of them he had well kept hands and manicured nails, a cleanliness that did not quite reflect the sweat and labour in which men should be earning their living according to God's Word. Moreover, he wore clean and smartly cut suits every day of the week; light ones in summer and darker ones in winter. In the salon he would take off his suit jacket and wear a short white coat over his freshly washed and meticulously ironed shirt, and he kept scissors, a comb and pins in the pockets at each side.

His hair was black, shiny and cut short and was parted on the left. He wore thick-rimmed dark glasses, with lenses that were, even then, slightly tinted so that you could never clearly see the colour of his eyes, a melancholic brown. He and Aunt Maria did not have children and that was probably why her aunt was also meticulously groomed and had her hair dyed a deep black without any grey streaks showing, unlike her sisters, so that she continued to be one of the most elegant women in the church on Sundays. Sometimes Aunt Maria even varnished her nails, although Anna had seen Johannes frown and he made a comment to Greta, who laughed nervously. Aunt Maria's house was very tidy and clean, and nephews and nieces were usually kept waiting outside when they knocked at the backdoor to deliver a message or a note from their parents, and they were only allowed inside the house after taking off their shoes. When they were the first in the family to acquire a television set, nephews and nieces would need to wash and scrub before being allowed inside, as a treat, to watch children's programmes on a Wednesday afternoon, and only if they had been invited in the first place, which did not happen very often.

The greengrocer just up the road from where Anna lived wasn't a relative, but he and his wife and two sons attended their church on Sundays and that was the reason they bought all their vegetables and fruit from him, although Anna heard her mother complain one day that another greengrocer, newly set up in the village, was much cheaper.

The new wife of the greengrocer's eldest son sometimes helped in the shop and she had very dirty hands with black-rimmed nails, but a clean scrubbed face and red cheeks. She kept a small box of sweets next to the till and handed them out to the smaller children. The second son was strange, and didn't want to know about his parents' shop, apparently. He wanted to be an engineer, he once told Anna. But every morning, his father dropped him off at a school in the next village, which, Anna was sure, was for children who weren't quite normal. Bert said he was stupid, this boy, but their mother told Bert to shush. However, she smiled at the same time, as if she'd been caught out.

Everything and everyone in this village were tied with invisible strings to one church or another except for a few heathens. Nothing escaped this inevitable religious pull, not even the trees and the animals, the cows in the fields, or the horses that would sometimes graze in the field next door when Anna was still quite small. The field had gone now and the farm had been pulled down. A new modern brick house had been built in its place as well as a school and later still, other houses joined along the street.

Anna pulled up her bike next to the house and manoeuvred it into the shed at the back. There would not be much to do, not on a Saturday night, and not on any other night for that matter, except for in the summer when they were allowed to go back outside after their evening meals and meet up with friends. Bert's bike had gone and so had Liesbet's. Bert would be at his girlfriend's house and Liesbet would have gone to see her boyfriend, most likely, although she usually helped Greta with getting things ready for Sunday, food that had to be prepared in advance and put in the cellar ready for heating up for Sunday lunch, and a tidying up of the downstairs rooms and kitchen.

She wondered what Bert or Liesbet would have to say if they knew that two twenty-year old boys, older than them, were friends with her and Gemma. Bert would think they were mad, of that she was sure, and she felt a touch of glee at outsmarting him. She could never work out Bert, he was always disdainful about his younger siblings, but then a few years ago he suddenly made them all sit up when he defended Greta against the anger of Johannes that flared up as they sat round the table.

They were having lunch and Johannes was very angry about something. Greta tried to calm him down but that always had the opposite effect and he suddenly, savagely, turned to her and said everything was her fault, she was the one who was always working against him and he raised his arm to hit her, ready to swipe his hand across her face. And then Bert, all of a sudden, stood up, throwing his chair backwards and holding onto the table, getting in between his father and mother and raising his own fists and jutting out his hips.

"If you dare hit her I will hit you!" He moved forward as if to grab Johannes by the shoulder or his jacket lapels, one leg in front of the other, pushing Johannes back so that he had to hold on to the back of his chair, not to stumble.

"Back off or I'll break your arm," Bert said again, his voice suddenly very cold and not that of a boy anymore.

God was being challenged in front of their very eyes and He didn't do anything. No walls came down, there was no thunder or lightning, just a piercing silence and a standoff. Anna felt the fork slip from her hand onto her skirt, leaving a wet, sticky feeling on her legs and she quickly grabbed it with her other hand before it slid onto the floor. One of her younger brothers giggled and Liesbet gave him a push with her elbow. They all stared as Johannes suddenly turned, shook himself loose from Bert, and walked out of the room, his face first red and then suddenly turning very white, his arms and hands shaking. He stood for a moment at the door and opened it.

"You're my son. How dare you!"

"I mean it," Bert repeated. "You cannot hit our mother. It's wrong."

"We'll talk later. You sit down and eat. All of you." He walked out of the door and closed it behind him, very quietly.

No one took up a fork or a knife in the silence that enfolded everyone and everything in the room like a blanket, taking their breath away. Their eyes darted from their mother and then to Bert, who did not sit down but stormed out through the side door, slamming the door behind him. They heard the backdoor and then there was another silence.

Greta didn't say anything except to shush the youngest children and then serve food with a shaking arm. She sat down and looked straight ahead of her, bit her bottom lip, fumbled with a fork and spoon and tried to feed Rienske, who refused to open her mouth. The others started to push the food into their mouths, deep, and swallowed without chewing. They kept their heads down when their father came back in and sat down to eat, his hands shaking and his face blotchy. When they finished what was on their plates, Johannes said the usual prayer, only his voice sounded hoarse as if he had a sudden cold.

From then on Anna felt admiration for Bert, for standing up like that and showing that Johannes wasn't all powerful after all, that he couldn't just bully their mother around, but Liesbet shook her head as if dismayed and Gerard and Stephan tittered, nodded at each other and disappeared outside without even lifting a finger to help clear the table.

No one ever again spoke about this incident and Anna wondered what would have happened if Bert had actually hit or hurt Johannes. Would he have been sent to an Institution just like Teake? What was the difference, really?

Johannes no longer threatened Greta, nor did he attempt to hit her again, at least not when his children were around, but you could see him swallow when he got angry and he would sometimes just walk out of the room when an argument flared up. The picture of Bert holding Johannes by his lapels was fixed inside Anna's skull, like a photo in an album that she kept opening at the same page. Sometimes, when thinking about it, she felt angry, but as much with her mother for allowing Johannes to threaten her and for not having stood up for herself with him. Anna wished she'd been big and courageous enough to hit Johannes, and from then on she would often feel the urge to taunt and provoke her siblings, or her father, just to see if they would hit, just to see how far she could go before someone would grab her and threaten her back.

No, Bert would probably not be at home that evening, he never was nowadays. He had withdrawn into his own life outside the house, at his College, and he only came back home for the weekends. During the week, he was in some kind of lodging in the south of the country where he was studying. It was too far for him to travel on a daily basis. He'd been banned from attending judo classes as punishment; Johannes said that it had been the judo that was making him aggressive. Anna suspected that Bert did whatever he wanted to do during the week. Perhaps Greta gave him the extra money to pay for his judo class, but Greta would not dare to stand up to Johannes. There was now an unspoken acceptance in the house, however, that Bert was grown up, he was nineteen after all. However, when he was at home for the weekend, he still attended church twice on Sundays, which was the rule of the house. Not attending church was one concession Johannes would not make, for as long as his children lived in his house. Bert, however, spent most of his time with his girlfriend's family and got on his bike early Sunday mornings thus avoiding church attendance. His girlfriend's family, the father a banker, the mother a dedicated homecare wife, lived in Gezel and they weren't Calvinist but Reformed Church, which was much easier going.

Once, when Anna asked Bert about a book by the Dutch writer Gerard Reeve that she knew he had hidden somewhere, he said, "You must be joking. You're far too young … if father finds out you'll be punished, and I'll be to blame again."

She felt snubbed and decided to ignore him from then on. She would find her own books in the library or borrow them from friends and besides, she was not that taken by those Dutch male authors writing about their father-son relationships and with their strident male voices. Jan Wolkers was another one of them, and she thought the family relationships he evoked even more oppressive than her own.

When Anna came into the kitchen, everyone was already sitting round the table, as if waiting for her, but she was not late; she checked the clock, not quite six. Her father was not there yet, fortunately, and her mother said, "Go and wash your hands and call your father, will you? He's in his office."

She called out loud, "Father, the food's on the table," from the corridor where she had left her coat on the rack. Someone had removed the coats from the chair in the room. The office was a small space off the corridor with an entrance to the shop. It was not much larger than a cupboard really, with a narrow desk and a lamp and a huge filing cabinet from floor to ceiling. Johannes followed Anna back into the kitchen room where they sat down and bowed their heads, when he said his prayer, and one after the other they quickly rattled off their own prayer in turn.

"*Dear Lord please forgive us our sins and bless this meal, amen.*"

Chapter Thirteen: 1965

The Netherlands

After November, in the months of December and January, Anna longed for frost, the kind of hard and relentless frost that would leave thick, flowery, grey and white leaf-like shapes on the windows when you woke up in the morning, and when, to keep warm in bed at night, you'd wear woollen socks, a thick vest underneath your flannel pyjamas and you'd hold a hot water bottle in your arms which you alternately placed at your back and then retrieved again in an embrace or pushed down to your feet.

When the frost persisted over days and even weeks, the canals and ditches around the village became skating rinks and the boxes with skates were brought up from cellars and out of attics. The boxes contained the Viking and Norwegian skates with their shiny mean-looking metal blades that were as sharp as butcher's knives and which had been covered in thick grease the previous winter. The attached leather black shoes had been blackened and carefully polished before they were put away, in preparation for the next winter. Other boxes or bags contained a bundle of the wooden skate walkers, with their shallow, blunter blades along the bottom, and these were for the smaller children, who, once the ice was strong enough, would scramble along on them, eager to show off and to convince their parents and older siblings that they also were proficient enough for the real ones, the Vikings. Once the skates had been taken out of their boxes, it was a matter of trying the shoes for size and hoping your feet had not grown too much so they would not fit anymore, or if they had, and it was clear that your own Vikings had become too small, you hoped that your older brothers or sisters had grown as much so that they would have to pass on theirs to their younger siblings. Then it would be them who needed new ones, for which they might well have to wait until St Nicholas Day, or their birthday. And bad luck if your birthday was in July or August.

When fifteen, Anna got her own pair of brand new Vikings for the first time, as a St Nicholas gift early in December, and she prayed for frost and it seemed that God was listening to her and everyone else for that matter, as it froze relentlessly throughout December and January and into February.

When a winter promised to be cold and frosty, a few farmers would flood their fields with water from the canal that was pumped across the road through pipes, enough water to cover the grass and ridges in the fields and turn them into skating sites. Tall masts along the edges of the field would be fitted with lights, the thick black wires dangling in between from one mast to the other. A small wooden hut was erected higher up on the grassy berm that would serve as a café and had a warm stove attached to a gas cylinder. When you tired of the skating and of the running along the tracks competing for speed and showing off, and then in need of a break, you could rest there and buy a hot chocolate, tea, cakes and fried sausages on thick slices of bread.

The major skating rink in the village was constructed this way and there were separate tracks for the grown-ups and experienced skaters on the outside, and on the inside a straight track from one end to the other for the younger ones or grown-ups who were still learning how to skate on their wooden runners that were tied under their shoes with thick orange and green and brown striped ribbons. Trousers and socks got frosty and wet from the powdered ice that was everywhere, shot up loose by the screeching blades.

That year, Anna was in love, as much with her new high Viking skates as with one of Bert's friends, Ted. Just like Bert, Ted was far too grown up to bother much with her and her friends, but on the ice even the older boys were in high spirit and they were less gruff and catty than usual. They didn't seem to mind her being around them, now that she'd got proper Vikings and had joined the core local group of respected and grown-up skaters. She showed off how proficient she was, going at speed and keeping up with some of them for fast rounds. Every time she glimpsed Ted her stomach turned underneath her thick layers of jumpers and jacket, and she wanted him to ask her to do a fast whirlwind skip around the rink, hand in hand, as couples did. She felt quite weak at the knees when she thought about what that would be like, him touching her through the thickness of their gloves, holding hands.

The sky was black, beyond and behind the glittery yellow balls of lamplight that grew fuzzy at the edges all around the skating rink. The fairy tale lights, together with the swishing noise made by the skaters in their thick jackets and floating scarves, their striped hats and gloved hands, and the cool clear smell of ice and frosty air, created a magic land within a glassy self-contained world, walled off from the rest of the universe, which was hidden in the darkness beyond and had become illusory. All that existed was this fairground with its own rules, where skaters were the kings and queens and princes and princesses who strode along, gloved hand within gloved hand. Some of the younger boys were pushing wide brooms along the paths to keep them clean of the snow and crumbled and powdered ice, produced by the violent braking movement of the high steel blades when their owners turned them with a sharp rectangular movement so that they would come to a halt. The boys would be rewarded with a pat on the back, "well done, boy" and a mug of hot chocolate. A different God ruled this icy world, or perhaps there just was not one at all here, on this small piece of earth, where secular rules applied and where the air you breathed was pure and devoid of morals, and where laughter sounded clear and musical and shouts, mirth and happiness spread unhampered through the clean thinness of its vapour, carried along by the warmth of the golden coppery light, to disappear into the shadows and darkness beyond, leaving behind a promise of goodness, a world without devils or sin, a world where you could be at one with yourself and your friends, unblemished and blank as the ice and the air around the odourless frost.

Anna, her cheeks glowing, pulled her woolly hat over her ears. Her scarf trailed behind when she made a run for it on her skates. Some boys and girls held hands to tow one after the other, going at a fast pace, then the boy would link both his hands behind his back, and the girl would grab them fast to be pulled along, screaming with the fun of it. Anna showed off all she could, aware that some people were watching her, her fast stopping movement after a run when she created a V-shape of icy particles that jumped out sideways leaving a powdery heap behind, her easy, long strides, her steadiness and hands behind her back just like the best of the boys as she skated at speed. She was one of the best. Surely Ted could see that?

She wanted to be the only one that he saw, a sudden jolt in her belly, a spasm that made her head ache as she whirled around. She wanted to have someone, just like the others had; she wanted to hold hands and she wondered what it would be like to be kissed by Ted. She'd seen them in the dark, those couples, groaning with their mouths stuck together and their smacking release, and something had happened to her seeing Ted, and all she wanted to do was the same as whatever those couples did, somewhere in the dark where no one could see them.

Ted was tall with dark brown almost black hair, which was curly and cut short around his neck and ears and sat on the top of his head like an unruly mop. On some days he had the beginnings of a beard as if he had forgotten to shave. He often wore tight, sporty looking outfits that made him look even taller than he was. His lips were thick and his cheeks fleshy but pale, and she tried hard to imagine what it would be like to snog him, to feel that stubble of his on her cheek. She shivered at the thought, looked around quickly, afraid that someone might have read on her forehead what she was thinking. Further away, Liesbet, looking her way, stood with a group of her giggling friends, eighteen year olds and ready for marriage, high on the adoration of boyfriends, and Anna quickly turned her back. She imagined the delicious secretiveness of Ted kissing her. Would he put his tongue in her mouth? She'd read about that even though it was never quite clear what actually happened. She'd smirked about the detail with Gemma and once even with Liesbet, and they giggled and grinned whilst pouting their lips before collapsing in a heap at the thought of how ridiculous it all was. But here on the ice and in the cold and glassy air, it seemed so very enticing. She wanted to know what it felt like and she didn't want her father to know, as he would forbid it.

She threw back her head, her face glowing with the cold and the frost and she slapped her hands together, to warm them. Her gloves were coarsely knit woollen ones and the cold air seeped through. Ted wasn't even looking in her direction and she decided to join the queue at the hut for the hot chocolate. Liesbet had gone there with her friends, and she behaved all girly, laughing and having fun. Her boyfriend, a lecherous looking, thin and tall classmate of hers, tried to snog her but Liesbet pulled away, "not here!" She hissed, as if he was trying to molest her in public, and she looked around to see if anyone had noticed. Anna grinned at her.

They went out again, four or five of them, formed a long chain all holding hands and their laughter disappeared in the darkness beyond the first lantern and then they popped up again in the magic circle of the next light, pirouetting around the few couples standing in groups and talking. It was almost time to go home, past eight, and Anna was unsure whether she would go back out again on the rink after she had her hot drink.

Bert and Ted and two other boys she didn't know came into the hut, laughing and talking and Bert said, "Well, that's it for me. I've still got some studying to do, we have a test on Monday, must go now," and he sat down next to Anna. He'd be off to see his girlfriend, who didn't like skating.

"Are you going home too?" he asked.

"No, I'm just off for another round," she said resolutely. She turned to Ted. "Coming? I dare you — I can go faster now with my new skates!"

Ted laughed, looked back at Bert who shrugged his shoulders as if it had nothing to do with him.

"Well, why not, one more. I haven't got anything else to do."

Anna put her protectors on the blades, walked the few steps across the frosted path to the rink, took them off again and was away, ahead of Ted. She pulled at her hat whilst on the move and picked up speed. She heard him behind her, his skates a regular and lengthy swish, and he grabbed her hand from her back and they went together, hand in hand, faster and faster. She kept up, felt the warmth of his hand through her woollen glove like a burning coal and fell in with his movement, right leg, left leg, long strides until they had the joint rhythm and the skating rink was suddenly full of light, the long stretch ahead, then turning to the left and back again towards the café. They didn't talk, just moved and he said, "You're good! Catch me."

He pulled away swiftly with long strides, looked back laughing, but she kept up with him and once more she put her hand in his, on his back now, and this time she moved behind him, while he led and she saw Liesbet at the side, who watched her and put up her hand, as if to acknowledge her.

Flushed and breathing hard, they came to a stop, holding their feet pointed inwards to break and coming to a halt just away from the light. If only he would now make a move, she wanted him to kiss her, to hold her there and then, wanted to be held, but he let go of her hand and said again, smiling, "You really are good. That was great fun."

And then he turned. "Must be off now, see you around sometime."

She went back to the café and sat down on one of the wooden benches, next to an elderly couple who had taken off their skates and were trying to get their feet back into their shoes that they pulled out from underneath the bench. The hut was crowded and noisy with people taking off their skates, having one last hot drink of chocolate or tea or coffee, before going home. Only a few people were left on the rink, the couples that would snog and cuddle and hold each other before they rushed back to their homes and parents, before curfew. Liesbet came in.

"You did great," she said. "I saw you with Ted. He's fast with his long legs. I saw him again just now, I think he's got a girlfriend, she's there with him." She pointed at a group of people moving away from the entrance of the hut.

"Yeah," Anna said. "He's okay. Just having a bit of fun."

She saw Ted bending his head to a girl with long curly and blond hair. She was much shorter and was without skates. She was talking to a group of people and she smiled up to Ted and then he kissed her, quickly, as he put his arm around her shoulder.

Anna pulled off her skates roughly and rubbed her cold hands over the thick socks on her feet, to warm up her fingers, senseless with cold now, so that she could tie the laces of her shoes. Her feet were cold as well and she wanted to get away as quickly as she could. The din in the café was far and distant, like a radio that was tuned to its lowest, but was at the same time overpowering and she had to shout so that Liesbet could hear what she said.

"You go ahead, don't wait for me. I've got my bike."

Liesbet smiled and nodded, Liesbet knew that she fancied Ted, at least fancied the imagination of Ted. And Liesbet allowed her boyfriend to pull her up from the bench and walked out with him.

Anna's bike was amongst a tangle of bikes left at the side of the road and she hauled it up. The road was quiet, Liesbet and her friends had disappeared into the darkness ahead, she could just make them out in the distance and heard their muffled voices and then they were gone. The few streetlights on this country road into the village were set far apart and Anna pushed the dynamo against the front wheel of her bike so that light flickered up, both at the front and the back, as she started pedalling, but it went out again when she slowed to walking speed. Enveloped by the darkness, she wondered where in this world, so cold and frosty, Hell could possibly be. If it were anywhere nearby, the fire would certainly melt the ice. She imagined God sitting in his iciness beyond the darkness of the sky above her and away from the light of the skating rink. She could see the stars, small and pitiful on the black dome above her. Where did He keep his Hell? Was it somewhere deep inside the earth? Was that what causes the lava in some countries when there was an earthquake? Was that where Hell was? Perhaps He was warning her, sending her a message to make sure that she couldn't have what she wanted, that He would forever prevent her from jumping out of His power and that she was caught. He surely was making sure that she couldn't have Ted, whose family didn't go anywhere near any church at all as far as she knew.

She came to a halt and stood, holding the handlebars of her bike as she looked up at the sky, and her body was as still as the frozen iciness around her, quite immovable. An elderly couple walked past her, looking at her curiously.

"You all right lass?" the woman asked.

"Yes," she said and looked away, making sure that they wouldn't see her face and recognise her.

The couple walked on, muttered something to each other, but she didn't hear.

*

She didn't see much of Ted after that evening except once or twice when he was with the same girl, and the spasms of longing seemed to have been just that; spasms that were

202

overtaken by indifference, a dream lost. He faded, but bits of him and the memory of her feelings that night stayed in her stomach, in her head, everywhere in her body and became part of an overall yearning she had for something that was beyond and outside of her reach, that would always be beyond what she could have. God would probably make sure she stayed where she was, *He* would not let go of her the easy way.

She cycled to school every day, sometimes with others, sometimes alone depending on timetables, and she covered mechanically the twenty-five kilometres or so each way, along the river with the wind blowing, and sometimes there was hail and sleet or rain and she would come back, cold, wet and always empty, searching for a way out of God's gripping and taunting hold. She wondered whether He was real, whether what she was worried about day and night, the thing that was always at the back of her mind, actually existed. She did not dare to think too hard about it, as even doubting could get you into Hell and beyond redemption. God was jealous and He could simply send all kinds of horrors her way; He was vengeful and cruel, without mercy. That was clear from the Sunday sermons that warned the churchgoers of even contemplating doubt. It was easier to try and avoid thinking about it, which was one way of being blameless.

On Sundays, her father played the organ, with ponderous fingers that milked the keys dry of any love they might have wanted to express, and to Anna's ears they regurgitated the notes, void of any beauty or mercy. His fingers growled the thump-thumping of the true Believer who knew how to gratify God and give Him a plateful of His own wisdom, dished up by means of an interpretation of Bach that left no room for doubt. Her father pulled the hand stops, moved his fingers across the two layers of keys, and slammed his feet hard down on the

203

pedals. Sometimes, he invited them to sing a psalm, but now his older children more often than not found an excuse to leave the room or simply were no longer there at all when he played, he had stopped trying to engage them the way he used to.

For a long time Anna hated the ponderousness of the organ, the murdering of the cantatas and fugues and Mozart and Bach, and it was only much later when she rediscovered classical music, away from the imposition of Hell and eternal damnation that she was able to peel away the arrogance of the Calvinist believer, who wanted to impress that music, like everything else, was God-given, and as such would always have the message of eternal pain and torture, unless you accepted and believed unquestionably, and then you would be rewarded with eternal happiness, even if not yet, not here. What kind of happiness would that be? And why should you have to give up and live a constricted life that was dull and boring in order to live forever after? To do what? What was the point of living?

All that time that she lived at home with her parents her father played his interpretation of truth across the scales of his organ, across the white and black keys, emphasizing the judgement of eternal damnation by pushing the foot pedals harder. As the years passed, however, he seemed lonelier in his attempts, and a doubt and weariness began to accompany his keystrokes. He would sigh and signal a sense of loss, as if he had done all he could and which somehow or other just proved to be short of expectations. Whose expectations? Anna wondered. How could he be so sure that there was a God who had all these expectations?

*

The world around them had expanded; news from other cities, from the world beyond their own country, reached out to them in different ways. Some people in their village acquired televisions, and the radio began to broadcast pop music if you could find the right station. In town, you could now buy a variety of pop magazines, with photos of Elvis Presley, or the Beatles, the Rolling Stones, the Beach Boys and of film stars, like Brigitte Bardot in her short skirts and bikinis, or Marilyn Monroe and her pout. The insignificant village world became even smaller, and somehow with the entrance of this other, outside world, the threat of eternal damnation diminished leaving only a dull ache and worry somewhere at the back of Anna's head.

"Can't buy me lo…oo…ve," Stephan and Gerard crooned. Away from home they flicked through magazines they borrowed from school friends, their own pocket money never stretching far enough and which would be cut altogether if Johannes knew that they were spending it on vile magazines. They listened to the songs on the jukebox in the ice cream parlour in town and they played the music at school parties when no parents were present, only to revert to the demure and well-behaved brood their parents imagined they were, the moment they heard the footsteps on the path or a car door slam. The twins' school friends seemed to be able to get hold of everything that was forbidden and although they wouldn't always allow Anna to be around with them, sometimes she slipped in, came along, and they didn't notice she was there, or perhaps they didn't care.

Johannes tried but was unable to stop it, this deluge of unwanted and godless information that overpowered his and God's authority. With the twins, Anna sang and hummed, "This land is my land, this land is your land", with a conviction that denied their own helplessness, and their uncertainty at what this land might be and who they were meant to share it with.

Anna read whatever she could put her hands on. She was thrilled and shocked by the books by Gerard Reeve who wrote about sex between two men, she was not sure what that would be like, she barely understood what having sex was about, except that you needed to be married and then it would produce children. Reeve was prosecuted and she followed some of the accounts in papers that she read in bookshops and then put back again. None of it entered her father's house. She read but didn't like Jan Wolkers' book much. She shivered at the description of his deliberate cruelty to cats and insects. All she was ever able to do to was step on a spider when it scuttled across the bedroom floor or perhaps she'd stand on a worm in the soil outside. Wolkers was too preoccupied with men and their roles, with his relationship with his father and his brother and his survival and this should chime with her experience but it didn't. He just didn't have a clue about what it was like to be a girl and in all this he saw his mother as just another appendage, like they all did. Anna didn't really want to read about Jan's devices to survive within poverty and within a Calvinist family. His was a man's world, and because of this far removed from hers. Nevertheless, she liked the way he described things as they were, to the point, and the book was so very unlike the books that lined her father's bookshelf at home, or the books her mother read, the country novels about God-fearing couples who overcame all kinds of trials set by God and lived happily after until they died and went to heaven, and this was clear from the big smiles and the hallelujahs when they lay on their death beds.

Anna liked the writer Anna Blaman best, simply because she was a woman and didn't comply with her father's expectations. Reading Blaman's books, Anna realised that there were alternatives to being a man and woman couple, that Anna

Blaman loved a woman. The thought was thrilling, unlike that of two men being in love. When in preparation for entrance to the Gymnasium, she received additional tuition from a lecturer over the summer holidays and he suggested that she resembled Anna Blaman, both his wife who sat with them and Anna looked shocked. "Don't say that," his wife said and he grinned.

For Johannes, all his efforts to steer away the relentless invasion of new books, godless music and different opinions, were without avail. Johannes and his children were attacked and swamped by a world that he could no longer come to terms with and could no longer explain even to himself, let alone his children, and the best he could do was watch and pray, and tell Greta that some or all of this intrusive godlessness was her fault, because she was too lenient, always too easy on their children, never strict and angry enough.

"How can you?" Johannes would say. "How can you allow them to do this? Why are you leaving it all to me?"

No, Greta should not indulge them, should not always rely on him, Johannes, to establish right from wrong. And so Johannes continued to try to keep God and the Devil, rules and regulations, inside a box that often contained a joker that upset the neatness of his collection.

*

On Sundays, they always went to church twice, together with all the other churchgoers, their aunts and uncles, their grandfathers and grandmothers, friends, cousins and cousins twice removed, nieces and nephews, and they all prayed before and after their daily meals, when the head of the family read from the Bible after the main meal and sometimes also after breakfast and their lunch. God was like the next person hovering somewhere with you wherever you were, invisible but nevertheless in the room with every single one of them. It hurt to think how He did this, this trick of being everywhere and nowhere, of seeing everything and nothing, of knowing everything but keeping quiet about it. And outside, Death would be waiting, but not simply dead Death, no, this was agonising Death, suffering Death, burning Death, a very unpleasant deadness, unless you obeyed the rules. And the only way to find out whether or not He was there waiting for you, to catch you and throw you into Hell and eternal damnation, was by finding out whether all this was really true or whether someone or everyone was lying through their teeth.

Anna decided that she was going to find out once and for all and then it wouldn't matter either way. She was going to find out whether God was there, hovering, and she would challenge Him and be done with it. At night she prayed her own prayer, not the set one that they'd rote learned, the Our Father. No, her prayer ran something like this.

I challenge you God, do what You say You do so well in the Bible, coming up to people, letting them know that You are there somehow, giving signs. Mostly these people are men though and I'm not one of them, you see, I'm a girl, female, different and inferior in your eyes, not part of You. I am the Eve that upset your creation and led men into temptation and I don't know why that should be so. It seems unfair. You never take us seriously, do You, let alone someone like me, a girl, who is the middle child in a large God-fearing family. The church, the Sunday sermons they're all about men, aren't they; men who serve you in church, who must serve you and who must be taught a lesson. Us girls, we don't even need lessons, don't need to struggle, we only have to do the washing up and be good daughters and then good wives and mothers; men will take the decisions for us, won't they, and decide what's good and bad. That's what You really think, don't You? Fathers are given authority in Your name; they must bring us up in Your image and they must make sure that we do the right thing and behave properly and never ever imagine that we might want to do something different, not be a wife or a mother or a sister but something else and I don't know yet what that is. I don't like You God, because you clearly don't like women or girls, do you? You let fathers and men be the bosses, the masters, headmasters, breadwinners, elders in the church, wherever they are because You and they are one and the same in this worship, we are the bit of Your creation that's falling foul. We are ignored.

I'm frightened. I'm tossing and turning and I'm frightened that You will suddenly strike me dead and I'm in Hell because I'm thinking all these things but I must think them because that's the only way I can find out whether You are actually out there somewhere and serious.

My father and my mother, I can hear them. They are going to bed, their bedroom door closes and then everything's quiet again. They do exactly what they think You tell them to do, and they are very frightened of You too. I know that, because they keep things away from us and from me, books and magazines and all that and we must not read them otherwise they will make us bad, and they will go to Hell too, for not teaching us properly. But then there must be lots of people who write them and read them and how do You keep track? Where are these people, how do they live and what is that other world that I don't know anything about, that I am not allowed to know anything about?

All's asleep, all's quiet, there's not a sound, all's dark and empty, only You lurking somewhere, and the Devil, waiting to strike me dead. But maybe You're not there at all. Maybe You're just something that parents and clergymen dream up to keep us all quiet, maybe they just don't know any better because they've never cared to find out? I've got to know you see, I've got to know and maybe it's better to be struck dead and then find out the bad way, than just not knowing or believing some tosh that has kept mankind busy and in their places for ages and ages, for all eternity as You call it. I can't live like this, I really cannot stand the claustrophobia any longer, the emptiness, the quarrels, the fights that my parents have and the fighting that we do, and half the time I don't know what for. It's as if they've just decided to do things this way, simply because they're frightened. Maybe I can be as clever as other people in this world and find out what the truth is. I'm not scared anymore. I will find out if nothing happens, because I don't think anything will happen, really.

I'm going to find out about the real world, the world we live in, not an imaginary afterlife in a Paradise that does not exist; I want to read books that help me to think, books that tell me stories of real human beings, not invented bible stories. You've just got to let me know. I think You don't exist, at least not in the way I'm being led to believe. I don't want to die yet God, but I can't just be scared the way I have been and so empty and confused and angry with nowhere to go or to turn. Just strike me dead if You really exist. I don't want this life, hating my father because of what he stands for, despising my mother for never standing up for us, for me, for being so frightened of my father, my father for only telling me what I cannot do, not really caring about me, just scared and dogmatic. You and my father seem to be colluding with each other, that is, if You do exist.

Men are everywhere. In church, the vicar, the elders and everyone of any importance are all God's messengers, so they say, and in authority; and the women, they just do the housework and support their husbands, look after children and parents. In this village, men have the shops, the bakeries and the farms and women help them but never own them and the men keep the books because supposedly they are in direct contact with God because they are true believers. They will get angry, and God agrees with them, and when things are not done right, they will strike a mother, who will not fight back but will only hold up her hands, a supplicant, frightened.

It's dark and I can't sleep. I should sleep. You haven't been around anyway and so all this is wasted breath, wasted time, wasted fear. I really feel quite empty but I cannot go to sleep even now, even if I don't think anymore that You will strike me dead and I don't have to be afraid or worried and I don't have to fight You anymore because there's no one to fight, except myself and the suffocating air around me. You've lost me and now I have to be clever about playing this right, because if my father finds out he'll try and stop me and he is almost as powerful as You are supposed to be, God, only less powerful now that I know there is not really anyone to back him.

I will have to try and find my way around, find out and eke myself out of this life, this environment.

You've cheated me all along; they've all cheated me, the schoolteachers and clergymen, the aunts and uncles, the doctors and everyone else, always colluding with You, telling me how thoroughly worthless I am in the scheme of things, and how I must behave, telling me that the books I want to read are wicked, cannot be read by children and implying that there's something inherently bad with girls and their bodies. Boys talk about fucking as if they know what it is, but God, I know I was afraid of even thinking about sex, something dirty unholy and not condoned by You. Just having the word in my brain, misty and unclear what it is about, used to make me feel wicked. Yet, I now like the thought of what I might do with my body, what my body looks like and how exciting it is to think about this. When we were little we played around, fooled around with our genitals, all these boys and girls, large families looking at each other and sniggering, but not anymore, because we are older now and there

211

is a real fear about what we don't know, what You are telling my parents to keep away from me and I want to know what it is.

I will live my own life dear God; I don't think You care anyway because You don't exist.

Chapter Fourteen: 1966

The Netherlands

Anna was not struck dead. When, after a bad night's sleep tossing and turning, she woke up the next morning feeling groggy and unfocused, life carried on as if she never had that prayer dream, or was it a conversation? A conversation with whom or what? She didn't know, but what she was sure of when she woke up was that all the commands and stories about a vengeful God who watched you day and night, all of that was a lie, a great big lie and how or why that lie had been made up she didn't know or understand. She guessed that it had something to do with obedience and a way of keeping children and women in check.

*

Anna avoided her parents and church adults as much as she could and ignored the demands to join in the catechism lessons, to join the church girls' club. She continued to attend all those annoying groups haphazardly, but often found an excuse about too much homework or another test or an exam for which she needed to prepare. She asserted she was unable to root learn the catechism, that she had not got the time — she had to focus on everything she had to learn at school, her sciences and her maths and her geography, history, languages, it was all too much. She hid prohibited books under the mattress, became loud in her commentary at the dining room table, expressed views that were slightly contrary to everyone else's but was also able to stop just at the right time, before being outrageous and thus punishable. She didn't talk about her decision and conclusions about God and religion with anyone; it was her secret, and one day she would escape from the box. When she stayed the night with one or another girl from school, after a birthday party or because of a late school session, she noticed the odd cracks in the façade of glossy fronts that all Calvinist families wanted to portray to the outside world. Sometimes, there were older siblings who no longer came home so regularly anymore, and never on a Sunday, but who seemed to have disappeared into 'the jungle of students' in Amsterdam, Utrecht and other places and who only returned home every so often for a brief visit to have their washing done or to make sure their allowances would continue. During these visits, there would be heated conversations behind closed doors, a father who shook his head like her own father did and a mother who expressed some kind of grief. "He's too young to be going off alone; he will come to his senses once he realises," but there was rarely an explanation.

Later, her friend would explain. "He's decided he doesn't want to go to church anymore," or, "he's got a girl friend and she isn't a Calvinist." It was rarely the girls that went off the rails though, rarely older sisters or female cousins, it was always the boys.

Although she and Gemma saw less and less of each other and Anna had stopped meeting up with Jasper and Teake, one day Gemma caught up with her again, as if they were still best friends, as if they had not ignored each other for over a year. Anna had tried to renew contact a few times, cycled to Gemma's house, but Gemma always proclaimed to be busy, in a friendly enough manner. She would let her in the house but

214

then inevitably made the excuse that she had homework to do, or that her mother wanted her to help her younger sister with homework. When Anna asked about Teake and what had happened, Gemma had simply ignored her, muttered something about having seen Teake but that things were unresolved, and had then changed the subject.

Anna shrugged her shoulders and was too preoccupied with her own life. One day she would be able to escape the village and leave it all behind; she would start her life and then perhaps they would meet up again and tell each other about what they were doing. All she needed now was patience; she sometimes held her breath until she gasped for air. She would not always be fifteen and not always be dependent on her parents. People moved away even from this village, sometimes. Hadn't Ted disappeared altogether? He was gone. Once the winter was over she never saw him around in the village and when she asked Dan he said, "He's joined the navy. Gone abroad, I understand." Well, that was Ted.

Best of all was that it had been agreed that because, 'the girl is so clever, she always has top marks,' her father thought she ought to continue learning at the Gymnasium, after finishing her secondary school. She'd been having extra maths and language lessons with a private tutor to prepare her for the switch. Johannes, against all odds, had decided that this was best for her.

"The girl has talent," he would say. And she knew that he meant that you must not hide talent under a bushel. The Bible was clear on that. There was nothing against being clever, even if you were a girl.

She knew that some of her teachers had been urging him and she was not going to mess up this opportunity. She wanted nothing more than go to that Gymnasium, as it would be her first step out — moreover, the Gymnasium, although with a general religious affiliation, was not a Calvinist school.

Gemma was also in the final form of secondary school and sitting her finals. She was doing well and wanted to join the teacher training college — she would stay with a family during the week, as the college was too far away to get to on a daily basis. It had all been arranged, and inevitably she and Gemma would grow apart even further.

But unexpectedly, here was Gemma catching up with Anna when she was cycling home on her way back from her last school exam in town. It was as if Gemma came out of nothing, a few kilometres before the village, as if she had been waiting.

"I want to talk to someone, someone who knows me and who knows Teake," Gemma said.

"How come? Have you finished your exams?"

Gemma, once her best friend, someone she had completely relied upon and someone she trusted, had become a stranger and the question seemed oddly inappropriate. They cycled on, not losing any speed.

"I've got to get back, I'm supposed to babysit for my aunt when I get back," Anna said. "What's up anyway?"

"Don't be angry. I know we haven't been good friends lately, but I've been very upset with the whole thing, what happened, you know, with Teake? I couldn't help myself. You didn't seem to care much."

Gemma sounded breathless. As if in agreement, they both reduced speed, cycling slowly now on the cycle track along the main road with only the sound of a car passing intermittently which then disappeared in the distance or round the next corner. A motorcyclist hooted behind them and screeched past, the driver waving an arm wildly for them to get out of the way or perhaps to wave at them, it wasn't clear.

"That's my brother," Gemma says. "He's really mad with that thing."

"Where do you want to go? Do you want to stop and sit somewhere to talk?" Anna asked.

"Don't mind. How are your exams coming on?" Gemma said.

Perhaps she wanted to show Anna that she was interested in what she did? Not like Gemma.

"I've taken most of mine and I think I'm alright. That's a relief anyway!" Gemma continued, as if unable to stop talking.

Anna looked at her. "That's not what you want to talk about, is it? What's happened with Teake? You still see him?"

Gemma looked straight ahead, no longer glancing sideways and avoided meeting Anna's eyes.

"Mmm… yes, he's okay, but there's something else." She lowered her voice, and then blurted out. "I think I'm expecting, I mean I'm pregnant and I don't know what to do!"

Her eyes were suddenly full, her face became red and blotchy and still she was looking straight ahead, her legs going round on the pedals as if on a pre-set automatic speed.

Anna stopped cycling altogether, pulled her bike to the side of the road, opened her mouth and then closed it again. Not a sound came out. Gemma looked back over her shoulder and then stopped her bike too, turned it and walked back to Anna.

How on earth could Gemma be pregnant? Invincible, straight Gemma who always knew what to do and how to behave, who was her father's good girl and her mother's treasure? How could Gemma be pregnant? What did she know and do that Anna didn't? How dare she do that! Anna stared at Gemma as she dropped her bike next to Anna's, her mouth still open; then she swallowed and still couldn't say anything.

Suddenly there was the sound of her own voice, angry. "I don't believe you — you're having me on. You haven't seen Teake for a year! How can you be pregnant? We're not even supposed to know about this until married! So how come you're all of a sudden so grown up?"

She grabbed Gemma's arm, and nearly pulled her over her bike that lay there. Gemma shook herself free.

"Let go of me! Well, I do know how to do it," she said. "And moreover, I've seen Teake many times since he left that stupid Institution. We've seen each other almost every fortnight, as a matter of fact, for the last year or so, that's why I had no time to keep in touch with you and I didn't want anyone to know. He's even met my parents and visited once or twice. There. Only my parents don't know that we've seen each other so often and where I go. They think I'm still meeting up with you regularly. They don't know we haven't seen each other for donkey's years."

Anna sat down on the grass at the side of the track, perfectly still and screwed up her eyes. She became aware of the sound of a fly and swatted it away with her hand.

"Well?" Gemma said. "Aren't you going to say anything? You're my best friend. I'm not sure what to do. I want to become a teacher, but I can't if I have a baby. I'll have to get married. I want children, but not now!" She sucked in a deep breath of air and kicked against the grass then dropped down on her backside, pulled up her knees and hid her head in her arms, sobbing uncontrollably like a five-year old. "What will happen to me?"

Anna looked at Gemma and then down at the ground. Here was Gemma, asking for her help and she had no idea what to advise her or even how to help. She was her best friend, or at least had been her best friend, and she didn't know what to do or say. *I'm helpless*, she thought. *This is what I want to get away from, the possibility of being caught out.*

"Does your mum not know? You'll have to get married I suppose … yeah. Or perhaps you can give it away…"

She couldn't think of another piece of advice. They usually got married, young couples in the village that had committed the Sin, and they had to confess in front of a church gathering before they could even get married. Then they lived with what they'd conjured up, their own choice, married life and living happily ever after, like everyone else in the village.

Anna suddenly knew with more certainty than ever that she would not get pregnant, never! She would keep boys well away from her until she knew what to do to stop that from happening. There must be something you could do because it was only them, the churchgoers that had these large families, the Catholics as well as the Calvinists. Other families seemed quite capable of either not doing it too often or they had some means that prevented them getting pregnant, because they had neat, small families of two or three children only.

Gemma was almost a year older than she was and at sixteen probably could get married. Anna suddenly felt relieved that she had stopped taking the tablets given to her by the gynaecologist and subsequently by their GP, whom she still visited regularly, and who every time again prescribed another six months worth of tablets which she duly put in the dustbin. She didn't have nor wanted periods. She wasn't ready for them, wouldn't want the sex, and she would keep her body under control. Just as well Ted didn't want to know. Anyway, most girls didn't have intercourse until they got married anyway, so why should she? She'd never get married.

Anna moved closer to Gemma, who was still crying. Gemma pulled a handkerchief out of her coat pocket and noisily blew into it. A few passing cyclists looked at them curiously but carried on, some shouted a friendly 'hello' but they ignored them.

"I suppose you could have it stopped?" Anna ventured.

She had heard of abortions. They were supposedly most wicked and from the Devil of course, the worst thing any girl or woman for that matter could do and it would be a deadly sin, one for which you went to Hell straightaway. She no longer believed that, but nevertheless the implications of an abortion or what that would mean were beyond her. She shivered with the unknown of all of this, whom could they ask? Was that thing in Gemma's tummy actually a child? Talking to their mothers would be almost worse than talking to their fathers, because mothers would simply tell their fathers and vicars and elders anyway, and then the fathers would blame the mothers. And then it was back with God and eternal damnation unless you married in church and confessed publicly that you had sinned.

"Does Teake know?" she asked, when Gemma didn't respond to her suggestion of a termination.

"No, I haven't told him. I kept hoping it would go away, that my period would start, that it was a mistake. But I haven't had a period for two months now, so… Then I saw a doctor, not ours. I made an appointment with that new one in Henen; girls in my class go to him. He takes on new patients and I said I needed to see someone confidentially. He's alright, doesn't really care much for our church and all that…" She shrugged her shoulders. "He said I would have to tell my mum, though." She sighed again, a deep shivering sigh from her stomach and clear phlegm came out of her nose, which she wiped away with a hard arm movement across her face. Her coat was smeared.

"I'm not even sure if I want to tell Teake. I just don't know what to do anymore!"

She started crying again, big tears now down her face, and then blew her nose like a trumpet. She pushed the hanky into a ball in her fist, and continued to swipe it across her face. "I guess I've really messed up, Anna, I didn't think anything would happen to me because we aren't married … we just went a bit too far… Teake said … and I didn't really want it but it happened, and before I knew, it was done, and I just prayed it would not and then of course it has …"

She furiously spat out the words now.

The cycle path stretched away from them with the receding backs of a few cyclists in one direction and others coming at them from the other. The light was fading and a sullen greyness and greenish-grey shimmer was visible in the trees behind them, a darkness advancing to the road where they were. When the darkness reached them, they got up.

"You can't go home. Not like this. You've got to go to someone who can help you." Anna said.

Gemma shrugged her shoulders, pushed her hands deep inside the pockets of her jacket and took them out again to pick up her bike. They pedalled slowly, towards and into the village without saying much. Their legs didn't seem capable any longer to put pressure anywhere. As they turned into the road where Anna lived, Gemma again wiped her nose with the sleeve of her jacket, looked up and said, "I'm going to tell them. There's nothing for it. My mother will be so angry, but there's nothing else I can do."

She pushed hard on her pedals and moved away forcefully, kicked her bicycle dynamo into action so that all Anna saw was the red backlight disappear in the distance.

*

Anna cycled to Gemma's the next day, rang the front door bell, but when Gemma's mother came to the door, she barely opened it, just enough to say that it was not convenient and that Gemma could not come out. She shut the door again in Anna's face. When, after a few days she still hadn't heard from Gemma, Anna tried again. The house was quiet and Gemma's younger sister disappeared around the back when she saw Anna walk up the path. The net curtains in the front windows moved, but it was too dark to see anything. Anna propped her bicycle against a tree and rang the bell once more.

"Gemma's gone to see her uncle," her mother said. "She will be staying there for a while, so it's better not to come round again. Her aunt is ill and Gemma's going to help out. Didn't she tell you?"

"What's happened to Gemma?" Greta asked when Anna got home. "Do you know where she is?"

Her mother smiled a thin, vague smile and Anna said, "She's apparently gone to help out with her uncle and aunt. Her mother says that the aunt needs someone to help out with her children." She hesitated. "But I'm not sure why Gemma is there, she…" She couldn't find the words to finish the sentence.

Her mother was already walking away, towards the shop. "Can you tell Liesbet to put the potatoes on at five?" she said and then disappeared through the door, clicking it shut.

"What's happening to Gemma, do you know?" Anna asked Liesbet, later. "Why does no one want to talk about her? It's not true that she's helping out an aunt, I know it isn't. She's supposed to go to her teacher-training course and she isn't back yet. She's expecting a baby, or at least she was. Why does no one want to talk about this?"

Liesbet opened her mouth. "What?" she said, and then shrugged her shoulders. "Don't know about that. People are

222

talking, always talking. Her family clearly aren't saying anything and there hasn't been anything about it in the church, no announcement, you know."

"How do you mean, an announcement? A wedding announcement, a confession announcement, what?"

"Either. They say she's helping out an aunt who lost a baby but I don't know. Why don't you try and ring her?"

When Anna telephoned Gemma's mother to ask for a telephone number to ring, she said that the aunt didn't want to receive telephone calls. Why didn't Gemma ring her, or send a letter? She had just disappeared. And no one was talking. It was as if she had never existed.

Chapter Fifteen: 1967

The Netherlands

How had it come to this? Anna tried hard to remember the moment when she and Paul had become an *item*, as she tried to wriggle herself away from him. At one point, some time back, Paul's friend Tom had been chasing her. Sure, he was not as attractive but was clearly smitten with her, you could see his hormones chasing around his body, desperate for a girl. She'd caught Tom whisper to Paul once when he thought no one could hear him, "I'm feeling so randy! Look at her." Had he even known what he was talking about, she wondered, embarrassed at the smut he uttered.

In church, Tom found a seat next to her, upstairs where they were away from parents and adults, and he had tried to hold her hand, which she kept well away from him in her lap clutching a pair of gloves or a bag. After a few months of continuous rejection and Anna clearly trying to avoid him he had finally given up and then, somehow, there was Paul who was interested in her. Only he'd been much less forthright, hadn't taken anything for granted, and when they stood outside clustered in groups after a church sermon or before going to their catechism classes, they had talked about books they both read. She'd been surprised at their easy understanding. There had not been any of the kind of pressure imposed by Tom, and they'd laughed about how they managed to read books, listen to music and do other things that were frowned upon by adults.

Once, when they sat in the back row upstairs, during the Queen's birthday celebration, a whole group of them, the twins, two of Paul's sisters, friends of Paul's and of Tom's and of sisters and of brothers, only Gemma was missing but they never talked about her now, all in that back row of hard benches in the church, where the only attraction were the lead windows, colourful with greens and yellows and reds as long as you didn't try to figure out what the pictures were about, the crucifixion and other gory details, men in prayer positions, men following a Christ-like figure, women on their knees, and when the organ was pumping out the glorification of God and the Queen, and they were sitting there all curled up inside with their emerging sexual desires, the dirty talk and the groping hands, Paul slowly and surreptitiously got hold of her right hand and pressed it. She hadn't pulled her hand away.

The vicar had droned on with his special sermon thanking God for Queen and Birthday and she hadn't heard a word of what he said. They'd sung the psalms, with the organ piping out the 'glory hallelujah', and she'd felt that stir again, similar to when she had wanted Ted to touch her. She sat with Paul's hand holding hers and wondered what he would do next, what she would do to keep him interested. She'd made sure that when he looked sideways he would see her straight posture, her slim knees and bare long legs. She'd teased him along by withdrawing her hand slightly, testing him, whilst singing loudly along with the rest of the congregation.

She'd been tempted and had forgotten her resolve. Paul was alright; he was attractive. After Gemma's disappearance over two years ago and the hollowness left inside with the disappointment when Ted ignored her and the realisation that he'd gone away, she'd kept herself aloof from the village crowd. But she was seventeen now and wondered if it might not be nice to have a boyfriend after all, to be less of a loner and to belong somewhere, to be an item with someone. She wanted some of that, whatever it was that they were all so preoccupied with, her brothers, sisters, their friends and even Gemma before she disappeared.

She had tried to get in touch with Gemma, but Johannes and Greta avoided talking about her, and when she'd tried to find out from Gemma's brothers, they had also refused to talk and had repeated the same lie that she was helping out at her aunt's. But some of their friends raised their eyebrows and winked, as if everyone knew what was really going on. What had happened to Gemma's baby? What had happened to Teake? Had the vicar and elders contrived to ban Gemma from the village and the church? Had she confessed, perhaps?

One of Gemma's brothers took pity on Anna and told her that Gemma was at a teacher training college, somewhere near her uncle and aunt's, where she would stay until she got her Diploma. Anna didn't believe any of it, but there was no way she could find out, and it was very odd that Gemma had just stopped communicating with her. Why hadn't she written a letter or sent a card? It seemed so odd also that she no longer came home, not even for the holidays.

Anna had thrown herself on her schoolwork, determined to meet the challenge of the Gymnasium, which had accepted her. She liked her new friends, the more so because none of them were from the village. Johannes wouldn't let her stay over with them though and so she continued to be the outsider, the one that never attended the parties, the one that always got on her bike at the end of the school day and cycled back the twelve kilometres to her home, never part of a group. She'd soon finish her exams, and once she was eighteen no one would stop her.

And now she and Paul were in this room of her cousin's, lying full stretch on a sofa and Paul was holding her tight, almost suffocating her, hot in his high-necked collar which pressed against her nose and she felt his hands move along her back, under her jumper and on her bare skin and then he fumbled with her bra. The room was dark with only a small pathetic sidelight on in the corner. Who had turned off all the other lights? She couldn't remember. It was very quiet and even Paul's breathing was now barely audible, except for a groan every so often, and then his teeth were in her neck, sucking, and his hands were hard and grasping, grabbing at her and she felt him getting hard against her. His moaning turned into a grunt whilst she lay still, not wanting to move, trying to disentangle the conflicting messages whirling through her mind, whilst her body became stiff and unyielding.

As always, her brain took over. She couldn't let this happen. If she did, she'd end up like her cousin Mary for whom they were babysitting, and who had had to bring forward her wedding after the humiliating public church confession of having committed a Sin against God. Or she'd end up like Gemma, kicked out by her parents and never heard of again; she'd end up like so many others, stuck in a house with babies, dependent on Paul as a husband. No, there wouldn't be any babies in her life, not in this village; there would not be prams and dull housework, forever and ever after. If she gave in to this, she'd never know about anything else beyond the claustrophobia and prison cell of the village. She didn't want this, didn't want to be married in church with a big belly and a sermon about the sins of the flesh and about the Almighty and Forgiving God, her parents smiling sheepishly and her father saying, *'too clever by half – how could you do this to us?'* First there would be the vows, then obedience, and all there would be left for her for the rest of her life was to be the helpmeet to her husband, to Paul.

She moved herself away with a jerk, pulled herself loose from him, and almost immediately there was the sound of a key in the lock and the front door opening with hushed voices in the hall beyond the sitting room.

"Gosh, it's dark in the house. Where are they?" There was the sound of a laugh and a giggle, the higher pitched voice of her cousin, and the deeper voice of Jos, Mary's husband.

"Well, at least the kids must be asleep, it's so quiet. Let's see what they're up to."

They sat up quickly. She pulled her jumper back, relieved to be away from Paul, her bra was only just covered, hung over her stomach but she pressed it back and straightened her skirt.

Paul looked at her briefly; his face was red and his straight, dark hair a messy blob on top of his head, the angular features shadowed in the half-light. How handsome he was and how totally at her mercy. But she could not afford to be merciful. He swung his legs off the sofa just as the door to the living room opened and Mary and Jos stood in the doorway, Jos flipping on the light as he stepped into the room.

"So, you had a good time, eh?" He laughed and winked at Paul.

Mary giggled again, nervously, but she wagged her finger at them. She was a cheerful looking woman of about thirty, who had lost her girlish and trim appearance, showing a bulge around the waist and stomach, a few wrinkles around her eyes and mouth and her blond hair cut short in preparation for the inevitable perm that the women all seemed to aspire to in this village, once they were over thirty.

Mary was a happy woman. She probably could not imagine any different life she might want. No, Mary was happy with her house, her husband and the two children upstairs, her new furniture, her new teeth, acquired ten years ago, prior to getting married. Her father had paid for the dentist, making sure her new husband would not have to pay for patching up bad teeth or for fillings, and so she had them all pulled out, the good as well as the bad, and now had a sparkling set of fixed dentures. Anna recoiled when she thought about what someone so young might look like without her own teeth, with teeth in a glass of water by the side of the bed, like her parents.

Jos patted Mary on her backside. He still had a boy's face, at thirty-two, but he was doing well in his job in an engineering company and his wife and children didn't want for anything.

"Don't tease," he said. "They're only having fun, just like we used to."

Anna shivered even though her face was still glowing with the heat of Paul's jumper and she felt the sweat, prickly along her back. She grimaced, ignoring their open-faced attempt at eye contact, and looked down in an attempt to find her shoes that had been pushed under the sofa.

"The kids were fine. I read Bob a little story and he went off to sleep just like that. Frank had his bottle at about nine and I changed him. He was happy. We must be going now. Did you have a good time?" She rattled it off as if she had practised what to say, like a speech.

"Good," Mary said. 'You want a coffee? Or does your father want you back at home?"

"Yeah, I'd better get back. He'll be up and he will worry you about it tomorrow if I don't get back before eleven. You know what he's like."

They stumbled to the hall, pulled on their light summer jackets against the night chill and waved another goodbye, promising they would baby-sit again.

They walked back to Anna's house, stiffly, without saying anything. Paul grabbed her around the waist, pulling her to him. He wanted to prolong the intimacy, and wanted her to yield. The streets were deserted and the village was asleep; the houses all in the dark and only the light of the street lamps cast their shadows on curtained windows and dark front doors. They'd soon left the new housing estate behind them and were on one of the main village roads. A few cars were parked along this road, like so many faithful dogs waiting for their lucky masters to come out in the morning. Paul stopped and tried to kiss her again, holding her face, and pushing his tongue deep into her mouth. She didn't respond and kept rigid and aloof, and shivered in her jacket.

"What's the matter?"

"Nothing." She pulled herself away and looked down at the asphalted road as if searching for something, and then started to walk again, fast now.

"I'll be going back to college on Monday," he said. "I can hardly wait until we're both finished with school. Won't be long now!"

His voice was full of an enthusiasm that she didn't feel and she was reluctant to accept his assumption that they had agreed what would happen next. They had never talked about this; about what each of them would do after they'd finished their exams. Paul would be ready to take on a job managing a farm, somewhere, anywhere, either in the village or further away and she would have her Bacc, as good as an entrance card to university and the world would be at her feet. She'd be a girl with the kind of certificate that very few girls in the village would have, probably none. They reached her house and she came to a dead halt in the middle of the street and faced Paul. "I'm leaving."

"What do you mean?" He looked at her with raised eyebrows, his face white in the light of the streetlamp.

"I'm going to Amsterdam. I've got a job. In an international company."

He opened his mouth but closed it again, as if he couldn't find the sound of his voice. Then he tried again.

"Well, Amsterdam's not far. We can meet for weekends as we do now."

"You've got to understand, Paul. I can't stay here. I don't want to get married. There has to be something else. I don't want babies. I hate the church and everything that goes with it."

Her voice was loud and echoed along the silence of the street. She balled her hands into fists and pushed them hard into her jacket pockets. She repeated as if she had only just made the discovery. "I hate it all!"

She pulled herself away from his hands, which again tried to grab hers, turned and ran to the front door almost crying now, and then before she opened the door, her hand on the doorknob, she turned back once more. The trees stood still, shivering lightly in the night air, and there was a faint rustle as if in a premonition of colder weather coming, a storm perhaps.

"It's not about you. You've got to understand this. None of this has got anything to do with either you or me. It's this shitty place, this prison. I've got to find out what it's all about! Life!"

He was hurt, she could see it, and he held up his hands, palms up, as if begging her.

"I wouldn't hold you back," he said. "We can go and live somewhere else. We don't have to stay here. I don't even know where I'm going to get a job yet. And if you don't want babies yet then so what? There must be ways we can avoid having them." He held his head slightly up, looking at the night sky and then jerked at the collar of his jacket, swatting away an invisible mosquito or a fly perhaps.

"That's just it. All you think about is that you need to get a job and the rest will just fall into place. You don't understand. I don't want us to be a couple, I want freedom. I want to find out what all this is about! Just let me go. You'll find someone. I'm not what you think I am. I'm not what you all want me to be!"

He walked up to her where she stood at the front door and grabbed her arm, held it very tight, and then pulled her to him, as she tried to escape, moving her face sideways.

"I want you. What am I going to do? You are my girlfriend. I'm in love with you. I want to marry you … and … I just don't understand any of this. What's made you change your mind?"

"You don't know what you want any more than I do." She spat it out. "We're both as uncertain as each other. We're only doing what everyone here expects us to do. What everybody else around us is doing. Pairing off. You're eighteen and talk about marriage! I'm still seventeen. I don't want any of it. Never wanted it … you're hurting me."

She pulled herself free again and refused to listen to him. She was afraid that she would not be able to explain herself clearly. She was afraid to see his hurt, she was afraid of her own callousness, and she slipped away from the front door to the back of the house where the kitchen door was unlocked and pulled the door shut behind her. She took in a deep breath. She could hear Johannes in the front room behind the closed curtains — had he peeped through a slit, had he seen their quarrel?

She put her head round the door, which was slightly ajar. "I'm back. Just going to bed now. Good night."

She went upstairs before he could answer or ask her anything. She knew it was past his bedtime, that it was too late for him, but then he didn't have to sit up and wait for her. All he wanted was to make sure that they were safe and well tucked up in bed, and he wanted to prevent anything unthinkable happening, such as what had happened to Mary.

Liesbet was asleep already, on the top bed of the bunk beds. Not much longer. She'd be married soon. Anna slipped out of her clothes in the dark, there was a faint light coming in from somewhere outside through a crack in the curtains. She searched for her pyjamas and found them folded under her pillow. She pulled the blankets over her so that they covered her head, but it wouldn't stop her brains churning like her mother's new centrifuge, in which she piled the sheets and the towels and which rattled when it was turned off and lost its speed gradually. Her body felt alternately hot and cold; she could still feel his hands, feel his body; she saw his red face, the expression of total shock. She didn't care about him, she was selfish, callous, and her sister and sometimes her brothers said so too. She didn't love Paul anyway, of that she was sure. It had always been the curiosity of what it would be like to have a boyfriend, being with someone and not standing out as the loner who was unable to attract anyone, like all the other girls.

She imagined Paul standing outside, waiting for her to come back to say that it was all a mistake. Then, realising she was not coming back, he would turn and walk away, perhaps forgetting about the bike he had left at the side of their house, but then he would realise anyway and would come back for it. He'd unlock the bike and jump on it and then speed away as fast as he could, blindly. He'd know better than to knock at the door and demand to be let in, although for a split second she worried that he might do just that, and tell her father what a miserable bitch she was and how she had treated him. But he would know that her father would only be annoyed at being kept up even later, and that he'd not be able to do anything for Paul unless she agreed to it. They could not force her to marry, could they? No, Paul would try and talk to her tomorrow. He was not catching a bus until late afternoon, to go back to his college. She'd need to have a plan. It would be easier if they never saw each other again.

She pulled the blankets tighter around her and eventually fell asleep, restless but relieved, as if a great burden had been taken off her.

*

Jos locked the front door after Anna and Paul left, took off his shoes and walked back into the sitting room on his socks where Mary had flopped down on the sofa. A cushion had fallen on the floor; the others were flattened and out of shape. She bumped up one of them and replaced it carefully at the end of the sofa. "Gosh, Anna really does take herself seriously, doesn't she?"

Mary carelessly tugged her legs underneath her, pulled her much patterned and colourful skirt over her knees and bent over to the low coffee table in front of her to pick up a half empty packet of cigarettes. She lit a cigarette with a square silver lighter that was left in a large ashtray in the middle of the table. She inhaled deeply and carefully blew out the smoke from between her full lips; her lower lip had been bitten and looked scarred. Her white, long-sleeved blouse was creased and had a red wine stain just below the V of her neck opening. She looked down at it and sighed.

"Will you have a look to see if the boys are alright? I'm knackered, shouldn't have had any wine really, I can't seem to take it any more, don't get enough sleep nowadays."

"That's okay, I'll go," Jos said, hugging up his trousers as he left the room again.

She heard him tiptoeing up the stairs and when he came back he grinned at her. "Bob's upside down, back to front and a total mess, but fast asleep. He's such a hoot really when he sleeps, as if he's still very busy. Frank's fine as well, a bit smelly but I don't want to wake him to change him now."

"Let's leave them, come and sit for a bit. Have a cigarette and then we'll go up. You've got to get up early don't you?"

"Yes, I'm afraid so. Five-thirty. But I'm sure Frank will have us up by that time anyway."

He sat down next to her on the sofa, lit a cigarette as well and they sat quietly, without talking for a while, until Mary said, "Do you think she's stuck up? Anna I mean. Does she really think she's too good for us? I was only trying to be nice, you know, helpful. Give them an evening away from their parents, and somewhere warm. You know what we were like when we were courting." She smiled.

Jos, even after ten years of marriage, was not very good at keeping his hands off her, would not have taken no for an answer, but then she never wanted to say no to him anyway. They'd been madly in love and she had promptly got pregnant, but then they had wanted to get married anyway. They'd just married a little sooner than they'd bargained for. Both her parents and his had been very good though, and after they'd gone through the public confession part in the church, had helped them set up. And then Jos, of course, had a good job and she'd been working in her father's bakery, in the shop. She'd been only too glad to get out of the crowded family home and into this newly built housing estate at the edge of the village.

"Ah well, what's it to us?" he said, yawning. "Come on, let's go to bed, I've got to drive to the factory tomorrow, a big repair job."

"I'm just sorry for Paul. He's such a nice boy and she really doesn't deserve him. That's what I think. She's always pretended to be different, actually they all pretend in that family, really. They're stuck up, even though they know they aren't any better than the rest of us. Well, with a father like that, what do you expect?"

She hauled herself up from the sofa. "He's so religious he falls right off the edge and my aunt really suffers. She's never been able to cope with all of it and it shows. She's got far too much on."

She stubbed out her cigarette in the large blue and cream ashtray. She pulled up Jos, and giggled again with the wine and the tiredness. "Let's go up then. You're tired I can see that. We shouldn't really go out in the middle of the week. It'll break us up for the rest."

"Ah well, I know. But it was great to see Roger wasn't it? He won't be able to come again for another six months, not until they get married."

Roger was his brother who worked in Switzerland on a one-year contract. He was an engineer and the pride of his father and mother. They were a close-knit family, not from the village. Jos' parents moved to Armitan only after his father had retired and they wanted to live somewhere quiet and away from the busy and overcrowded west of the country.

Mary much preferred Jos' family to her own. They were easy going, much less concerned about the rights and wrongs of what people thought and how they lived and they weren't concerned about going to church twice on a Sunday, so different from her own relatives. Even though her parents were less overwrought than Anna's father was, they were still strict in their interpretations and tended to be on the heavy, worrying side whenever something happened. She sighed again. What could you expect when you had such very large families? She was determined to avoid that, and so was Jos for that matter. They had their own methods now to make sure that she wouldn't get pregnant again. Yes, they were a young family but that family would stay small, they would make sure of that, no matter what the church and parents and family proscribed. Of course she believed in God and of course she was sure that He was there and made sure that the world went round and all that, but she also read the more worldly magazines. They had a television and she no longer believed that God watched her every minute of the day. In fact she did not even think about it very much, never had. Shame about Anna though, she seemed so troubled, she thought too much. Johannes should never have let her go to that Gymnasium.

Chapter Sixteen: 1968

Amsterdam

Anna had drunk too much, the room was definitely rotating and would not keep still, but she giggled as Kees pulled her towards him. She stumbled but he held her up, one arm around her waist, the other grabbing at her shoulder. The music was deafening, some couples were clutching and kissing, others moved wildly to the beat, twisting and rocking. Anna was sweaty in her thin, sleeveless mini-dress. It was nearly midnight and the party was in full swing, the windows wide open. Surely someone would ring the doorbell soon and tell them to be quiet, but no one seemed concerned.

The party was on the top floor of the building but the whole house, from top to bottom, was booming with noise and music. It was a warm summer's evening, and when they came in she had dropped her thin jacket somewhere on a heap of clothes just inside the front door. Kees had disappeared into the crowd of people almost immediately on arrival, into what seemed to be the sitting room, and she had stood at the edge of a group of people in the small entrance hall, peering into another room that had been cleared of all furniture, where couples moved in rhythms dictated by the boom of the speakers, sometimes loud and wild and sometimes slow and soft. She didn't know anyone there except for Joanne, her friend from work, who she spotted at the other end of the room dancing with a large bald man in jeans and a loud orange tee-shirt, but Joanne didn't see her. Anna enjoyed the slow intoxication at these parties, although the wine was cheap and by now the beer was lukewarm. She enjoyed the clusters of people in their casual dress, all happy and noisy and the music so loud that there was little conversation possible that made any sense at all. She loved the dancing and the accompanying groping, depending on how drunk she was; this was the third party in less than a month.

Kees, a native of Amsterdam, was a designer in the company she worked for, and someone or other on his vast list of friends and acquaintances was always throwing a party on Fridays or Saturdays. Within days of joining the company, Kees had chatted her up even though he was at least six or seven years older. He seemed busy chatting up all the younger girls in the company, but his attention for her had lasted; he fancied her, she could tell.

After six months in Amsterdam, Anna still went home occasionally, for a weekend when there was no party and she had little else to do, and then she was forced to travel back early on the Monday morning. Johannes would not allow her to travel back on Sundays if it was possible to catch an early bus and train on Monday morning, even if that meant she had to get up at five in the morning and he drove her to the station to catch the early train to Amsterdam. He still expected her to go to church twice on Sunday but she went without objections or creating an argument, always leaving the house at the last minute and slipping in just before the vicar and elders entered from a door at the front to take their seats in the side pews. She'd sit down at the very end of the very back row of the church without looking around, avoiding eye contact with anyone that might know her and who might want to talk to her,

239

and at the end of the sermon and the last psalm and prayer, she got up quickly and jumped on her bike which she had dropped just outside the entrance. She never met with Paul or Gemma; they were no longer there when she was. At home, where only the younger brothers and sisters were now, no one talked about Gemma. Liesbet had married as well as Bert and both Stephan and Gerard had moved to other towns, Stephan for a job and Gerard to finish college at a specialist technical design institute. They were rarely home when she was, and they never tried to coordinate their visits.

When he realised that Anna had found and accepted a job in Amsterdam, her father immediately organised accommodation for her through his church connections to make sure that she was 'safe and well-looked after, without getting lost.' He was unaware that she had, meanwhile, moved out of the room in the house of the kindly lady who had been bewildered when Anna announced that she had found other accommodation on one of the canals in town, 'because it was cheaper and more convenient.'

She had first met Kees through the company tennis scheme, and being a proficient player he had offered to teach her, held her arms and hands to show her the right posture and the feel of the racket, let his arm slip around her shoulder to press her into the right position and then met her after work for drinks. Now he regularly took her to one or other party.

Kees was thin and at least a head taller than she was. He was a crowd pleaser, always trying to engage his friends in one joke or another, but his work was highly regarded by the bosses who praised him. His designs were used for science books and he shared a large office with five other designers, who all whistled when one of the administrative assistants walked through to drop off a note or letters or to pick up work to be considered by one of the managers. When she walked through their office for the first time, Anna was embarrassed by the whistles, but now she was used to it and like the other girls, she played to the audience with her short skirts and tight shirts. This was the sixties and they were living in Amsterdam, where girls were equal to boys and where doctors would hand out the new pill without asking questions. She'd talked to Joanne, who was on the pill and who had given Anna the address of the friendly doctor, but Anna had not dared yet to go there, feeling shy and afraid. What would she say if this doctor asked if she had a boyfriend? What about not having had periods for as long as she could remember? Besides, she had not slept with anyone yet and felt confused about whether or not she might get pregnant if she did.

Nowadays, no one whistled when she walked by the office of the designers, carrying envelopes and files. They knew that Kees had his eyes on her. She also knew that he'd soon want more than simply hold her hand and she wondered when he'd make his move and what she would do.

Kees pulled her away from the group of people out of the room and she giggled again, leaning into him. He kissed her sharp on her mouth. She realised that he was tipsy too and there was a hardness about him, no longer the charming, harmless man who played at being her boyfriend. He arched her back and groped at her bottom and legs, pulling up her skirt. The din around them drowned out what he said, and she just nodded and let him push his hand inside her underwear, squirming at the same time as she laughed. They were in the shower room, where a dingy, blue shower curtain with green and black mould at the bottom was drawn from one wall to the other, hiding the cubicle and the shower hose. To the side was a cracked toilet with the black, hard plastic seat up. It needed flushing. A wall rail held a dirty blue-grey towel, frayed at the edges. Kees clicked the lock shut behind them and then pulled up her skirt and suddenly he was in there, with a sharp gasp.

This is what she had been fighting over with Paul, had avoided for so long. This is what they had been hiding from her, what she was not supposed to do until she got married, and she wondered what all the fuss was about. She wanted to hold on to Kees, wanted him to say something. She wanted him to put his arms around her, but he pumped into her, in and out, groaned and was already pulling up his trousers again. They had fallen around his ankles and she vaguely thought this looked slightly ridiculous and then wondered what she looked like and pulled down her skirt, quickly.

"Better get out of here," he said. "There's someone banging on the door, they'll want to use the loo."

He pulled at the skirt of her dress and straightened it. "I'll go first, see you out there." And then he was gone, slipped through and clicked the door shut behind him, and she tried to find the lock but her eyes wouldn't focus properly and then the door opened again widely.

"Beg your pardon," someone said, "but can you hurry. I'm desperate for a pee." The man, his two faces blurring and sharpening as if seen through a camera that wouldn't focus, looked at her and grinned. "Had a good time then?"

She tried to look at herself in the small mirror above the sink but again saw two faintly ridiculous, red faces that skidded over each other in slow motion, as if floating in a blue-zoned space. She adjusted her underwear, pulled the top of her dress in place and managed to splash some water over her face, then patted it dry with a dirty towel, covered in stripes of blue and brown and full of grey spots that hung on a plastic peg fixed to the back of the door. She left the bathroom and the same man who had talked to her earlier rushed inside behind her, pulling at his trousers as he closed the door behind him. Kees was standing with his arm around the shoulders of a pretty blonde girl, who looked at her curiously. Her curly hair was thick and hung shoulder length, cut in a sharp straight style. She had a pale but fresh complexion with just a tinge of maroon lipstick and big blue eyes with pupils that were shiny against their whites. She wore an expensive looking silk shirt over tight black trousers that showed off her slim body and legs. There was no sign of drunkenness or even of having had anything to drink at all. She held a tumbler with what looked like plain water. Anna swallowed and turned round and saw her friend Joanne, who grabbed her arm and said, "I've been looking for you all over the place. Are you all right? I've got a taxi coming, you want to share?"

Anna looked around towards Kees who was still with the blonde girl and now in animated conversation with someone she recognised from work.

"Yes," she said 'I'll come with you." She took a step and nearly fell over.

Joanne laughed, "We'd better get you out of here before you collapse. Had too much to drink now, haven't you."

*

From then on Kees avoided her, and when he was on the tennis court the blonde girl was with him and they played mixed doubles with another couple Anna had not seen before. She asked one of his colleagues about the girl, casually she thought, and he said, "Oh, didn't you know? That's his fiancée Irene; they're engaged to be married."

When she was next home, her father asked her whether she had met 'nice people' through the church in Amsterdam. She shrugged and said she worked hard during the week and yes, she'd been to coffee with a few people, but they all lived quite far away and it was not easy for her have regular contact.

"Aren't you a member of the girl's catechism club?" he asked.

Surely he had to be aware that she had no contact whatsoever with any church member or meeting in Amsterdam?

She didn't answer and ignored further questions, ignored her mother's vacant smiles, and ignored everyone else and most of the time pretended to be engrossed in a book. The world she lived in had moved into a different space from that of her parents and her siblings and of her childhood and the two worlds had become irreconcilable. Wasn't that what she'd always wanted?

Recklessly, Anna went up to Kees, as they happened to leave the building at the end of the day at the same time, and invited him to her room for a chat, she said, and a cup of coffee, and this time she slept with him, properly, on the single bed. She curled up to him and he said he loved her and that he wouldn't see Irene again. She would give him time though, because he also loved Irene who was very possessive about him.

Anna believed him and they carried on seeing each other until she realised how careless and stupid she had been. She was pregnant. One morning at work, she was violently ill and colleagues whispered. She said she hadn't eaten properly, had eaten out and must have picked up something.

The world around her suddenly lost its glossiness, her make believe and exciting existence felt frayed. She wondered what Kees would say and whether she would in fact tell him at all and what he would do if she did.

Even if he hadn't realised it, she thought, Kees had helped her rid herself of the layers of fear, of God and the Devil and

Hell and damnation. Their relationship, if that is what it was, had encouraged her to peel away the final layers of Calvinism that were still wrapped around her brain and her body, invisible to the outside world, like so many old and dirty bandages that had suffocated her for too long. For the first time in her life she was not afraid of her body, nor of sex, but at what cost? She had defeated herself.

She'd been stupid, so very stupid, caught out again, but not by God or the Devil this time but by her own thoughtlessness. She should have gone with Joanna to that doctor as she'd told herself she would. But no, she'd assumed that she was infertile. She had stopped taking the green tablets years ago and had not really thought about the consequences, imagining she was immune, a non-woman, and a non-mother, who could simply ignore what all girls were so afraid of. Only her periods had started again and she had done nothing about it. And now they'd stopped again and she was caught. God had found her out after all.

She stopped Kees on the tennis court as he came out of the changing room in his all white outfit, smart and without a care in the world. "I need to talk you Kees. Something has happened."

The girl Irene was suddenly there next to him, in an equally stylish white tennis dress, her blonde hair pulled back with a wide black tie. Kees put an arm around her shoulder to let her know that he was not the least bit interested in whatever Anna wanted to talk about. Irene pushed Kees's arm aside however and said, "I'll be on the court in a minute. Just leave us for a moment," and he wandered into the pavilion.

"Kees and I are getting married, you understand? What do you want to talk about? Kees has told me about you and has promised to stop the relationship. Kees is mine, always has been."

Then after a silence in which she studied Anna carefully, Anna said, "I'm pregnant".

"Is that it? You think you've got him now do you? Well, you can get rid of it. I'll find you a doctor. No one need ever know, not even Kees."

Anna was alone. She no longer wanted to talk to Kees. It had all been a mistake, her own. Now she knew what it had been like for Gemma all those years ago. There was no one to go to, no one who would be able to help her, who would want to help her for that matter, except for this strange girl, Irene. If she walked away she would have to take care of herself, but she had no idea how.

Irene made the appointment with a doctor she knew. He was family of some sort and was willing to help young women who, he said, 'had made a mistake,' and he would make it a legal termination. Irene would fill in the appropriate forms; she would help her through the procedure and the investigative meeting and she would pretend to be an older sister. However, Anna would have to agree and understand that she, Irene, would never want to see Anna again after all this was over. She would pay the bill; they would get a special deal because of her connections.

On the rare occasion that she came across Kees during the next few days and week, he avoided looking at her as if they'd never met before, just as Irene predicted. He no longer tried to catch her eye when he walked past the administrators' office at work, or made a comment when she passed through the design department full of boys and men who still whistled at the girls in mini-skirts. She no longer went to the tennis court, and told her tennis partners and colleagues that she had hurt her arm and needed a rest.

When it was done, when the foetus had been sucked out of her and there was nothing and nobody left for her to stay for in Amsterdam, let alone in the rest of the Netherlands, except sour memories, hurt, and her own muddled tears at night, she searched and found a job in London. She could move away and leave God and Devil and her unborn child behind. The only person she told of her move to England was Bert, who was too busy with his own budding family, two children already and another baby on the way, to take much notice of what she said or of the implications for their parents. He himself had very little contact with them, he said.

No one knew about the abortion but Irene and she was certain that Irene wouldn't talk. Perhaps Kees did know after all, but Anna no longer cared.

She wanted to start again and forget; she had to reinvent her life. The shame in Holland, where everyone would be prying was too much. She no longer wanted to think about the emptiness, about the fear and the nothingness that took possession of her afterwards, after the deed was done; her crying fits, the dark lonely nights. She told herself that she had defeated God, that He could no longer punish her. However, now that He was gone from her life for good she was left with an emptiness that was deeper than any sea or ocean she could imagine. It was as if she had dived into living water without knowing what was underneath the surface, like the boy Hans who drowned when he showed off on that bridge when they were children. How long ago was that? At least she had come up alive, even if damaged. She would heal though; she would escape and not drown.

The job interview in an Amsterdam hotel was pleasant. The man and his wife had a company in London and wanted someone who was fairly fluent in English as well as Dutch and who could take care of the secretarial duties, answering telephones, typing letters in Dutch and in English, taking shorthand, someone with initiative and she convinced them that she was the girl they were looking for. After all, she had been top in her English class, had taken additional classes in Amsterdam as one of her bosses in the company was English and she had taken care of all his correspondence.

"What's your name? What shall we call you? It says Johanna Katarina here on the form, but I assume that is not what you go by on a day to day basis," the man said jovially, smiling and encouraging. His wife nodded.

"Katie," she said. "Call me Katie, that's fine."

*

Two months later she crossed the Channel to England on the ferry from Hook of Holland with all her belongings, which fitted easily into two suitcases. She was barely twenty years old and to all intents and purposes an orphan with no home to return to. As well as the work permit, the company had arranged a furnished room for her in a London house not far from their offices. Neither Johannes nor Greta knew that their daughter had run away.

As the ferry began its crossing from the Hook with seabirds noisily following, dipping in and out of the water for fish that were thrown up in a merry-go-round by the motor of the ferry and for the bread, that was thrown across the railings by passengers who laughed out loud and shouted at each other over the noise of the water, the birds, the wind and the motor, Anna stood at the railing and shivered in her thin blue raincoat that flapped across her legs in the wind and stared at the land that had been her home and was now disappearing steadily in the grey watery distance. Then resolutely, she turned and went below deck to read a newspaper she had bought before boarding.

Student protests had moved from Europe to Mexico and America and were being put down with massive force. It had all passed her by, this political upheaval and rebellion — she had been too busy and preoccupied with her own rebellion against God, family and imposed morality. She was not sure whether she had won or whether her own protest had broken her heart and sullied her life for good, just like the police batons had broken down the students and workers demonstrating against an unjust war.

She put away the paper and closed her eyes. She was too tired and worn out to try and understand the rest of the world now. She was going to start a new life, one that had no links with her previous one.

Chapter Seventeen: 1978

Neshnafad

I have nearly completed my notes on Anna, and I sit here on my balcony and stare at these pages full of scribbles in my cheap notebooks, the ones that I bought in the bazaar when I could still go out on my own, before all this unrest started. It seems so long ago now, when I could freely wander about this town, without feeling stared at or in danger of being assaulted or spat at. Even now I think that probably would not happen, but we're all uneasy at the change in mood, and local people are much less friendly, especially the ones that don't know you; the men that sit on their haunches outside their shops and houses, by the side of the street, staring at the passers-by and mouthing while they slip their fingers endlessly across their prayer beads.

I no longer go out on my own, and only venture out with my friends, with Betty and with Rosa, and usually a man, Mike or someone else's husband or a brother or a cousin, comes with us. It's the males who give us the much-needed sense of security in this increasingly male dominated society, fuelled by the anti-Shah mood.

I don't want to leave this life in Neshnafad, not yet, despite the increasing unrest. We are happy here, we still have fun, we have our tea parties and communal dinners and we still listen to music and walk around the compound and sometimes onto the university campus across the road. We play tennis on the private courts at the back of the compound, even if we are pregnant and not very agile, but it doesn't matter, as nobody will be watching us there. We bake cakes and celebrate each other's and our children's birthdays. My cakes are inedible; I've never had the patience before for baking cakes and so why would I succeed now? But it doesn't really matter. No one cares as long as you try and it looks good on a plate.

My girl is growing in my tummy. Even though we have not had a test done, I just know it's a girl, the daughter I long for. At my last check up, the gynaecologist reassured me that everything was fine and that there shouldn't be any complications.

I regularly sink into a dreamlike state, conversing with my daughter and I ignore what is going on around me. Even though I carry this extra little person, I actually feel as if I'm weightless, and for the first time in my life I am completely indifferent to what I look like or what impression I make. I have become immune to the rest of the world and neither God nor the Devil can reach me where I am now.

At night, there are the power cuts, and all we can do is use a kerosene lamp to try and read by in the sitting room and then go to bed early, finding our way around with a torch. Without electricity the pumps don't work and there is no water up here in the compound above Neshnafad, so Mike fills up the bath and every conceivable container we have with water, when, for a few hours in the middle of the night, the pumps all of a sudden work because someone has decided to give us electricity when we are asleep. I carry on teaching some of my private English lessons, and help children whose parents are desperate for them to have opportunities that will help them, when they want to leave for 'Amrika or Engelestan' for a better life. With the Shah retrenching and unwilling to listen to the voice of his people, and to the clergy, the mood in the country is becoming more and more threatening towards anything '*farangi*' or foreign; there is also a sense of desperation.

Early in March, just before the Nou Ruz celebrations – the Persian New Year - when we are already in Tehran, my waters break and my daughter Anahita is delivered in a private hospital, away from the mayhem. It is still safe, even if there is a hushed silence and staff are on the alert. Despite the unease and the dark atmosphere in the town and on the streets, Mike and his parents have managed to cajole a private gynaecologist into taking me onto his patient list here in Tehran so late in my pregnancy, and because of Sharrokh's status I receive more care than the average Iranian woman could ever dream of. But then, I am in no mood to feel concerned about that, or guilty. I am petrified when I enter the hospital and don't always understand what is being said or what I am being asked to do. All I want is to be safe and deliver my baby girl, my daughter.

"Oh. It's a girl," one of the nurses says, when she hands me the baby. She looks disappointed, and perhaps expects me to be sad, but I beam and cannot wait to hold her, my little girl. Mike stands by helplessly and just smiles, embraces me and the baby, and says he's just gone through the worst twenty-four hours of his life and is so relieved that we have both come through. He holds our little girl as if she is the most precious thing he's ever looked at, until she suddenly screams, loud and indignant, and he jumps and quickly passes her back to me, and she is quiet again. We both laugh, relieved it's all over, and astonished at what we have produced.

'Anahita', I say to Mike and he nods. Yes, she is our little Anahita, our female guardian 'angel of water.' She heals and is wise, I am healed and I feel wise just because I have her. She is the Greek Anaitis for us; she is divine. She is what I have been waiting for, the female confirmation, the opposite of the Devil and God; she will heal my hurt and has already done that simply by being born. I will give her everything that was denied me; love and care; a life without fear; a living without gods and devils. I will show her how to be a woman, beautiful and unashamed.

I have always been intrigued by the story of Anahita, a hymn to the waters in Avestan. She is the goddess who nurtures crops and herds and she personifies a mythical river as great in bigness as all the waters, which flow forth upon the earth. I have chosen the name carefully, as a shield to protect my daughter from all that is ugly and wrong, and also to protect myself. So similar to my grandmother's name and yet so far removed from the person she was.

Although Mike leaves for Neshnafad two weeks after Nou Ruz, their New Year's Day in early spring, to get back to work, I stay with my in-laws in Tehran until I feel well enough to travel the long distance by car. The mood in Tehran becomes uglier by the day, but I miss the signs. I am too preoccupied with my little girl, who demands all my attention, and leaves me little time to sleep, let alone read newspapers or listen to what people say. I am lost in this country, and everyone around me makes sure that I don't wake up from my dreamlike state, my total ignorance of what's really going on.

I have no clear recollection of the Nou Ruz celebrations that year, although the Haft-e-sin table in the house must have been decorated, laden with sabze and sir and sib, the greens, the garlic and the apple, as well as love and affluence and other good wishes, like beauty and old-age. Guests must have come and gone, but I am excused from all visiting and from receiving visitors. I am still recovering and am feeding a little baby and

253

the family and servants hover around me as if I am a terminally ill person who must be pampered and taken care of. I am a queen, and my daughter is the little princess that will heal everything that is hurtful.

In the two weeks before he goes back to Neshnafad, Mike sometimes looks at me and the baby as if he wants to ask me something, but then closes his mouth again, smiles and kisses me on my forehead before he leaves the room. He sits with Anahita on his lap for hours, and she is quiet and comfortable when he holds her. We both miss him when he leaves for Neshnafad at the end of the two weeks and Anahita looks around as if she is searching for his familiar voice.

In the middle of May, when I feel quite well again and walk around the house and the little yard to strengthen my muscles, Mike comes to collect us so that we can travel back together to Neshnafad by car. Mike's mother hovers and advises us once more about what to do and what not to do and where to stop and where not to stop and how to take care of our Anahita. There is an undercurrent of unease and worry all around but I am not paying much attention.

"Wear your scarf all the time," she says, as she did that time when we undertook the journey for the first time, so long ago now.

We smile and let her fill up the car with food and last-minute presents, admonitions and good wishes, and we set off early in the morning with the sun coming up in a clear blue sky. The trip is exhausting, more so than I want to admit, even to Mike, but eventually we arrive and I manage to sleep in the car, on and off, and in between feeding Anahita, who seems to be aware of the seriousness of this trip and is very quiet all the way.

Betty beams when she sees us, her growing stomach visibly pregnant. "Hi you, so glad you're back. I'm off in a week's time," she says. "Let me see your precious little one. I can't believe it. I'm so thrilled for you, a little girl. Just keep fingers crossed mine is a girl too."

Rosa is withdrawn, and has a perpetual frown in the skin of her forehead. "Things are not going too well," she says. "I just hope this country isn't going to the dogs." She shakes her head. "Nevertheless, I'm glad you're back and at least I have some company when Betty goes. We need each other like water."

It strikes me that perhaps our world is not as rosy as I imagine it to be. Did my in-laws try to warn me, us? Were we too preoccupied with our own lives, our Anahita, to notice what was going on? Is our new life in our new home less secure than we want it to be?

The reality is that the Shah is still trying to keep control, even though it seems to me that a revolution has started and there is no return to the old days, whilst the alternative, the mullah-led opposition by the Khomeini believers, now begins to feel like a worse but inevitable alternative. Mike continues to reassure me that all will be fine. But how could I ignore the signs? How can I bring up our daughter in an atmosphere that will condemn everything female as ultimately seductive and therefore sinful just because of her gender? But perhaps it will not come to that, perhaps Rosa is just pessimistic, unnecessarily so, and Mike is right.

I sleep little. Anahita wakes me up at regular intervals and my days and weeks are spent in a dreamlike, exhaustive state. Mike tries his best to make everything as comfortable as possible for me, he goes out and shops, brings back little gifts, a bunch of flowers, a shopping bag full of meat and vegetables that mean I don't have to go anywhere for days on end. I am oblivious to his needs and don't notice the slow withdrawal, the times when he tries to start a conversation and I cut him short, telling him about the wonderful new things I have discovered in our daughter.

Even I cannot deny it though. Khomeini's influence on the lives of Iranians becomes increasingly obvious. The locals trade in cassettes with his sermons and exhortations, they listen to them and talk about them, and our husbands come back with the tales of what is happening in Tehran, in Qom and in all the other places across the country, including our own town. The revolution is happening while I am preoccupied with Anahita and her needs and care. Suddenly, there is martial law and life becomes quite ugly. Betty has left. We have waved her out, crying, wondering whether we will see each other again.

"I don't know how I feel," she says. "I'm sure glad that I'm getting out of here, but I worry about Behmand. Please look after him. I wish he would come with me, but he's obstinate; he thinks his country needs him. As if…" She puffs, and tries to hide her anger and emotion.

We reassure her, of course we will look after Behmand and we will invite him to dinner and make sure he is not lonely, but she needs to make sure she has that baby really quickly and come back with it.

We don't want to consider a long-term interruption to our lives, or even a complete change to our lives. We tell each other that it will pass, this revolution, and that we will all be back here in Neshnafad and we will pick up where we left off.

*

On the day martial law is declared, our town is in turmoil, and Rosa's husband is called to the local hospital to help look after the injured in the fighting that has broken out in and around the town. Rumours fly about like so many bees escaping from a smoking beehive. Someone has been shot, no, a whole group of people have been shot at, they were rioting, they were looting, they were innocent bystanders, they were a couple and their two young children. We don't know what is true and what isn't. Our safe and happy world is slowly crumbling, other forces are taking over and we can't stop them. We become painfully aware that we are mere visitors in this country, and neither I, nor our daughter, are really part of it, let's be honest. We don't belong, and are intruders unless we submit to the new rules and a different way of living that will be dictated by males and will re-establish everything that I have fought against all my life. Unfortunately, I feel that I have nowhere else to go, that I am homeless without my life in Neshnafad. This town has become my home. I have given up my other ones, first of all by rejecting my birth country and then by leaving my adopted second country, England. Iran has become my home, for better or worse.

"It's probably better if you don't go out for a few days," our husbands say. "We'll go and get the shopping, or at least we should come with you, if you insist on going out."

"Women must wear the chador and they must be accompanied by male relatives," the wise, religious men say and they add that "Women shouldn't work. They should stay at home, cook, bring up the children, look after parents and grandparents, and keep the house clean. They don't need to go out on their own."

An avalanche of advice and musts and cannot do's come at us and even then multiply. Then there are the counterclaims of other groups of revolutionaries that tell us that women will be freer, there will be fewer restrictions and this is not about us being locked up in the house. Rather, this is about a dictator, the Shah, being ousted and there is no intention to curtail anyone's freedom, there is only the wish to bring back true freedom. This, we want to believe.

We agree that the Shah has gone too far, that the country is not ready for such an all out westernisation, that the Savak is a nasty institution and that Iranians should be allowed to take care of themselves, without the insidious interference of America or other western powers. It is whispered that a cinema fire in a town in the north of the country was a plot to discredit the Islamists, no it was to discredit the Savak; it was started by the Savak; no it was started by Islamists who wanted it to look like it was the Savak. We don't know who or what to believe. All we know is that the Shah's power is slowly but certainly crumbling and that it is not clear who or what will come in his place.

Chapter Eighteen: 1980

Neshnafad

Everyone knows what's happening of course. It's insidious. We were promised that the revolution would bring freedom to all of Iran's people, that there would be free elections, that there would be freedom for the press. All lies.

I'm busy packing my suitcases. When I went to the embassy and asked the Dutch authorities for advice on what to do they said I should leave the country immediately. They would soon be packing their own bags. I said I couldn't as I have a little girl who is Iranian and she has no papers to leave Iran or enter Holland. Would I have to leave her behind? Is that what they suggest? The official I spoke to left the room and said he'd be back. When he returned he gave me some papers that would need to be signed by both Mike and I, and he said I should come back the next day with the signatures. Mike signed the paper without any questions and now Anahita can travel on my passport as my child, without Mike accompanying us. I will leave in a week's time. Mike has decided to stay.

*

All through this time I have been teaching, a few private lessons to children in their own homes here in the compound and when I teach, Mike takes care of Anahita. When I come back late one afternoon he says, "Anna is you, isn't she?"

"It's a novel," I say.

"But it's not fiction."

I refuse to answer or comment. I am angry that he has read my notebooks without asking me. He has been snooping in my drawer, behind my back.

"Have you had an abortion?" he asks.

"What is it to you?" I reply sharply. "We never talk about each other's past, so why would we start now? What's the purpose of bringing all this up?"

"You are my wife. You are the mother of my daughter. I have a right to know," he says.

"I've never asked you about the girls you slept with before you met me," I say. "For all I know you're the father of a number of children."

He is indignant and looks very hurt, throws up his arms and sighs. "It's not about that. It's about whether I know who you really are. It's about whether you are telling the truth."

Why is he suddenly, after all this time, so interested in my past? Why is he secretly going through my things? I thought we had an unwritten agreement that we would never ask and never pry. It is as if this revolution and the politics and attitudes that go with it bring out the worst in all of the men here; as if, however liberal they used to be, these edicts by Khomeini and his cohort rub off on them and suddenly make them sit up and think that they also ought to have some influence on their wives' and their sisters' behaviour and morality.

We don't talk much anymore. I'm glad he's signed the papers for Anahita, but I wonder if he would have done that had he known. He could still stop me from going; he could stop me from taking Anahita. I am very afraid. Our world has shifted and we are no longer in the same space and I feel sick inside.

Behmand is none to happy now about Betty being away and not coming back soon. Whereas before, he agreed that it was the best thing for her and that life in Iran would become difficult and unbearable for women, especially foreign women, now he is agitated. He still has not seen his newborn son and wants him to be in Iran. Betty has telephoned and written to him to get out of Iran whilst there is still the opportunity, but he refuses and says that his wife's place is with him, no matter what. She should adapt to Iranian culture, whatever that is nowadays, just like he does. At least Betty's son is American. My daughter is Iranian, and so I am very dependent on whether or not Mike will agree to my leaving the country. I am glad that he is not using her in our silent but on-going disagreement.

Mike says again that he cannot accept the fact that I have lied to him. I say, "But I never lied to you Mike. We were happy together, we still are happy together, don't you agree? You never asked about my previous life and I didn't tell you. Neither have you told me all about yours."

"It changes everything," he says. "It's not right. You are not what you say you are. How can you abort a child?"

"Have you read all my notes on Anna or just this part?" I ask.

When the next day I tell him that the Dutch Embassy has advised me to leave the country in the light of the occupation of the American Embassy and the failed attempt to rescue the Americans, he says, "That's probably a good idea. You will be safer in The Netherlands. But I'm staying here."

I am devastated that he doesn't want to come with me. I beseech him, tell him that it will be dangerous for him in a country as a non-Muslim. He doesn't agree and says that he wants to stay because he doesn't want to become a nomad again. I think that the reality is that he wants me to be away, that he wants to reconsider our relationship. I think he can't bear to be with me and despises me for having had an abortion. He has shut me out and even started to sleep on cushions in the sitting room, rather than share the bed with me. He says it's because he needs his sleep and I'm restless with Anahita during the night.

We will go to Tehran in a week's time and then I'll travel to The Netherlands. I have no idea what I will do there and I haven't decided on where I'll stay. Bert has sent me a telegram to say that I'm welcome to stay with him for as long as it takes. I really want to go back to England and have contacted Tessa who says I should try to find a job in England, she'd help me.

My notebooks are packed in one of the two suitcases that I'm allowed to take out, together with a couple of toys for Anahita and essential clothes for both of us. I am homeless again and feel sick at the thought of returning to The Netherlands. I don't want to have to discuss God again, not with family nor with anyone else.

Chapter Nineteen: 1999

Oxford

My dearest Anahita

David will give you this letter after I'm gone. I know that we have spoken on the phone quite regularly these last few months, but I want to tell you again how proud I am of you. I love you with all my heart and you should know that you are very special.

You will be twenty-one when you read this and I so very much wish that I could be with you to celebrate your birthday. Of course, you know that too and I console myself with the thought that David will always be there for you.

You mentioned in one of our conversations that your Aunt Taraneh who lives in Canada not far from you has been in touch. I'm aware that we haven't talked much more about this as my illness made it difficult for me to talk extensively and you clearly did not want to upset me in any way. I want you to know however that I would not want to stop you from re-establishing contact with your father's family. Not only are you an adult and quite capable of making your own decisions and arrangements but also, although I lost contact with your father's family this does not mean that I feel hostile or that I would want to prevent you from getting in touch with them again. They are your family.

Parents often try too hard to protect their children from whatever they consider might harm or hurt them. Perhaps I did this unwittingly, afraid of possible hurt. Before you left for Canada you said you wanted to know more about my family as well as your father's. You were angry and accused me of being secretive and uncommunicative. I was surprised and I've thought about it, what you meant. My own parents were very uncommunicative in the sense that it felt as if they did not want their children to have a separate existence from their own, as if they had to mould them just so. They could not accept change and a different world and it felt that we, their children, simply had to accept their way of life, without explanations. But theirs was a time when Europe was full of damaged and lost people, families and strangers, so soon after the war. To them and their generation, the world was a very frightening place; and where better to hide than in their religion and small village existence with strict rules and regulations, what better way of trying to keep out the reality of this vast world around them, a world they did not understand? That's what they tried, anyway.

However, I'm digressing. Before I became ill and before you left for Canada, you asked me about my childhood in The Netherlands and I never really gave you more than the bare minimum of information, just enough for you to recognise the names of your uncles and aunts, so that you could pick up contact with various cousins, should you wish to. I don't have a lot of contact with my siblings, your uncles and aunts, not because there is an enmity between us now, but because I have always felt we have little in common to talk about, except for old hurts. Perhaps that is partly to do with my desire to bury it all and forget about it, I have mulled it over too much and my years in England have been the happiest years of my life, with

David and you. There has been no need to rake up the past; our lives here have been complete without the need for doing that.

For you to understand better my ambivalent feelings towards The Netherlands and my family, I am passing to you with this letter a cd that contains notes I made for a novel on a girl called Anna; I never completed the book. The girl Anna resembles to some extent your mother, me. You will read in these notes that Anna had an abortion, barely out of her teens. Although in these notes my own family environment has been fictionalised, it does reflect to a very large extent the reality of an upbringing in a suppressive and repressive Calvinist environment during those post war years in the middle of the twentieth century. Once I had written these notes, and after my return to England, I decided against trying to get them published as a book but rather to keep them as a story that I would hand to you, one day, to help you understand why I may not have wanted to talk about my childhood but would much rather focus on what we have in the here and now and in the future. Unfortunately, as it has turned out, life won't allow me much more of a future and so I need to hand to you my notes, so that you will know what happened.

Your earlier anger and demand for explanations and for more information about who you are and where you come from made me realise that I must hand my notes to you. They will help you understand, and hopefully you will feel less angry about what you call my secretiveness.

Nowadays, there is no shame attached to becoming pregnant outside marriage, or to have an abortion for that matter, not in the west anyway. However, when your father discovered and read these notes, my notes on Anna, he was very upset when he guessed the truth: that I had been pregnant before I knew him, and that I had an abortion. I have never found out whether he told his own family about this, after you and I left Iran just after the revolution. If so, it may have been the reason why they haven't been in touch much. Communication with people in Iran is much easier nowadays, the telephone system is better and I am told that e-mails are the future of mass communication all across the world. When I lived in Iran we did not even have a telephone in the house and snail mail was exactly that: it took a long time to arrive. I admit that I have not tried to contact the family again, after the death of your father, and I don't really know if they know about the abortion. It may well be that Taraneh will raise the subject with you, when you meet and I would rather you find out from me.

Your father died so soon after I left Iran with you. He may not have spoken about any of this with anyone, about my notes and my admission. It is unlikely that he did, as he was a very reserved person, something I only became aware of once we had moved to Iran. Still, it has always been a mystery to me why I was not informed of his death until so much later, until well after the Iran-Iraq war, and why there was so little communication from his side of the family. Not knowing of his death at the time, I despaired and assumed that he had decided to turn away from me. I was unable to contact him, there was never a response and in those days of mayhem and confusion, with the newspapers revealing more and more atrocities, and then the Iraq-Iran war, I became very frightened. When I eventually received the news from Taraneh, his sister who got in touch with you, I was devastated. It would not have been too difficult for his family to contact me, I'm sure, and I have found it very difficult to forgive them.

When you were a child, I did not think it was necessary to burden you with the details and I wanted you to remember your father, and us as a couple, as loving parents who adored you from the day you were born. You have never known him, as you were too little when you and I left Iran in such a hurry. Your father and I were very happy together, first in England and then in Iran, we loved each other to bits.

Mike's death was a tragedy, although I still don't understand why he was out demonstrating that day and got himself killed, when he knew of the dangers. Taraneh said it was a stray bullet, and that remnants of the Savak were responsible, but I don't know whether that's the truth. It may just as well have been the Muhajideen, those so-called freedom fighters in their early days.

Even though your father's parents were good to me when I lived in Iran, it was also quite clear that they were never happy about our marriage and that they would have preferred it if your father had married an Iranian woman. I was their disappointment, and this may go some way to explaining their subsequent attitude to me and to you. I believe that once we had left the country and when life in Tehran became so very difficult for them, for their daughters as well as for Mike, they simply had no energy left to worry about us. They wanted Mike to stay and perhaps hoped that eventually I would return to them, with you. Then, when Mike was killed so suddenly and so shortly after you and I left, there probably seemed little point for them to keep in touch, they were unable to leave the country and travel to Europe and had great difficulty keeping their heads above water and avoid being picked out by Khomeini's men. Remember, that they belonged to a minority religion in a Muslim country, and everyone was paranoid at that time. Later, I think they did travel to England again, but we never made contact. I had moved in with David and I don't think they would have been able to cope with that. Taraneh and her family moved to Canada before the borders closed altogether during the war with Iraq.

Had circumstances been different, I'm sure that your father and I would have been able to work through our differences. I don't think that he would have remained angry with me about not having talked about my abortion. I like to think that he would have understood what happened to me, why I did what I did, once he'd fully read and absorbed Anna's story. We did not have that time together, however, and it has left a great hole inside me.

You asked me once what I consider to be my home country, my real home, The Netherlands, England or Iran? This was important to you, as you often used to wonder out loud what your own home country was and you often said you felt a bit of a nomad. You have your Dutch passport because of me, you were born in Iran and have an Iranian father, but you have spent the best part of your life in England. You went to an English school and then you chose to go to Canada for your university studies. I have wondered why that was, that decision to go to Canada. You said it was because they offered a good and respected course, but I think you needed to get away from us in England, from me in particular, to try and find yourself perhaps within the muddle of an extended family scattered across the world.

Homelessness is a sad existence, and I would not say that I have felt homeless or an exile these years in England. David and I have been very happy together. He is a good stepfather to you, even though we decided not to get married, for various reasons.

Although I have frequently been back to The Netherlands, during the last few years especially, and I have picked up contact again with my siblings, your uncles and aunts, I still have a love/hate relationship with the country and find it difficult to reconcile current liberalism with how it used to be, the narrow-mindedness and rampant fundamentalism, the claustrophobia, quite similar to present day fundamentalism as you find it in some Muslim countries all over the world, and also in the religious fundamentalism in Ireland for example, the Catholics versus the Protestants. Fundamentalism always is hardest on females and children, even though it's usually the men who rebel and are loudest in their cries for war; men are often at the forefront of rebellion against perceived fundamentalism, nevertheless it is always the women that bear the biggest burdens and we, women, should be more vocal in our protests.

In The Netherlands, during the time of my own childhood rebellion against the religious fanaticism in which I was brought up, there were many Dutch male writers challenging their fathers, especially Calvinist fathers, but there were so very few females openly defying what was imposed on them by church and bible. Look also at what happened in Ireland where pregnant girls were sent to convents. In The Netherlands and in the Calvinist Church, a girl who was pregnant was forced into first making a public confession in church and then into marriage, and if that did not work out for one reason or another, the girl would be sent away somewhere, as in Ireland, and their babies were taken care of in the family and sometimes adopted by another religious family. The shame of being an unmarried mother was just too much to bear and was also considered to be a fundamental sin, one that a girl would carry with her for the rest of her life.

My abortion deprived you of the sibling you always wanted; however, had a child been born you would probably never have been born. Strange to think about that, isn't it?

Do I consider England to be home from home? I suppose so, although as I get older I have begun to feel more alienated from the country I live in, and my real home is the house I live in with David. Our lives here, yours and mine, have been good, with David and his children, your 'step siblings', as you like to call them, fondly. We have made our home here together.

I feel grateful that I found my first teaching job, with Tessa's support, here in Oxford, and so I was able to look after you and stay away from the country of my birth, that I loathed. Tessa and Ben have been my lifelong rocks and I owe Tessa more than I can tell you. Then I met David of course and we fell in love and decided to live together. The rest you know.

Friends and colleagues in England have always been very helpful, even though on the odd occasion I still felt as if I was an outsider, however hard everyone pretended I was not. I could never engage in jokey conversations about what it felt like to attend primary school here or what we read there or how influenced I have been by an English neighbourhood or friends. The first twenty years of my life will forever feel soiled, something that is no longer part of who I am now, nevertheless I cannot escape it. It's been a part of my life I much rather not speak about – my notes on Anna should do the talking for me.

Iran could have become our home I guess, yours and mine and Mike's; that was the intention when we moved there, but it never worked out. We had no say in it.

My darling Anahita, I want you to be happy. I don't want you to be homeless or feel an outsider in the way I did, wherever you are going to be. The world has opened up and is opening up even more and you can make your home wherever you want. Please forgive me my previous secretiveness.

Your loving Mum, Anna.

About the Author

Corri van de Stege was born in The Netherlands where she attended secondary school before moving to England and completing a philosophy degree at University College London. She lives in rural Norfolk in the east of the UK, and after a successful career in education and as a management consultant she is now a full time writer and book blogger. *Half the World*, a memoir of living in Iran before and during the 1979 revolution, is her first book publication and *Notes on Anna* is her debut novel. She is also working on a collection of short stories that she has been writing over the years. The author is a keen traveller and with most of her family and friends living abroad there is always an excuse to take a trip somewhere.

Notes on Anna can be bought in eBook and print versions from Amazon, Barnes & Noble, and other online and physical bookstores worldwide as well as the publisher's online book store. Further information can be obtained from the author's site and blog on http://www.51stories.com

Now you are at the end, the author hopes that you have enjoyed this book and would welcome any feedback or questions on any aspects of the story, characters or settings. Please support the author by providing a review on Amazon, Goodreads, Twitter or any other favourite book site or social media

Author Twitter: http://twitter.com/corrivandestage
Author Linkedin: Corri van de Stege
Publisher information and online bookstore:
http://www.creativegateway.com